FRENEMIES AND LOVERS

A FAKE-DATING AGE-GAP STANDALONE
ROMANTIC COMEDY

40 AND FABULOUS
BOOK 1

MICHELLE MCCRAW

lazy dog
books

CONTENTS

1. Flipping Angels	1
2. Fashion Emergency	11
3. It's Not Me. It's You.	19
4. Smacked with My Own Hubris	27
5. Frenemyship, or Is It Frenmity?	37
6. A Waste of a Perfectly Good Hookup	45
7. Go Forth and Calculate	53
8. Getting Old Isn't for the Weak	59
9. We Have to Stop Meeting Like This	73
10. Bigger Balls	81
11. A Proposition	85
12. We Sell It	93
13. Cuffing Season	105
14. I Play It Balls-Out	111
15. The Perfect Amount of F–You, Brad	119
16. Falling for My Fake Date	125
17. My Epic Mistake	133
18. Welcome to Crone Life	147
19. A GD Goddess	157
20. Zombie Bride	171
21. #CoupleGoals	179
22. It's Not Serious	183
23. Cake? Totally Overrated.	187
24. Fifteen Minutes	193
25. A Doublè Black Diamond	205
26. Zero Chill	213
27. A Cinderella Story	221
28. The Power of Puppies	229
29. A Modern-Day Pee-wee Herman	239
30. A Fashion Crisis	245
31. The Leading Lady	253
32. I Overthink It	259

33. A Family Meeting	263
34. A Twenty-Year Mistake	275
35. F*** the Rules	281
36. I'm Incorrigible	287
Epilogue	295

EXCERPT FROM BOOKS AND HOOKUPS

1. Couples Are the Worst	303
2. When Do You Get Off?	313
Acknowledgments	321
Credits	323

*I see you out there. You're over forty. Or fifty. Or sixty. Or any number that makes people think you're invisible.
You're not, you incredible firebird.
This is for you.*

1
FLIPPING ANGELS

CARLY

To-do list—October 22
✓ Request limit increase for credit card
✓ Pick up client's gowns at boutique
~~Take gowns to client~~ Give Audrey Hayes a piece of my mind

Everything about the Jones-Hayes mansion in Presidio Heights was exquisite, from the graceful curve of the staircase leading to the front door to the delicate amber spider mums spilling over a planter on the doorstep. The first time I'd come here, I'd stood on the doorstep like a slack-jawed noob, listening to the doorbell's lovely, melodious chime. To a girl who'd grown up in low-rent apartments, it sounded like angels singing.

I banged the side of my fist on the heavy wooden door. Audrey's flipping angels could shove their tiny harps where the sun didn't shine.

The door swung open, making me wobble back on my two-seasons-ago Jimmy Choos. The pretty, smiling young woman who answered wasn't my frenemy.

She was her daughter, Natalie, a stunning blonde in her midtwenties, about the age I'd been when I'd entered her mother's social sphere. But Natalie hadn't bumbled her way in like I had. No, Natalie had been born into San Francisco's tech royalty.

No one would kick her out the way they'd done to me.

"Mrs. Winner. Would you like to come in?" As Natalie pulled the door wider and stepped aside, her high-waisted beige trousers swished. Her periwinkle-blue silk blouse was Brunello Cucinelli, if I wasn't mistaken. Natalie was the youngest of Audrey's children, but she had the best sense of style, vastly superior to her brother's. I would *not* think about him today. Not while I stood on his mother's doorstep.

"It's Ms. Rose now." I stood as tall as I could on the doorstep. "Or just Carly. Is your mother here?"

"She's in the conservatory. Shall I show you to her?" Her phone buzzed in her hand, and she glanced at it.

My phone hadn't rung in weeks. Except for today's call to cancel my job. I sucked in a deep, calming breath through my nose. "No, thank you. I know where it is."

"Great. See you later." She bounded up the grand staircase, leaving me in the foyer.

I'd been to Audrey's home often enough to be able to find my way around. I used to come with Brad for formal events and dinner parties. One time, when we were on the friend side of our frenemyship, she'd brought me to the conservatory to show off an orchid she'd coaxed into a pink bloom so ethereal I thought it might crumble like sugar if I touched it.

I rounded the pedestal table in the center of the foyer with its enormous arrangement of alstroemeria and stalked through an arched doorway into the hall that led to the back of the house.

My heels echoed off the Spanish tiles as I passed the doorway to the dining room. Audrey usually held committee meetings there and presided over them like a queen in her armchair at the head of the table. I strode past her private wing, the black and white powder room, and her husband's office.

Finally, when I smelled green things, I flung open the French double doors that led to the glass-enclosed room. I slowed my steps, watching for wet places on the tile. Avenging furies didn't fall on their asses.

Everywhere I looked was verdant. Trees grew from pots that two people could fit inside. Leaves the size of an elephant's ear nodded in the gentle breeze from a fan. Graceful pink and white flowers cascaded from hanging baskets and planters. Although it was autumn outside, here, it was spring.

"Audrey?" I called.

"Over here."

I followed her voice toward the trickling fountain in the center of the room. She sat in a rocking chair facing the garden outside. She wore yoga pants, a simple white T-shirt, and a man's plaid flannel shirt—in her signature color, red—thrown over like a jacket. She'd tied a matching kerchief over her blond bob.

I'd never seen her dressed casually before, not even when we'd gone to the rainy, muddy groundbreaking for the library their family foundation had funded. Without her Dior 999 lipstick and couture armor, she looked as small and fragile as one of her orchids. But I knew the truth.

As one of the most powerful women in the city, she could bar anyone's entry into the upper echelons of San Francisco society.

And today, she had put up her metaphorical keep-out sign in front of me.

I balled my fists at my sides.

She wore no makeup, and her unmasked wrinkles made her look almost as old as she was. With four grown children, I knew she had to be in her sixties and not forty-five as she'd claimed for the past ten years.

I was forty-five. And I was not going to think about her children right now. Especially not her second son.

There was a small bench beside her, but fury kept me on my feet. I stomped up and towered over her, planting my hands on my hips.

Her pale lips opened in surprise. "Carly, what are you doing here?"

The nerve! As if she didn't know exactly why I'd come here madder than a wet hen.

I took a deep breath. When I was this angry, my Texas twang tended to pop out, but I wanted to inspire the fear of god, not laughter.

"What you did was low, Audrey. We used to be friends." Sort of. "Before..." I swallowed down the words *my divorce* and, even worse, *my downfall*. "We worked together on more committees and galas than I can count. You know I'm a hard worker, professional and talented. I'd have done a good job for Bianca and started to build my business. There was no reason for you to go behind my back."

"Behind your back?" Audrey shook her head slowly, her diamond earrings glinting in the afternoon sunlight. "Whatever are you talking about?"

"Bianca Waddingworth." I parked my fists on my hips. Feigning ignorance was beneath her. "I was supposed to be styling her for her birthday party tonight. She texted me to cancel because *you* told her to."

"Me?" She planted a perfectly manicured hand on her chest. "Why would I do that?"

"You're trying to kick me to the curb." A fresh wave of anger tightened my throat. "News flash: you're too late. Brad already took care of it."

"It seems like something you could have predicted," she said in that cultured voice of hers. "Since he left Eleanor for you."

Why did she have to be right? Brad hadn't told me he was married when we met. And I was positive his new fiancée hadn't known we were still living together when she knocked on my door eighteen months ago. But if I let Audrey distract me with that disaster, I'd never get my point across.

"All I want—"

"Hey, Carly, a question for you while you're here." Natalie's voice at the door to the conservatory startled me. She was barefoot, and I hadn't heard her approach. "If someone is sixty-something and in decent shape, what type of gown would you recommend for a formal party? She's a yoga nut, if that helps."

I paused. That could have described a dozen women in her mother's social circle. "Good arms, then," I mused.

"That's right. And she's a blonde."

That narrowed it only slightly. But I had a sneaking suspicion she was asking for styling advice for the woman who'd backed out of paying me to do it. Still, Natalie was a nice girl. I only wanted to jerk a knot in her mother's tail. "An A-line. Sleeveless, of course. In red."

Natalie approached me, looking down at her phone. "Here's a red sequined gown. But which shoes?" She showed me a photo of a pair of glittery gold pumps. "These?" She swiped to show a pair of strappy black sandals. "Or these?"

"Does she have a neutral dress shoe? Something beige?" I asked.

"Good idea." Natalie tapped on her phone. "She should've asked you to style her."

"Who?" I gritted my teeth.

"Bianca Waddingworth."

She did. And then she canceled. But that wasn't Natalie's fault. It was her mother's. "Maybe next time," I said with a sweet-tea smile, hoping my tone didn't sound as strangled to her as it did to me.

"Will these work?" She flipped her phone around to show me a photo of a pair of rose-gold rhinestone-spangled sandals.

"Perfect."

"Thanks. I'll let her know."

Damn it, I'd just styled Bianca Waddingworth. For free. *And* let Natalie take all the credit. I sucked in a breath, but the conservatory's moist air weighed heavily in my lungs.

Natalie looked between her mother and me, her gaze lingering on my fists jammed onto my hips. "You two okay?"

"Fine, thanks." I broadened my smile.

"We were talking about Carly's styling business," her mother said smoothly.

"Nice. I'm sure you can refer lots of clients her way, Mother."

"Perhaps Carly's style would be better suited to a different type of clientele." Audrey's smile was brittle. She muttered low enough that only I could hear, "The kind down on Capp Street."

I sucked in an outraged breath.

The doorbell chimed, and Natalie glanced down at her phone. "I lost track of time. I'll get the door, but then I've got to go." She pecked her mother's cheek. "See you at the party. Will we see you there, Carly?"

Pain speared behind my right eye. "No, I'm not on the guest list tonight."

Her cheeks went red. "Oh. What about the gala at the Merchants Exchange?"

"A gala?" I repeated. The event would be chock-full of potential styling clients.

"On November first. You should come. Is there room at our table, Mother?"

Audrey looked like she'd sucked on a lemon. "I don't think so, darling. I'm sure Carly would prefer to sit with the new wives."

Because after nineteen years of marriage, I was still a new wife. An interloper. I balled my fists.

"Still, you should come, Carly. You haven't been to anything since..." Natalie grimaced.

The doorbell rang again.

"Saved by the bell!" Natalie said, trotting toward the exit. "Really, you should come."

Across the room, a buzzing erupted from a phone resting on a wireless charger. Audrey ignored it, so I did too.

"I don't care about being invited to parties anymore." Staying home was preferable to facing down my asshole of an ex and his fiancée. "But I do care about making a living for myself."

Audrey pursed her lips. "I heard your divorce settlement was less than ideal."

Heat licked across my forehead. I wished I could go back and shake my twenty-five-year-old self, the one who'd blithely signed away any future interest in Brad's business ventures. The ones I'd supported through dinner parties and networking for almost twenty years. But even if I didn't have his money, I still had my pride, and my dirty laundry was none of her business.

"I came to talk about my clients. I need women like Bianca to hire me."

She rose from her chair. She was shorter than me, but fire ants are small too. "Why do you think I had anything to do with Bianca canceling?" Her pale-blue eyes glinted.

"Of course you did. You've always had it out for me. You and the other first wives." I'd never said it out loud, not to Audrey or any of her cronies. But it had been true since the day I walked into that first party on Brad's arm, so much younger than his friends. Back then, she terrified me. Now, I was old enough not to give a damn about what she thought of me. I only feared what she could do to my business. "You're kicking me when you think I'm down."

I straightened my spine. I'd show her, and all the other first wives, that even without Brad, I was a force to be reckoned with. Someday, Audrey's circle would beg me to style them for their parties. "I'm not down. Far from it. I'm going to show you, and everyone—"

"Mother?" A familiar voice echoed down the hall, sending lightning up my spine.

I couldn't keep the images from my mind. His sexy saunter as he approached me that night in Monterey. His outrageous suggestion that I meet him in his hotel room. The way his face lit up when he opened his door to find me standing there.

His handsome face, slack with pleasure, as he groaned my name.

"In here, Andrew," Audrey called. She raised an eyebrow. Her son could move his eyebrows independently too. "You were saying?"

Shit. I couldn't face him. Not in front of his mother. Not after I'd left him asleep in his hotel room six weeks ago without a word. His heavy footsteps echoed on the hallway tile.

I held up a finger. "Do. Not. Mess. With me, Audrey. I might not have Brad's clout anymore, but I've got plenty of fight left in me."

I whirled and wrenched open the glass-paned door that led out to the garden. Heedless of the damage to my shoes, I scurried down the gravel path and around the side of the house, out of sight of the conservatory windows.

Tessa waited for me in her SUV. When I yanked open the passenger-side door, my middle fingernail snapped, shooting pain up my hand, but I didn't pause as I hopped into the seat. "Floor it!"

Even though we'd been friends for only about six weeks, Tessa trusted me enough to do what I asked. She whipped the BMW into reverse. I missed the roar of a gas-powered engine, but the whisper-quiet electric motor did the job. Seconds later, we flew down the hill, away from Audrey's house and the peril her son represented.

"So, how'd it go?" She flicked her auburn hair over her shoulder and swerved around a corner.

"Not like I planned." I checked the rearview mirror. "You can slow down now. I think we got away."

She decelerated only slightly as we merged onto California Street.

"What about the shock and awe?" she asked.

"Fizzled into turn-tail-and-run. *He* showed up."

"Andrew?"

"Shh!"

She rolled her green eyes. "We're alone in my car. No one can hear us."

"I'm trying to forget it ever happened."

"Carly. He's thirty-something years old—"

"Thirty-two."

"Old enough to make his own decisions. You're consenting adults. There's nothing wrong with it."

"Nothing wrong?" I plucked my blouse from my sweaty chest. Stabbing at the switch, I lowered the window to let cool air blow over me. "His mother can destroy my career. In fact, she may have already started. Do you think she knows? Is that why Bianca canceled on me?"

Tessa shrugged. "Fuck them both. You don't need those bitches to be successful or happy."

"Don't I?" Women like Bianca and Audrey could afford my

services, and I was comfortable styling them after years as their peer. In fact, that gala would be a perfect opportunity to prove it.

"Turn here," I said. "We're making a stop."

She jerked the wheel and flew around the corner onto a side street. "Is it a revenge plot? I'll work out your alibi. I'm an excellent accomplice."

"Not that kind of revenge. Park here."

She parallel parked the car in three moves. "What kind of revenge are we getting at a boutique? Are you going to hide a stiletto in your, um, stilettos?"

"No! It's the kind where I show up to a gala I can't afford." Maybe this wasn't a great idea.

"Ah, and you look like a million bucks and everyone wants to hire you so they can look fabulous too."

"That's the plan." I got out of the car, and she met me in front of the boutique.

"Find me a dress, too, and I'll go with you. And to pay for your styling services, I'll buy your outfit too."

"You don't have to do that," I protested.

"But I want to." Linking her arm with mine, she walked toward the store.

I blinked away the sudden moisture in my eyes. Tessa was worth a hundred Audrey Hayeses. And this afternoon, I wasn't going to worry about my dangerously-close-to-the-limit credit cards or what my frenemy would do if she found out I'd slept with her son.

2

FASHION EMERGENCY

ANDREW

```
From: Andrew Jones
To: Oliver Bond
Sent: October 22, 6:01 am
Subject: Saturday's video
```

Hey. Don't forget, we're filming Saturday at the Arboretum. Subject is Fibonacci sequence. I've got this one. All I need is for you to show up on time (no sorry excuses this time) and hold the camera.
- A

Get in, check on Mother, grab a fern, get out.
Avoid comparisons to my brother.

Steeling myself, I strode into the conservatory. One billionaire executive wasn't enough for my mother. She wanted a matched set, no matter what *I* wanted.

I wouldn't repeat the mistake I'd made at brunch last

Sunday. When I mentioned my job, she'd started in on my lack of career progress and then my checkered dating history. I didn't have the energy for that today, not after an email from the client down in Monterey had reminded me of the night I'd tried—and failed—to erase from my brain.

I held my breath as I passed the sunny corner where Mother grew lilies. They always made me think of my dad's casket covered with the stinking things.

"Mother?"

When I reached the center of the room, a fresher aroma hit my nostrils, sharp and tart like a green apple. It reminded me of a night not long ago when I'd buried my face in silky skin and breathed it in. My fantasies had come true when I'd held a dream of a woman in my arms. In fact, I had feared it had been a dream when I woke up alone, the citrusy perfume that lingered on the pillow the only remaining proof of our night of passion.

I shook it off and approached my mother next to the fountain. I kissed the cheek she offered. The scent wasn't coming from her. Like always, she smelled like Chanel No. 5. Maybe she had a new plant. I scanned the flower-packed room. I'd never find the source.

"What are you doing here?" she asked.

"I texted I was coming over, remember?"

"Oh." Her pale lips turned down. "I forgot. With your brother's news—did I tell you they did a full-page spread on him in *Buzz Bizz?*"

Only about a dozen times at brunch on Sunday. "You did."

"We're so proud." She glanced at the door to the garden.

Eyeing the pink splotches on my mother's cheekbones, I asked, "Are you feeling all right?"

"I'm fine." But when she waved her hand, it trembled.

After Dad died, the conservatory had been my mother's refuge. How many times had I come in here to find her, elbows-deep in dirt, fussing over one of her plants? Too many to count. Sometimes it had been hard to pull her out even when one of the girls needed her. I tried to never need her, but my sisters had been too young to understand that adults grieved too.

As hard as I'd tried back in the dark days, I'd never been strong enough to hold our family together on my own. We couldn't lose Mother too.

I scanned her face for signs of fatigue. "Are you taking your blood-pressure medication?"

"I take it every day. Remember, I'm the mother here."

"Of course, but—"

"Close that door, would you?" Mother pointed at the French doors that led outside.

Maybe she was overheated. I walked to the door and locked it, scenting that new perfume again. "Was someone here?"

"Carly Rose. You'd remember her as Carly Winner, Brad Winner's ex-wife."

I froze, remembering impossibly soft skin. Her rasping cry when she came. "Carly was here? Just now?"

"She left a minute ago. Ran out like there was a sale at Barney's."

I touched the door handle. One push and I could follow her, chase her down and ask why she'd left me alone in that hotel room after she'd promised we'd talk in the morning.

That would be pathetic. Clearly, I'd been only a fling. For her, our night together hadn't been the earth-shattering moment it had been for me. I'd been foolish to hope I was worth staying for.

Besides, talking about it would break her rules. It didn't matter that I couldn't forget her any more than I could forget the derivative function.

I composed my face into a neutral expression and turned

back toward my mother. After clearing the tightness from my throat, I asked, "What was she doing here?"

"Insulting me, can you believe it? Some nonsense about ruining her business." Mother sniffed.

I chuckled, but when she didn't smile, my stomach tightened. "You'd never do that, right?"

"Of course not. We're friends. Of a sort." She dusted off her hands and examined her French-tipped nails.

I narrowed my eyes. They'd always been in the same social circle, but they'd never seemed warm to each other. Carly usually ruled over one end of the party while my mother anchored the other like two oppositely charged poles.

"Hey, Andrew." Natalie's sneaker squeaked on the tile as she wheeled in a rolling cosmetic case, a dress bag looped over her arm. "I need a favor."

"What else is new?" I reached out to tug a lock of my little sister's hair. She dodged my arm.

"I need you to drive me to Bianca Waddingworth's place."

"She literally lives down the street." I glanced at her sneakers. "You can't walk there? I'm only here to pick up something for my video, then I have work to do."

"I wish you wouldn't waste your time making those videos," Mother said, her lip curling the way it did whenever I talked about my YouTube channel.

I unclenched my jaw. "I can make the videos and still get my work done."

"But you'd advance so much more quickly if you weren't always goofing off with Oliver. You should be at least a vice president by now. Then you could champion your causes any way you wanted. Like your brother, for example…"

I turned away to examine a fern to keep her from seeing my flush while she chattered on about my perfect big brother, Jackson, his multibillion-dollar company, and his charitable foundation.

He'd been away at college when it all happened. He hadn't found Dad slumped over his laptop in his office. He hadn't watched Mother and our two little sisters fall apart. He hadn't had to trim his focus to the essentials. He hadn't been dogged by fears of dying too soon and leaving people behind unprotected. So, my brother had carried on our father's legacy of success by founding his own software company.

I didn't begrudge him his success. Much. I could never take the kind of risk he had. It was much better to work for someone else, a company that provided benefits, a company that didn't depend solely on me like we'd all relied on my dad until one day he was gone.

I unballed my fist and ran a fingertip over the fern's frond. When Mother launched into another rhapsody on my brother's company's stock valuation, I said, "This fern displays the Fibonacci sequence here in the frond pattern and these little shoots. Can I borrow it? I'll return it unharmed at brunch on Sunday."

"Not one bruise on it," she said. "It's an elfin tree fern. They're endangered in their native habitat."

"Andrew," Natalie said in a wheedling tone. "That ride?"

"Down the street to the Waddingworths'? Fine."

"We have to stop at Neiman's on the way."

"On the way?" I yelped. "Neiman's isn't on the way."

"I meant we're going there first to pick up her dress. Then to Bianca's. She had a fashion emergency. Mother promised I'd help. Now hurry up. The store closes at six."

I sighed. I wouldn't get started on my work until after seven and on the script for Saturday until, at best, nine. But I'd been wrapped around Natalie's finger since she was born. "Fine. What happened to your car?"

"Oh, you know." She waved a hand. "Foreign cars."

"I drive an Audi," I grumbled.

"Not everyone can be as boring as you, Andrew." Leaving the case where it was, she fluttered over to kiss Mother's cheek. "See you at the party."

Mother stilled her with a touch on her arm. "Who's your date tonight?"

"One of the van der Poel twins."

"Which one?" she asked.

"Not sure. Does it matter?"

"Technically—" Mother began.

"Bye, Mother."

My sister swooped out like a butterfly. I offered Mother my arm and escorted her (and Natalie's case) out of the conservatory.

"Have fun at your party tonight," I said. "Don't forget what the doctor said about mixing wine and your medications."

She waved off my warning. "You could come too. I'm sure Bianca would love to have you. Her daughter Bella is home from college now."

I hummed noncommittally.

"She's always held a torch for you."

"She's, like, twenty-two, Mother. Have you forgotten how old I am? I'm thirty-two."

She waved her hand. "An age difference like that doesn't matter."

"It matters to me. Girls her age don't know what they want. I'm looking for someone more...mature."

She narrowed her blue eyes at me. "You're in your thirties, Andrew. You need to settle down soon. You can't afford to be so picky."

"I'm not picky. I date a lot of women."

"And you always find fault with them. No one's perfect."

For a moment, I'd thought Carly was. Until she'd left me without so much as a note.

"I know. I'm waiting for someone special."

She huffed. "Don't you want what your brother has?"

Not really. I didn't want a whole company to worry about. Or kids.

I wouldn't mind getting some recognition from my family. But that was petty of me. I forced a careless grin onto my face. "Sure. If Alicia's looking to ditch my worthless brother."

"Worthless?" Her right eyebrow shot up. "His company's valued at—"

"Andrew!" Natalie flung open the front door. "Fashion. Emergency. Move it!"

Relieved not to have to hear about my brother's superiority yet again, I pecked Mother on the cheek. "See you Sunday."

"I'll give Bella your regards."

I already had my hand on the door. "No, thanks."

I wasn't ready to date anyone, not even a nice girl like Bella. My heart was still too raw from the tenderization Carly had given it with her stiletto heel.

3

IT'S NOT ME. IT'S YOU.

ANDREW

```
From: Victor Lynch
To: Andrew Jones
Sent: October 25, 2:26 pm
Subject: <none>

Come see me when you have a minute.
Victor Lynch, Chief Financial Officer
```

*B*eing unexpectedly summoned to the CFO's office on a Friday afternoon is never a good sign. As soon as I saw Vic's email, I locked my screen and stood, stretching. I'd been in my closet of an office all day hunched over my keyboard, working on my latest financial model. It was a hairy one, likely to take another week or two of development before the next round of testing.

My office didn't have a window—windows were for vice presidents, not quants—but I glanced across the hall, through the open door of Reva's darkened office, to the view outside.

Clouds covered the sky, and a few halfhearted raindrops hit the window.

Usually, my boss protected me from the executives. I remembered seeing Reva this morning before I went heads-down into my model. Maybe her kid had a volleyball match today, and she'd left early.

Shoving my hands into my pockets, I trudged out my door and down the long hall toward Vic's corner office. The markets in New York had been closed for over an hour, and the office's atmosphere felt easy, relaxed. My coworkers leaned against desks or doorframes, chatting about weekend plans. Mei, the marketing VP, strode toward me, her laptop bag on her shoulder.

"Have a good weekend, Mei," I said.

"You too." She stopped. "I bet you've got some wild plans." She waggled her eyebrows.

I chuckled at her joke. "Not really, unless you consider working on a model wild." I'd never volunteer that I planned to spend Saturday recording a math video for kids and Sunday editing it. Most people at the bank frowned on my hobby.

She chuckled. "Working on a *model*." She walked away.

"No! That's not what—never mind."

At the end of the hall, Vic's door was open, and I leaned on the frame. "Hey, Vic. Is now a good time?"

He looked up from his screen, his forehead a stack of wrinkles all the way up to his bald crown. "Yes, yes, Jones, come in, and shut the door."

Uh-oh. I shoved off the doorframe and plodded across the rug to Vic's desk. I perched on the edge of one of his guest chairs.

"Reva left us this morning," he said without preamble.

I blinked. My boss hadn't said a word to me about leaving. "Left us? Is she okay?"

Vic's bushy eyebrows lowered. "She went to another bank. Security walked her out."

"Oh, shit." I'd missed all the drama with my headphones on. I'd have to call her later.

"Oh, shit is right. Do you have any idea how much time it takes to recruit a VP of finance in San Francisco? We're talking weeks, if not months. I need you to take on some of Reva's responsibilities while we search."

Reva's responsibilities seemed to center on checking on me and the rest of the quants, reporting our progress to Vic, then urging us to speed up our model development because Vic wanted it faster. It sounded like a pain in the ass, but I was the dependable one, the one you could ask to pick up extra work. It had started way back in elementary school when I'd seen my brother do the opposite, always slacking, and I wanted to be the good example, the one who didn't give my mother migraines.

I opened my mouth to say, *sure,* but that wasn't what came out.

"Wait." My mother's disappointed expression flickered through my brain along with her reminder that my veal pen down the hall wasn't an office befitting a Jones, regardless of how much I liked my job. "Are you considering internal candidates for the VP job?"

Vic raised his eyebrows. "We would if we had anyone qualified."

Swallowing, I forced out the words. "What about me?"

"You?" He leaned back in his chair. "But you're a quant."

My jaw tightened. Sure, I often referred to myself as a quant, but I didn't love it when others did. It was dismissive, like calculations were all I was capable of. "Who better to lead the financial engineering department than a financial engineer?"

He narrowed his eyes. "And you're…" He waved his hand in a circle. "Flighty."

I reared back. "Flighty? All I do is work."

"You've got a side hustle. You don't even try to hide it. People can see your face in those videos."

Damn it. Mother had been right again. Still...

"The videos I make on the weekends are my business. They don't affect my work."

"Regardless, the perception is that you aren't one hundred percent invested in the bank. It would help if you..."

I leaned forward. "If I?"

"If you looked more stable. Look at your brother, for example."

"What about him?" I growled through gritted teeth. When we were kids, I'd had to cover for him when he'd accidentally set fire to the neighbors' lawn with his trebuchet experiment and when he'd failed to hide his stash of weed on cleaning day. Now he'd turned the tables on me.

"No one took him seriously until he settled down. He married that consultant. Pretty, and boring as hell. Now he's got a family, and he works hard. Everyone respects him. Last month, he charmed a hundred K out of the board of this bank for his foundation. Genius."

"I can't believe you're telling me I have to get married to advance."

"I'm not telling you that." Vic splayed his hands wide. "But this is a client-facing role. You can't hide in your office all day, then party all night."

"I hardly party all night." Most nights, I fell asleep in front of a televised soccer game. Alone.

He snorted. "Then you're doing bachelorhood wrong. Before I got married, I was out every night until the bars closed. I had my fair share of walks of shame." He gazed into the middle distance for a long moment until he shook himself. "In this role, you'd be meeting with customers as a representative of the bank.

All I'm saying is that you'd be an easier sell to executive leadership if you acted like a banker."

All I did was work and make nerdy videos with my best friend. How could I have time to party even a quarter as hard as my brother had before he met his wife? Or as much as Vic had?

But if Vic did an external search, I'd never get Reva's job. "What if I were seeing someone?"

Vic's expression turned calculating. "Are you?"

"Ye-es." I hated lying, especially at work.

"Someone appropriate?"

"Of course! She's a paragon of stability." If I was going to lie, I might as well go big.

"It's serious?"

I went all in. "Very."

I watched him mentally calculate the savings on an executive search firm, not to mention the time it would take to vet and interview external candidates. "We have a meeting with a client in two weeks. Bring her. If you're still dating her at the bank's New Year's Eve party, we'll talk. In the meantime, I'm assigning you two of Reva's projects."

I gusted out a breath. "Thanks, Vic. You won't regret it, I promise."

"Hmm." His eyes flicked back to his screen. "I'm sending you the details on those projects. Review them by Monday."

"On it, boss." Sensing my dismissal, I stood. Reva had complained nonstop about Vic's demands. No wonder she'd gone to a competitor. Still, it was my best chance at finally meeting the Jones family expectations. "Thanks again."

A grunt was his only response.

∾

On my way out of the building a few hours later, my laptop felt heavier with the details of Reva's projects loaded into it for review over the weekend. I stepped into the elevator thinking about how I had to do the Fibonacci video in one take, two max, if I had any hope of assimilating Reva's projects by Monday morning.

"Hey, Andrew." The soft voice came from the corner of the elevator.

"Winnie! Sorry, I didn't see you." I scanned her face. She'd gotten rid of the braids, and her hair was in one of those voluminous twist-outs now. Maybe that was what made her seem larger and more confident.

She chuckled. "What else is new?"

"Hey, I wasn't that bad of a boyfriend, was I?"

She quirked her full lips. "Not until the end when I failed your test."

"Test?" I remembered a vague sense of disappointment around our breakup, but I'd lost the details.

"Andrew." She put her hands on her hips. "We dated for three months, and you never took me to meet your family. Once I figured out you went to your mother's for brunch every Sunday, I made sure I was free in case you wanted to invite me. It wasn't until I gave up and said I'd go out with friends one Sunday that you asked me. Then you said I wasn't there when you needed me."

"Oh." I cringed. "That sounds terrible. I'm sorry."

"It's okay. It got me into therapy, which was fantastic for me."

Yikes, I'd sent her to therapy?

"Serves me right for dating a player," she said.

"Me? A player?" First Mei and Vic, now Winnie?

"You dated, like, a dozen people in the three months before you asked me out."

"I did?"

She rolled her eyes. "We called you Andrew the Appetizer. Because all you gave anyone was a taste."

"You and I dated for three months. That was more than a taste."

She smiled wryly. "That's why it hurt so much when we broke up. I thought I was the exception."

"I'm sorry. Again." But talking with Winnie had given me an idea. "Hey, would you like to go out for drinks? We can catch up." *And I can ask if you'll pretend to be my girlfriend until I get this promotion.* It wouldn't even be that much of a lie since we'd dated before.

"Oh." She wrinkled her nose. "I don't think so. You see…" She held up her left hand and waggled her fingers. An enormous diamond sparkled on her ring finger.

"You're engaged? Congratulations."

The door opened on the ground floor, and I waved her out ahead of me.

She paused in the lobby. "Can I tell you something, Andrew?"

"Um, I guess?" I rubbed the back of my neck.

"Therapy helped me see our relationship in a new way."

"It did?" My shoulders crept up to my ears. This couldn't be good.

"Yeah. It wasn't me. It was you."

Uh-oh.

"You're a nice guy, Andrew, but you never trusted me enough to let me in. I know how important your family is to you, and it was a huge red flag that I never met them."

I set my hand on my chest, like I could protect my heart from the darts she was throwing at it. Family was the only safe space for me, and I rarely invited others into that sanctum. Especially not someone I'd dated for only three months. "Sorry?"

She rolled her eyes. "It's okay. I'm better now."

I grinned even though it pained me. "Good for you, getting therapy."

"Yeah. Especially since that's how I met my fiancée."

"He was another patient?"

Winnie's eyes sparkled. "*She* was my therapist. She saw the real me and loved me for it. But don't worry, I changed therapists."

"I'm glad you're happy."

She laid a hand on my arm. "I hope you find happiness, too, Andrew."

"Thanks."

I watched her walk away. Who had time for happiness? I had to dig into Reva's projects, catch up on my own work, plus record, edit, and post a video.

Then find someone to pretend to be my girlfriend.

4
SMACKED WITH MY OWN HUBRIS

CARLY

To-do list—November 1
✔ *Pick up dress from cleaners*
✔ *Hair and makeup mood: fierce*
Rub Bianca's and Audrey's noses in it

It's funny how, even if you don't miss a person, you can still miss the concept of them. For example, when I walked into the ballroom at the Merchant's Exchange, I didn't miss Brad at all. I didn't miss his constant searching for networking opportunities, or his tight grip on my elbow as he towed me toward dull strangers, or his too-loud laugh that made me cringe.

But after entering formal events as part of a couple for the past twenty years, I missed having an arm to clutch or at least another target for some of the attention because every eye turned to me as I stood there, alone.

I used to get admiring looks, back when I was young and

confident in my beauty. Now, I felt the whispers of, "Why is she here?" and "The nerve," deep in my bones.

My racing heart took me back to my last pageant, Miss Teen North Texas, when I wore a daffodil-yellow gown of fluffy tulle, and my mother hissed from the wings, "Shoulders back!"

Rolling them back, I stood straight on my towering heels and resisted the urge to check that the draped neckline of my black Dior slip dress had behaved itself and stuck to the fashion tape on my boobs. I propped a hand on my hip and scanned the faces the way I'd run my hand over a rack full of gowns, searching for the right one.

But the wrong one pricked me like a pin left in a seam.

"Carly, what a surprise." Audrey glided up to me wearing an elegant burgundy velvet jumpsuit. "If I'd known you were serious about coming to the gala, I'd have sent you a ticket. I'm sure your finances aren't what they were."

From anyone else, those words would've seemed kind. But Audrey knew exactly how to tweak my pride.

"It's a business expense," I said. "I'm here to network. You can't have dragged my reputation through the mud to everyone here."

Her red lips turned down. "That again. If you'd like to accuse me in front of everyone, I'm sure the emcee would let you borrow his microphone." She whirled on her black patent kitten heels and stalked away.

My jaw clenched when she stopped to talk to Brad and his new fiancée, whose white lace Oscar de la Renta gown was an exclamation point against the clump of black tuxedos.

I panned to the other side of the room and smiled with relief. Unsurprisingly, Tessa had pulled her hermit act again and blown off the event, but my friend Lucie stood next to the buffet table, piling shrimp onto a small plate. Lifting my chin, I strode toward her.

I'd warm up by talking to my friend, then I'd work the event like I planned. I gripped my beaded clutch stuffed with my flashy new business cards, which were die-cut into an hourglass shape to look like a strapless dress.

A waft of fresh, clean air cut through the fog of perfume. An awareness made the back of my neck prickle.

My gaze locked on the back of a man standing nearby. Broad shoulders narrowed to a trim waist. His sharp black tuxedo pants hugged a taut behind. The suit itself was nothing special, a run-of-the-mill Brooks Brothers, but it fit him like a dream.

Oh, no.

I tipped my gaze up to his slightly too-long sandy-blond hair as he turned to face me.

I'd pulled fifteen hundred dollars out of my fuck-you-Brad account to attend this gala, and spiteful irony had thrown this man into my path again. I'd planned to dazzle the crowd with the old Carly magic and convince them I still belonged. More, that they needed me.

Hubris smacked me across the face like a Real Housewife.

Andrew Jones stood not six feet away, all muscular shoulders, chiseled jaw, and bottomless gray-blue eyes. His blond hair? I'd pulled it while he buried his face in my pussy. He had the power to upend my life by telling everyone I'd temporarily lost my sanity after a few glasses of chardonnay.

No styling client would take me seriously if they knew I'd slept with one of their sons.

I'd never meant to do it. Andrew had seemed sweet, someone you could trust to bring in your mail and water your plants while you were on vacation. Not that I'd ever asked him to do that. When I was married to Brad, our housekeeper took care of the plants and brought in the *Wall Street Journal* and *Financial Times.*

I'd never thought of him as anything more than the nicer of

Audrey's two sons until seven weeks ago when I'd spotted him across the bar in Monterey. He was no sweet kid that night. He'd gone and grown up in the ten or so years since I'd given him a purely platonic hug at his college graduation party.

When he'd peeled off his button-down shirt, I'd run a finger across his hard pecs. His voice went deep when he called me his fantasy come true. I'd been sore for two days, unused to a thirty-two-year-old's impressively short refractory period.

I'd lost my mind.

It was the only way to explain how I'd hooked up with Andrew Jones, a man who was thirteen years younger than me *and* the son of my frenemy.

His handsome face split into a broad grin. Those dimples—my kryptonite—dented his cheeks. He'd laughed that night. I'd laughed, too, more than I had in the lonely year before.

In his hotel room, he'd made me feel powerful and adored, like I was the only woman he'd ever cared about. Something reckless inside me wanted to reach out to him, to touch him, to see if my skin still sparked when it met his. I felt my lips curving into a reflection of his smile.

But tonight, exposed here in the ballroom, those gentle hands were dangerous. Those soft lips threatened my plans. My heart hammered, demanding I flee. But my feet stayed firmly planted on the carpet. Maybe they were right. Running away would only draw attention.

Two of his long strides brought him in front of me. "Carly, you look amazing, as always."

I focused on the sharp points of his bow tie. "Andrew, what are you doing here?"

"My mother asked me to come."

Ice coated my belly. Audrey Jones Hayes could *not* see me talking to her son. I glanced to the side, where a heavy curtain created an alcove by the window. But dragging Andrew behind a curtain would look more suspicious than talking to him in the middle of the ballroom.

I stared at the center of his tie, trying not to think about the hollow behind it where I'd dipped my tongue that night. "It's great seeing you again, but—"

"That's what you want? To be strangers? After that night? You left without saying goodbye, without saying anything at all. And I couldn't call you because of the rules—"

"Shh!" I stepped closer and almost put a hand over his mouth. There were people everywhere, people who'd love to pocket the currency of a juicy bit of gossip like that. That's why I'd made rule two: we'd never tell anyone, especially his mother, that we'd slept together. The one he was talking about was rule three: it could only be one night.

"Dance with me." He held out a hand, palm up. "We should talk. No one will hear us on the dance floor."

"No!" I made the mistake of looking into his eyes. They were the color of storm clouds in spring, dark and dangerous. If I danced with him, everyone would notice the indecent heat in his stare.

"Come on. I danced with Bianca Waddingworth. No one will think anything of it. It'll look like we're networking."

My stomach clenched. I'd danced with dozens of Brad's business colleagues over the years. But I hadn't slept with any of them.

"One dance," I said. "And then we go our separate ways." I tore my gaze off his eyes. One dance was like rule three...with our clothes on.

His mouth was a flat line. "Then we talk until we've said what we need to say."

Damn it. I knew I should have left him a note, one that didn't leave room for a future. Or talking. But staring at his gorgeous, unlined face smiling in his sleep, his thick hair crushed into the pillow, the sheet pushed down to his hips, and all that skin on display, skin I'd tasted, I couldn't.

That was my mistake, leaving an open loop when I could have closed it and cut off any chance of an encounter like this. So I smiled up at him, the fake one I used to use on Brad's dull colleagues, and placed my hand on his. "I don't think there's much for us to say."

"We'll see." He swept me toward the dance floor and into his arms.

I kept a stiff distance from him, pressing against his palm and his shoulder to keep our chests as far apart as possible. I braced myself for the denunciation I deserved.

"You look beautiful tonight." The softness of his tone, like warm honey, was not what I expected.

"Thank you." My voice was as hard as my diamond earrings, the ones Brad gave me for our fifth anniversary.

"Of course, you're always beautiful." He leaned forward to whisper in my ear, and his hand tightened on my hip. Only a thin layer of silk—and my spandex shapewear—separated his skin from mine. "Especially when you come."

His words brought back memories of that night. I'd come again and again, each orgasm tipping into the next until he'd climaxed with a shout. And then, instead of rolling over and immediately letting out a rumbling snore like Brad had always done, he'd coaxed one more out of me with his fingers until I'd flopped back to the pillow, exhausted. He'd held me after, just like I wanted. Like I needed. My core clenched with an echo of those remembered orgasms, and I shivered.

I pressed his shoulder until he was a safe distance away. "We can't talk about that here."

"If not here, where? Can I take you for a drive?"

"No. I'm here to network, not to...to..." *Hook up,* my neglected vagina screamed.

"Okay, maybe after you're done networking? We need to talk."

"Why? What do we have to talk about? We agreed to pretend it never happened." My jaw tightened. "It was a mistake."

His expression had been so wide and open that night. We'd both laughed when he told me about the crush he'd had on me when he was a teenager. But now it shuttered. "A mistake?"

"It was reckless. And being together right now is even more so. That's why we made the rules." I glanced at the nearest couple, but they were too far away to hear. "It was only a fling for —for both of us."

It didn't matter that it had been the strongest connection I'd felt in a long time. The dozen years that separated our ages, plus the professional relationship I needed to maintain with his mother and her friends, forbade anything more. I never should have allowed myself even one night, but that terrible seminar had left me vulnerable. He'd smashed through my weakened defenses like the Kool-Aid Man.

"We agreed to reassess in the morning, but you left."

I winced. I'd been a coward. "There's nothing to reassess. Your mother would destroy me." A chill started at my scalp and dripped down the back of my neck. "Wait—is that what happened? Does she know?" I missed a step in the dance.

He steadied me, then shook his head. "What happened?"

"Bianca Waddingworth. I was supposed to style her, but she canceled on me at the last minute. Did Audrey tell her to do that because you told her we...we...we lost our minds?"

"No, I didn't tell her. She—" He winced. "She said you accused her of something she didn't do."

Frost erupted in my stomach. "Does that sound like something I'd do?"

He met my gaze. "No. But sabotage doesn't sound like something she'd do, either."

"Hmm." Audrey was a force. Was there anything she wouldn't do to protect her family?

"Why'd you leave?" he asked softly.

The words bubbled out of me without thought. "I couldn't stay."

"You wanted to?" His blue eyes practically glowed with hope.

I hated to snuff out that light. But I had to. "No. It would never work out. We're too different. Not just the...the age gap." I'd broken rule number one by mentioning our ages, so I rushed on. "Look, my divorce left me with almost nothing. The lifestyle I was used to, my old friends, even my self-respect, they're all gone. I need to rebuild my reputation and a life I can be proud of."

"And that life couldn't include me?"

He gazed into my eyes, and the intensity brought me back to Monterey. We'd talked and shared our secrets until it only seemed natural for my lips to meet his. My heartbeat slowed, remembering how strong and treasured I'd felt in Andrew's bed. He'd made me laugh. He'd made me feel beautiful.

Stupid heart. That was the last time I'd let it be in charge.

I'd come here to act like a professional, to grow my business. None of the women in this ballroom would take me seriously if I were screwing Audrey Jones Hayes's son. She'd make it her personal mission to destroy me.

I took a deep, bracing breath. "No. If the past twenty years have taught me anything, it's that I can only rely on myself."

The music hadn't ended yet, but he stopped moving and jerked his hands off me like I'd burned him. I stumbled to a stop.

"Then I'll leave you to your networking. Sorry to have taken up so much of your time." He spun on his heel and strode away, leaving me alone at the edge of the dance floor.

It was exactly where I wanted to be, according to my brain.

My heart disagreed, beating against my breastbone like it could race after him.

I turned and took a few wobbling steps toward the buffet. The farther I got from the dance floor, the surer my stride became. It was a good thing my brain was in charge.

5

FRENEMYSHIP, OR IS IT FRENMITY?

ANDREW

> Oliver: Hey, the Fibonacci video got 20k views!
>
> Me: Great
>
> Oliver: And we hit 100k subscribers!
>
> Me: Awesome
>
> Oliver: Wait, aren't you excited?
>
> Me: Yeah. Just…yeah
>
> Oliver: Want to talk?
>
> Me: Not right now. Call you tomorrow

First stop after having your heart broken? I recommend the bar.

After turning off my phone, I leaned against the wall, sipping whiskey. A few people approached but veered off when they saw my expression.

Unfortunately, my scowl didn't deter my mother.

"What are you doing over here? And why are you frowning like that? Smile." Mother swiped a speck of lint from my lapel. "You should be mingling. Making connections."

It was exactly the reminder I didn't need that Carly had chosen to make connections over reigniting the chemistry we'd felt in Monterey. The chemistry I still felt whenever I was around her. I'd fully intended to greet her coldly, to keep my feelings contained behind a thick wall until I couldn't feel them anymore, but they'd burst out like a high school football team through the cheerleaders' paper banner. All it had taken was a glance at the curve of her jaw, and I remembered how it felt to kiss her there. That night, I'd felt like anything was possible if Carly Rose cared about me.

But as it turned out, she didn't.

I needed to lock down my emotions the way I'd learned to do after Dad died. Emotions made me weak, and I never wanted to feel weak again.

"I need a minute," I grumbled. "I'm not fit for mingling right now."

"What's wrong?" My mother turned up her blue eyes to me, so much truer than my grayish-blue. I looked past her face to her neckline, which revealed the edge of the pinkish scar from her heart surgery three years ago.

I wouldn't worry her with my petty troubles. It was my job to protect her, to protect them all.

"Nothing. I'm fine."

"Hey." A slender hand snaked around my waist and squeezed my stomach. For one heart-stopping moment, I thought it was Carly, then I noticed the slim white-gold bracelet on her wrist, the one I'd given my little sister on her twenty-first birthday.

"Ugh. Get off." The loss of that momentary hope turned my stomach.

"Aw." Natalie released me. "Someone's grouchy tonight."

"He is, isn't he?" Mother said.

"It's a shame since he's danced with the two best-dressed women in the room."

"He hasn't danced with me." Our mother arched an eyebrow.

Natalie chuckled. "Aside from you, of course. I wish we wore the same shoe size. I'd snag those heels."

While they rhapsodized about designer footwear, I zoned out and sipped my whiskey.

"Who are these women Andrew danced with?" My mother's words caught my attention. "I was talking to one of Charles's colleagues."

"Carly Rose, of course, and Bianca Waddingworth. She looks fantastic, doesn't she? I can say it even though I dressed her." Natalie tossed her long hair.

"You did a beautiful job. I always thought you should have stayed in fashion school."

"Let's not, Mother. Anyway, that color is fabulous on Bianca."

What Carly said about Bianca Waddingworth stuck in my brain. "Mother, you didn't have anything to do with Bianca canceling on Carly, did you?"

"You think I'd do that?"

"No, of course not." I couldn't sync up what I knew about my mother with what Carly had said.

"Maybe Bianca had a reason to do it." Natalie was always the peacemaker of the family.

We turned at a too-loud laugh.

Brad Winner had his head thrown back, his arm around someone who—no joke—was around Natalie's age.

Mother's lip curled. "At least she's free of that millstone. He can be charming, but..."

What had Carly seen in him? Clearly, something she didn't see in me.

"Stop furrowing your brow, Andrew." Mother fluttered her hands at my face like she could smooth away the wrinkles. "It makes you look old."

I flashed her a smile. "Better?"

"Smile with your eyes, darling. That's better." She glanced over my shoulder. "There's the state senator. I need to speak with him about the education bill. Care to join me? I know STEM education is an important cause for you."

It was, but I was in no mood to schmooze tonight. "I'll catch him later."

Casting one more concerned glance at me, she strode purposefully away in her low heels.

"So." My sister turned on me. "What's with you caring about who styles who?"

"Me? I don't care. I heard something and thought I'd ask."

She snorted. "I saw how you two were gazing into each other's eyes while you were dancing. 'Heard something' my butt."

I rolled my eyes. "Fine. She said Mother trashed her stylist work. I wasn't sure what to believe."

"I wonder..." She frowned.

"What?"

"Mother *was* the one who told me Bianca needed help. Though that seems pretty underhanded, even considering their frenemyship. Or is it frenmity?" She wrinkled her nose.

"What are you talking about?"

"They've been frenemies for, like, ever. You know, they act like friends, but they secretly detest one another. So, friends-slash-enemies. Do guys not do that?"

"No?"

"Huh." She shifted her weight. Her pointy-toe heels made

my feet ache in sympathy. "Don't you remember? They always volunteered for the same organizations and were on the same committees. They played nice in public except for the occasional snipe. You have to remember the Vulgar Bikini Boat Party."

"The what?" How did she know all of this?

"Mother never stops talking about it." Nat tapped her finger on her lips. "Or maybe it's the whole first-wife versus second-wife thing. Carly was always trying to fit in with the first wives. She was a little younger than Mother—"

"Seventeen years younger."

She raised her eyebrows.

"Or so." I took a sip from my nearly empty glass to keep my mouth from betraying me again. "What was the deal with the boat party?"

Natalie leaned closer. "It was Carly's first big party, right after she married Brad Winner. No one must've told her how things worked because she scheduled it on Labor Day weekend. That was when Mother and Dad used to host a huge house party. Remember?"

"Right, Dad made a big joke of wearing that barbecue apron even though Mother had it catered."

"Yeah." A sad smile flitted over my sister's face. "Whatever happened to that apron?"

"Probably donated with all his other stuff. Anyway, this party caused a twenty-year feud because she stole Mother's weekend?"

"That wasn't the worst of it. Instead of a regular party at, you know, someone's house or a hotel or the arboretum, Carly hosted it on their yacht."

"*That* party?" It had been my pubescent awakening.

"Remember what she wore?"

"A white bikini." I'd said it too fast, and she smirked at me.

"Right. Everyone else showed up in garden party attire, and

she had the audacity to offer them swimwear. You can guess who took her up on it."

"Not me." I'd spent most of the party trying to hide my hard-on by sitting at a table with the van der Poel twins.

"Aw. You've always been such a loyal little Jones. But a lot of the husbands did, including Dad."

"He didn't—"

"No. I mean, I was too little to notice things like that, but I don't think he flirted with her. She had a little suit and life jacket for me, so, of course, I went in the water, and I remember Dad swimming with me.

"But I think what pissed Mother off was that Carly swooped in and did something outrageous. And then it got worse because every party the following spring was on a boat or at the marina. Plus, everyone begged her to repeat her yacht party the next summer. Carly hit a home run on her first at-bat. Mother both admired and hated her for it."

"For twenty years?"

"She has a long memory. So, be aware, you know? In case you, um...start something...with Carly."

"Don't be such a mom. I don't need you looking out for me. I'm the big brother here." I glugged my whiskey too fast, and it singed my throat. As much as I loved my baby sister, I wasn't ready to share what I thought I'd felt with Carly, or the pain of her abandonment.

If Carly was Mother's enemy, it was for the best. My loyalty had to be to my family, especially my mother. She held our family together. Though she wasn't one of those mothers who said it out loud, I felt her love at the dining table every Sunday. Every time I walked into a crowded ballroom and saw one of my siblings, that feeling of security locked into place. We Joneses had each other's backs.

I thought I'd found that same security outside our family

when I met up with Carly. We connected in a way I'd never connected with anyone else.

Until she'd slipped out of my bed in the dark and ghosted me.

Natalie punched my arm, not hard, but the way I'd taught her with the flat part of her fingers, her thumb on the outside. "Come mingle with me. We'll make sure Mother sees us."

I couldn't face the idea of speaking to another person, not after Carly had shot me down again, this time to my face.

"I'm gonna jet. Give my apologies to Mother?"

"You're not going home to sulk, are you?"

So what if I was? I was in no condition to impress anyone, not even for the benefit of the Jones family. My insides felt too raw and exposed. "Bye."

"Andrew—"

I turned and left the ballroom. I needed time to rebuild the wall I'd let Carly Rose demolish.

6

A WASTE OF A PERFECTLY GOOD HOOKUP

CARLY

I stared at my pale face in the ladies' room mirror. My eyes were wild, and the neckline of my Dior gown fluttered with the throbbing of my heart. Sweat glistened at my temples. I couldn't go back out there looking like this. No one wanted to hire a stylist who didn't have her shit together.

Closing my eyes, I tried to breathe from my belly, but my shapewear constricted my inhale. Was it worth it to fight my way out of the spandex in one of the stalls? What I wouldn't give for a full breath, a bar of chocolate, and a few minutes to chill out. To-do list be damned.

"Oh, hey!" A chipper voice startled my eyes open.

Shit. It was Brad's fiancée, looking gorgeous and glowy in this season's Oscar de la Renta and a giant Asscher cut solitaire ring perched on her finger. *Goddamn Brad.*

I rubbed a hand over my compacted belly and squared my shoulders. "Hi. You probably remember me from…from that day at the house. I'm Carly." I stuck my hand out to her.

I'd forgotten her name in the fog of shock that had settled

over me the day she'd shown up at my door. I'd been dressed for my hot yoga class, hair piled on the top of my head, no makeup. I was just slipping on my sunglasses when I'd opened the door to find a willowy, young woman standing on my doorstep, finger hovering over the bell.

We stared at each other for an eternity before she blushed and introduced herself. I shook her hand like an idiot. And then she asked if I was going to take the crystal with me in the divorce. When I remained in stunned silence, she asked if she could see it so she could decide if she'd want something similar.

Now she shook my hand again. "Hayley, but I'm sure you remember. Sorry about that. Again. I had no idea... You know how Brad is."

I chuckled because it seemed she expected it. I hadn't known Brad as well as I thought I did. I'd believed he still cared about me. Maybe we weren't in love anymore, and we'd been going through a rough patch—we'd weathered them before—but we'd be fine. I was shocked as hell that not only did he not love me, but he'd proposed to someone else without telling me he wanted a divorce.

"You look absolutely stunning," she said. "I hope when I'm your age, I'll look half as good."

Was that supposed to be a compliment?

"God, sorry, that didn't come out right. You're just so...so awe-inspiring, and I feel totally awkward around you. I would love it if we could be friends."

"Friends?" I blinked. The soon-to-be third Mrs. Brad Winner wanted to be friends with the second one? How would that work?

"We have a lot in common."

"Brad's dick, for one thing," I said.

"Well, yeah, but also, we both love fashion. Your gown is to die for." She reached out a hand like she'd touch the silk but then snatched it back. "I have to admit, I stalked you on Instagram when I found out you and Brad were still living together. Your look is fire. My friends would love it."

I'd done my share of internet stalking too. Hayley was a model, not as successful as I'd been at the height of my career, but she'd done a spread in *Elle* last year.

"Thank you. Your de la Renta is...also fire." I sounded like Steve Buscemi saying, "How do you do, fellow kids?" in that *30 Rock* episode I'd watched back when network TV was still a thing.

"Thanks." She smoothed the fabric over her belly in a movement that mirrored my own. What did she have to worry about at her age? I could bounce a quarter off her abs.

She glanced away toward the stalls and grimaced. "Sorry, you probably think I'm a creeper for following you into the ladies' room. I'm usually a little more chill than this. It's just"—she gestured back toward the door—"it's a lot, you know? Meeting all of Brad's smart, important friends. I don't know how you did it."

I remembered those early days. First wives like Audrey displayed an effortless elegance that had cowed me. At my first event, I'd thrown up in the restroom from an excess of nerves and champagne. Over the years, I'd learned the amount of hard work and determination required to establish and defend my place in the clique. "You get used to it."

"Do you?" She scrunched her nose. "I guess that's why you're here."

I chuckled. "Not really. I'm here to network. Not because—" But I couldn't tell her none of those women had stood by me in the divorce. I wouldn't be the one to crush her hopes of making friends in Brad's circle.

"These women aren't your target market. Your look is classic yet avant-garde. These women wouldn't know a new trend if it whacked them on the forehead...because of the Botox, you know?" She snickered.

I couldn't help touching the spot between my eyebrows where I had a line my makeup couldn't disguise.

"You should style people whose fashion inspiration isn't *Desperate Housewives.* My friends would love your style."

I shook my head. I had nothing in common with people Hayley's age. They wouldn't be interested in me or my work.

She smiled, tentative. "Think about it. And I really hope we can be friends. I'll text you, okay?"

"O-okay."

She was gone in a whirl of white lace.

I rechecked myself in the mirror. I'd never worn a Juicy Couture tracksuit, but maybe Teri Hatcher had worn something like this Dior back in the day. Hayley was wrong. These women were my only hope for a successful styling business. Only women as run-down and obsolete as I was would hire me. Which meant I needed to make the most of this fifteen-hundred-dollar networking opportunity.

As I stepped out of the restroom, Lucie grabbed my elbow. "There you are. You look like you could use a drink."

I relaxed my shoulders. I could spend a few minutes with my friend before I had to sell myself. Call it a warm-up. "Sounds great. How's the research going?"

"Total dud. No one wants to talk to a journalist. Or be seen talking to one. I've given out a few business cards, and I'll follow up on Monday."

"What are you asking them about?"

"My editor wants a piece on charitable contributions among the tech elite. With the way tonight's going, he won't cover the fee for a fancy-dress party again. So we need to take advantage of the open bar." She towed me toward the nearest bar but then changed course toward one with a shorter line.

"So...what were you doing hiding out in the bathroom with your ex's fiancée?"

"How did you know who she was?"

She rolled her eyes. "I'm a journalist. Research is my specialty. Hint: reverse image search is the best invention ever. Her Insta is incredible. Did you know she's friends with Helen Choi?"

"The actress? Wasn't she in that Netflix rom-com everyone was talking about last summer?"

"That's her. Anyway, why were you in the restroom when you could've been dancing with Andrew?"

"Shh!" I'd become friends with Lucie, Tessa, and Savannah the same night Andrew and I hooked up. They'd watched us flirt and nudged me—more like shoved me—to meet him in his room. The next day, our brand-new group chat had ignited with their questions, and I'd shared all the sordid details from our night of passion to my stealthy escape the next morning.

"What?" Lucie lowered her voice only slightly. "You can't throw a rock in this ballroom without hitting an Andrew or two. It's a stuffy name for a stuffy crowd."

"Please," I begged, glancing around. The shorter man in line behind us leered. I turned back around in time to step up to the bar and order a vodka tonic.

While the bartender poured our drinks, I muttered in Lucie's ear, "I'll tell you all about it privately."

"Fine."

After we took our drinks to a table on the fringes of the party, Lucie said, "So what happened with Loverboy? Are you two back together?"

"We were never *together* except in the euphemistic sense. And only one time."

"One time? That's not what you said before."

"One night," I said through gritted teeth.

"Total waste. We're living vicariously through you. Once you hit forty, it's game over. Or so I hear." She smirked. Lucie was the youngest of the four of us at thirty-nine. "I need details. You danced with him."

"I was afraid he was going to do something rash. He wanted to know why I left without talking to him."

"Don't we all," she muttered. "Are you meeting up with him later?"

"No." I thunked my drink on the table. "Why would I do that?"

She tapped a black-painted nail against her lips in a fake thinking gesture. "For the hot sex, obviously."

Heat erupted across my chest and raced up to my face. I almost wished I hadn't told her about it. But you couldn't keep that kind of stuff from your friends.

"We are not getting together."

Lucie shook her head. "Such a waste of a perfectly good hookup."

"You understand he could destroy me, right? One word from his mother, and no one—*no one*—will hire me. If I go without work much longer, I'll have to apply at Bloomingdale's."

"Working retail is the worst, especially at the holiday season. But how do you know? Have you talked to her? Has he?"

"We can't talk to her. Then she'll know. Cue the disaster scenario and spritzing perfume on strangers."

"Brad certainly doesn't give a fuck what anyone thinks. An age gap doesn't seem to bother *him*." She tipped her chin toward Brad slow dancing with Hayley in the center of the dance floor.

I remembered that move, dancing to a different beat from everyone else. It had made me feel like I was the sexy center of his universe.

It was a lie.

"Women in my line of work don't have that luxury. We

always have to care what everyone else thinks. Because other people can destroy us."

Lucie put her hand over mine. "Are you sure? It seems to me you've always played it safe. Brad was a safe choice. Your life as arm candy was safe. Now, if you'd risk it, you could find genuine happiness with Loverboy. The expression on his face while you were dancing was—" She shivered. "If you go for that sort of thing."

"That's exactly what I *don't* need. Twenty years ago, I fell for Brad's promise of love and security. I fooled myself into thinking Brad's success was mine too. Now, I'm focusing on my business and success on my own terms. It's my second chance."

She twisted her lips. "I was talking about being happy."

"When I have a schedule full of clients to style, when my phone doesn't stop ringing, I can call myself a success. Then I'll be happy."

She narrowed her eyes. "Will you? Will you really?"

I snorted. "Of course."

When I could stand in an event like tonight with my shoulders thrown back in real confidence, no more fake-it-till-you-make-it bullshit, then I'd be happy. Definitely.

But later that night, as I lay awake in bed, alone in my apartment, not even the familiar visualization of a phone that constantly rang with calls from clients could lull me to sleep. I tried to picture myself stepping into that gala tonight with the confidence of a full contact list. Everyone's heads would turn as they whispered about me, not whispers about my divorce, but whispers of admiration.

Did you hear she styled Helen Choi?
Did you see when that actress thanked her on the red carpet?
How can I get her to style me?

I stared up at the ceiling. It was a good vision. One that would make me happy. But like sleep, it was out of my reach.

7
GO FORTH AND CALCULATE

ANDREW

```
From: Victor Lynch
To: Andrew Jones
Sent: November 1, 9:26 pm
Subject: Client dinner

Good job today on the briefing. Looking
forward to seeing your work on the project.
The client dinner is Monday the 11th, 8 pm at
La Colombe Bleue. Don't be late, and don't
forget your date.
- Vic
Victor Lynch, Chief Financial Officer
```

"Maybe you should be on camera for this one." When I said it, my stomach clenched.

"What?" Oliver looked up from adjusting the tripod. We stood on the corner of Washington and Columbus. People mostly ignored us as they bustled past on Saturday at midday. "Why?"

"Because..." *Because my boss thinks these videos are unbecoming of a bank vice president.* But I couldn't force those words out. "Because you never take a turn on camera."

His right cheek crept up into a slow smirk. "I'm the brains of this operation. You're the pretty face. Besides, I never paid attention in trig."

"Trigonometry is easy. I'll write you a script."

He squinted up at the top of the Transamerica Pyramid, then at its shadow creeping toward our feet. "We'd lose the shadow before you were done."

"You *do* know trig! You know exactly how this works."

"You know this shit like the back of your hand. It's your passion. Why don't you want to do the video?"

I sighed and picked up the meter stick. "My boss."

"But Reva loves our videos. At that last foundation event, she told me she watches them with her daughters."

"She quit." I still got a sick feeling when I thought about it. Work wasn't the same without her. "Now I report to Vic, the CFO. Temporarily. Until they can hire a replacement."

"Who do you think—oh. Oh! *You* want the job?" He rubbed his chin. "You don't want that job."

"Coming from a CEO, that's pretty rich."

"You know I never wanted the position." He screwed his phone into the tripod with more force than necessary.

"Shit, I'm sorry." I'd been too caught up in my feels to protect him from the memory of losing his business partner last year. Oliver had loved his Chief Technology Officer role at their startup, but now he held the entire company on his shoulders.

"'S okay." He shrugged. "Our operations chief does all the work."

"That's not true, and you know it." I put a hand on his shoulder. "You're doing good work. Simon would be proud."

"You think so?" When he lifted his face, it was twisted in pain. "I'm terrified of fucking up what he built."

I squeezed his shoulder. "What you two built *together*. The company wouldn't have amounted to much without your ideas."

The tension melted from his shoulders. "Thanks, man. Not just for that but for everything else."

I knew what he meant. He'd come from an upper middle class family, and he'd been able to handle the venture capital funding, but when the money from their IPO rolled in like the waves at Ocean Beach, he'd been overwhelmed. After meeting him at a bank party, I'd straightened out his finances and set him up with the right balance of investments to keep him comfortable while also easing his conscience with charitable contributions.

"Thanks for helping me with my nerdy hobby," I said. "You've got to be the highest net-worth cameraman in California."

He squinted at the top of the building. "As your cameraman, I advise you to get off your ass and start rolling. You're losing that shadow."

I looked down. It had reached my feet. "Shit. Let me reposition." I shuffled back on the sidewalk until the shadow covered the bottom of the meter stick but not the top.

"I've got you in frame," Oliver said. "Ready?"

"Yeah."

While he counted down, I shoved all thoughts of my job out of my brain and remembered the drawing one of our young viewers had emailed us. She'd sketched squares in the Fibonacci pattern I'd shown in the video along with the spiraling curve through them, and she'd colored the shapes in pastel shades.

Fuck Vic. I was doing this for her.

"Welcome, math nerds! Today, we're talking trigonometry. What's trigonometry?" I screwed up my face in a fake confused expression. "It's the math of triangles." I paused for the cut where I'd explain the concepts of angles and ratios.

"And now I'm going to show you how we use trigonometry in real life. We're going to find out how tall this building is." I pointed at the Transamerica Tower. Oliver would splice in a shot of it later. "How would you measure a building that tall? There's no tape measure long enough. And don't say you'll look it up on the internet because we can measure the height of that building using this measuring stick, a laser measure, and trigonometry."

I demonstrated how to measure the height of the shadow on the stick, the length from the bottom of the stick to the tip of the building's shadow, and the distance to the bottom of the building.

We cut there. Later, I'd insert an explanation of similar triangles and the rest of the math, including the diagram I'd made. I'd have to do that as soon as I got home. Tomorrow, after brunch with my family, was for catching up on my extra work projects. But I wasn't going to think about all that. I had to keep my energy up for the kids.

I reset so the Pyramid was behind me for the end of the video. "And that's trigonometry, math nerds. Go forth and calculate!"

After he stopped the video, Oliver said, "See? You didn't want me to do that."

"You could've done it. You've got the right level of nerdiness." I dropped the laser measure into my backpack.

"I may be a nerd, but you're the one who geeks out about math. You're passionate about it. And the kids who watch. It's like you're talking directly to them. You love this shit."

Maybe that was why my stomach twisted at the thought of anyone else, even Oliver, speaking to our subscribers.

"I guess I do."

"And they love you. Our viewership is up enough that our check this month could pay both our rents."

"Fortunately, our day jobs pay our rent. That's why all the income from the channel goes to literacy," I said.

"Well, the literacy foundation is going to be thrilled this month, which is why you're going to tell Vic to shove it up his ass if he tells you to stop."

Could I do that? "But I need this promotion."

He snorted. "You could live off your trust fund for the rest of your life."

"No, I couldn't. I mean, technically, I could. But that wouldn't be living up to Jones family expectations. I'm already the black sheep since I don't have my own company like my brother and sister."

"What about Natalie? She's unemployed."

"She's the baby. And she's in school. If she gets her shit together before I do, they'll probably make me change my name to Smith."

He rolled his eyes. "Fuck your family if they can't accept you as you are."

"Hey." My scalp bristled. "Only I can talk shit about my family."

He held up his hands, palms out. "Okay, so what do you have to do to get this promotion?"

I checked that we had all our gear, then trudged down the street toward where my car was parked. "I've got to wow him with the two projects I picked up from Reva. Then I'm supposed to show up at a client dinner"—I winced—"with a date."

"I'll go with you," he said, bumping my shoulder. "As your platonic, bisexual date."

"Wow, um, thanks. I'll keep that in mind."

"Ah, you think Vic would prefer a date of the more traditional variety?"

I stared down the long row of parked cars. "I kind of told him I'm seeing someone. Seriously. I made her a female someone."

He snorted. "Mr. Love-em-and-leave-em is in a serious relationship?"

"It's not like that. I date people."

"You break up with them before they can break up with you. Classic Andrew Jones."

I remembered what Winnie had said. "Maybe you're right. When did you get to be so smart?"

"A year of therapy has given me perspective. But what are you going to do about this date?"

"I don't know. I only have a week to figure it out."

"You could hire an escort. That works in the rom-coms."

"Like a *Pretty Woman* thing?"

"I was thinking *The Wedding Date*. Who do you think is more fuckable, early 2000s Debra Messing or Dermot Mulroney?"

"Debra Messing," we said at the same time.

"Have you seen her recent photos?" I asked. "Still gorgeous."

"I do love a redhead." He bit his lip. "Maybe you should email her and ask her out."

"I've got to find someone I could realistically be in a serious relationship with."

"Guess you'll have to ask everyone you meet. Excuse me," he said to a pair of twenty-something girls paying at the parking meter. "Would one of you pretend-date my friend here?"

"Sorry about my friend," I said, gripping his arm and dragging him away. "I'm not that desperate."

He smirked. "Aren't you?"

"Not yet."

8

GETTING OLD ISN'T FOR THE WEAK

CARLY

To-do list—November 4
✓ Update website with discount offer (don't make it look too desperate)
✓ Pick up wine and charcuterie for girls' night
Do not be tempted to restyle my friends, who are beautiful as they are despite Savannah's tragic dye job

A real grin stretched my cheeks as I took in my three best friends lounging on my living room furniture. Although we were still getting to know each other, these women made me laugh every time we got together. I hadn't had friends like them in years, maybe ever.

The women in Brad's sphere had come to my parties, but they weren't my friends. Brad had gotten them in the divorce, just like my Peloton and the Jonathan Adler sofa.

Before my marriage to Brad, I'd had some fun times with my

modeling and pageant colleagues, but it was nothing like this. For one, those girls didn't stuff their faces with cheese.

"Oh. My. God," Lucie moaned. "This is fantastic. What is it?"

"Sarró de Cabra," I said, rolling my Rs. "I had it in Barcelona once, and I've finally found a cheesemonger who'll get it for me." I cut a small hunk and lifted it to my lips. It carried me back to Mediterranean sunshine on my shoulders, cobblestones beneath my feet, and the scent of spices in the open-air market. The cheese wasn't cheap, but my friends were worth the splurge.

"Try some, Savannah." Lucie held out a slice of baguette slathered with soft nevat.

"I shouldn't." Savannah sat on her hands. "I need to lose fif—twenty pounds."

Lucie appraised her frankly, scanning from her round face to her curvy calves. "You do not. You're gorgeous. Isn't she, Carly?"

"Gorgeous," I echoed.

"And Carly should know. She's our style expert," Lucie said. "Right, Tessa?"

Tessa repositioned her glasses into her wavy red hair before she grabbed a slice of jamón serrano. I noticed she avoided the dairy end of the charcuterie board. "Eat the cheese," she said.

Savannah took the bread and cheese from Lucie. She bit into it tentatively, then her eyes rolled back. "Heaven." She finished the snack in two more bites.

"Who told you to lose weight?" Lucie asked.

"No one. Me." Her cheeks flamed, and Savannah stared down at her leggings. "Jason did. On Halloween, he caught me eating a mini Hershey bar and asked me if I was going to hand out candy or eat it all."

I ground my molars. Brad had given me the same type of passive-aggressive criticism when we'd been married. But it wasn't my place to judge her marriage.

Lucie, apparently, didn't feel the same way. "What a douche! How long have you been married?"

"Thirty years."

"Shit, girl." Lucie tossed her curtain of mahogany hair. "How long has he been negging you?"

"Negging me? He's not negging... Oh. I guess he is. A little."

Lucie shook her head. "Tessa, what do you think?"

"One hundred percent negging. But I don't think Savannah wants us to criticize her marriage tonight."

"It's okay," Savannah said. "I know the seminar was garbage, but talking with you all has made me question things."

"Really?" I leaned forward. "What things?"

She was right about the seminar in Monterey being garbage. When the speaker told us we needed to treat our men like gods so they'd worship us as goddesses, we had walked out and complained about it in the bar afterward. We'd bonded. We even had a name for ourselves: the Goddess Gang.

These women had encouraged me to say yes to Andrew Jones's bold proposal, and still, only they knew my secret.

Savannah reached for a handful of smoked almonds. "My marriage, for one. My career, for another. I stopped working when my oldest was born, but my kids are grown. My blog is fun, but now that I'm an empty-nester, I think I need to, y'know, talk to people. Maybe I should go back to work as an administrative assistant. I used to be good at making copies, setting up conference rooms, answering phones..."

"Yeah. No one does that anymore," Tessa said. "But if you added a video component to your cooking blog, you could monetize it."

"Wait. What do you know about my blog?"

"I looked you up after Monterey. It's good. And it'd be even better if you added video. You could put it on YouTube and ClickClackGo."

Savannah snorted. "ClickClackGo is for my kids, not me. And the ads earn me a little, but it's barely enough to cover the costs of ingredients."

"You'd be surprised," Tessa said. "I could help you draw up a business plan. And I—I could find someone to give you seed money for the equipment."

Savannah waved her hand at her white leggings and pale-blue tunic that matched her eyes. "No one wants to see this. They want to watch young, hot chefs like Padma Lakshmi and Kelsey Barnard Clark. Not people like me."

"You're funny and engaging and kind. I'd watch you," I said, "even though I don't cook."

Savannah ducked her head. "No, I don't think so. Not like... not like this." She smoothed a hand over her generous hip. "I'm not beautiful and stylish like you."

"Beautiful?" I snorted. "My husband traded me for a newer model. Stylish is easy. All you need is a little update."

"Your ex is an idiot. But could you give me an update?" Savannah's eyes went round. "I thought I'd need a complete overhaul."

My fingertips tingled with possibility. Savannah might be a caterpillar with her helmet hair and cocoon-like outfits, but a few changes and an infusion of confidence would turn her into a curvy, blue-eyed butterfly.

"Are you sure you want my advice?" I asked. "Not everyone wants a critique of their look." We hadn't been friends that long, and I couldn't afford to screw up my new friendships.

She jutted out her chin. "People pay you to tell them what to change. I can take it. Like those people on *Queer Eye*."

"You go, girl." Lucie lifted her glass of wine. "You got this."

I narrowed my eyes at Savannah. "How long has your hair been that color?"

"All my life. When my grays started coming in, I started

dying it. But I'm naturally blond." She clutched at the ends of her long bob. "Why?"

Because you look like you're wearing a Green Bay Packers helmet. "The single color looks a little flat. I think some highlights would frame your face better. Or you could see what the gray looks like. Gray is trendy now."

"Gray?" Her blue eyes widened like I'd told her to shave her head. "But I'll look old."

I winced. Maybe I should've started with her clothes. "Okay, then try the highlights. You might like them."

"Gray." She wrinkled her nose. "I'll think about the highlights."

Tessa topped off Savannah's wine, then settled deeper into the cushion. "Do me next."

"Wait, you want feedback on your style too?" Could our friendship survive this?

"Give it to me," she insisted. "You're a pro."

"Fine," I said. "You're easy. Do you own any clothes that aren't black?"

"Nope. Black is the best. I could spill this entire glass of wine on myself and no one would be the wiser."

"Please don't," I said. Her black sweater and black jeans might be able to take it, but my wheat-colored sofa couldn't. "With your red hair, you'd look gorgeous in emerald green."

She curled her lip. "I'd look like a fucking leprechaun."

I shook my head. "You could try a cobalt or a deep purple. Those colors would warm up your skin."

"I thought you were going to tell me to wear makeup or some shit, not threaten my emo existence. You'll take my black pants off my cold, dead body."

"Your skin is beautiful, and you don't need makeup if you don't want it," I said.

"Especially with your eyes," Savannah said. "They're the coolest. Like jade."

"Thank you," Tessa said, fiddling with her glasses.

"Okay, my turn," Lucie said. "You going to tell me to stop wearing black?"

I bit my lip. I was oh for two so far, and I didn't think this would go any better. "No, your black is fine. Between your skin tone and dark hair, it works. I'd suggest you update your makeup, though."

"My makeup?" She widened her eyes. "It looks like everyone's."

"It looks like everyone's did in the nineties. Today, people tend to go with a fuller brow and softer eye."

Tessa nodded. "It's true. I wore makeup like that in the nineties. You look like my yearbook picture."

"Huh." Lucie lifted her phone and looked at her image in the camera. "A softer eye. And *more* eyebrows?"

"You could pencil them in while your natural brows grow in." *If* they'd grow in after decades of overplucking. "I could do your makeup for you someday."

"Could you do my makeup like yours at that gala? When Loverboy couldn't keep his eyes off you?"

"Loverboy." I let out my breath. Our friendship had survived my style advice. "Are you sure you're thirty-nine and not eighty-nine?"

"Deflect much? He looked at her like Ben Affleck looks at JLo," she informed Tessa and Savannah.

"He did?" Tessa asked. "Why the fuck didn't you stay and talk to him that day I drove you to his mother's place?"

"What?" Lucie and Savannah said at the same time.

"She ran out the back door like a bank robber. Made me her getaway driver. All because *he* was there."

My cheeks burned. "I couldn't face him."

Lucie's eyes looked preternaturally wide with her heavy eyeliner. "You totally should have stayed and tested rule number three."

"Which one was rule number three?" Savannah asked. "The one where they don't talk about the age difference?"

"No, that was rule number one," Tessa said. "Three was only for one night. I think Lucie means rule two, not telling anyone."

"*Especially* his mother," I said. "I didn't trust us not to give it away. You saw what happened at the gala when we danced. I was not okay."

"You think his mother would have an issue if you dated?" Tessa asked.

My laugh bordered on hysterical. "An issue? I'm a dozen years older than him. Of course she'd have an issue. I'm her peer. Or her rival. She made my client cancel. I'm sure of it."

"Why does his mother have it in for you?" Savannah asked. "I thought you were friends."

"Sort of," I said. "We used to be on charity committees together. But she was friends with Brad's first wife. Plus, I can be a little competitive." My mom had taught me when I was six that as nice as most of the other pageant girls were, they were my adversaries. Winning had always been the priority over making friends.

Even more important than winning? The appearance of it. Win or lose, I carried myself like I wore the tiara. In my twenties, that perspective was still stuck in the back of my mind.

The first time I met her, Audrey Jones had wowed me with her elegance and confidence. The party had been at her home, and she'd taken my arm and introduced me around. I'd been so naïve to have thought she liked me or that things could be different with friends outside the pageant and modeling world.

It wasn't until after I'd married Brad six months later and thrown my own party that I'd learned how she really felt about me. She took one look at what I'd thought was a unique event on Brad's yacht and muttered, "How vulgar." I'd fallen back on Mom's advice about not making friends, and my competitive nature wouldn't allow me to take the insult lying down.

"There was a bit of a rivalry," I said. "We were always trying to one-up each other with our parties."

In those days, backed by Brad's money and power, I'd been brave enough to stand up to Audrey, to let disdain curl into my voice as I cut her down with artfully veiled criticisms and threats. Perhaps if I'd been softer, friendlier, she and her cronies wouldn't have ditched me when Brad did. Now I needed them to keep my business afloat. The last thing I could afford was a full-blown war with Audrey Jones Hayes.

"But wouldn't she try to like you if she knew you and Andrew were together?" Savannah asked, her blue eyes round and trusting. "I'm always nice to my sons' girlfriends."

"If Audrey Jones Hayes finds out I slept with her son, a canceled styling appointment will be the least of my worries. She'll ruin me. Regardless, we are absolutely not together."

"That's too bad," Savannah said. "You two had outrageous chemistry. Are you sure you couldn't work it out with him?"

"No." He was young and good-looking. Women had to be knocking down his door to date him. He'd forget me soon enough.

Fucking Brad had.

"I'm not looking for a man," I said. "I've been there, done that. I have the scars to prove it. I'm laser-focused on my business right now. This is my second chance. My ex always talked about his work as his legacy. And I supported him and his business for years. Now I'm going to build my own legacy. I'll show him. I'll show everyone."

"What does success mean to you, Carly?" Lucie had pulled a

notebook and pencil from her pocket. Her pencil hovered over the page.

"I guess..." I drew on the image that comforted me when I woke up in the middle of the night. "My phone ringing all the time with calls from clients."

"What are you writing, Lucie?" Tessa asked.

Lucie mumbled something about inspiration.

Savannah patted my knee. "I'm sorry about Andrew. He seemed like a nice guy, like he'd make you happy."

My face heated. He'd made me happy, all right (more than once that night). I couldn't afford that kind of temptation.

"What's that?" Lucie looked at my front door, where an envelope had just slid under.

"Must be my upstairs neighbor," I said. "They're always mixing up our mail."

Lucie scurried over to pick it up. She held the corner between her finger and thumb like it was covered in toxins. "Are they serious?"

"What?" Sweat broke out along my hairline. Was it a collections notice? I wasn't *that* late with my credit card payment. I was running out of designer handbags to sell.

"Looks like an invitation." She held the thick envelope out to me. "To your ex's wedding."

I took it from her. The heartbreakingly familiar return address on the back flap, the script made out to Ms. Carly Rose and Guest, and the thick ivory paper all told me Lucie had guessed right.

I took a sip of wine, then slipped a finger under the flap and pulled out the contents one by one. The wedding was on Christmas Day in Barcelona. Barcelona? Had he chosen it on purpose to hurt me? I flipped through the papers until I found a slip of thinner, light-blue paper with a handwritten note:

I really hope you can make it, friend!!! XOXO Hayley

She'd signed her name with a looping Y with a heart sketched on the end of the tail.

Ugh. I swallowed the last of my wine then held out my glass. Tessa refilled it.

"So," Lucie said, "will you go?"

I set down the wine to keep from chugging it. Go? To sit and watch Brad erase my happy memories of Barcelona and replace them with something painful? To be stared at and judged for having nothing to show for the past twenty years of my life?

"No, thank you." I stuffed a piece of cheese into my mouth and didn't even taste it.

Tessa narrowed her eyes. "I think you should."

I held my hand over my mouth to keep the cheese in. "What?"

Lucie said, "Nope. That shitstain doesn't merit a transatlantic flight."

Savannah frowned. "I don't know. Maybe you need it for closure."

"Closure?" Lucie exclaimed. "I'm pretty sure a whole-ass divorce is all the closure she needs. She's gone through enough on his behalf. No need to watch him marry someone else."

I swallowed. "Exactly!"

Tessa said, "Lots of potential clients will be at their wedding. Showing up looking fabulous could build you up in their eyes."

"And..." Savannah twisted her lips. "That note from Hayley breaks my heart. I think she needs you there."

"Hell, no!" Lucie burst out. "She was screwing Brad while Carly was still married to him!"

Tessa shrugged. "You don't owe Hayley anything. Go for yourself. Or don't."

"But, Carly," Savannah said, "I think you remember how hard it was when you first joined Brad's world."

Shit, that hit me right in the chest. I remembered exactly how it felt to be the outsider.

But Tessa and Lucie were right. I didn't owe Brad or Hayley anything. I needed to focus on myself, on my mental health, on my goals. Letting Brad humiliate me and sully my memories of Spain wouldn't help with that. Going would only shine a light on my failed marriage. I hoped people might forget I'd ever made the mistake of marrying Brad. Then I could move on and be known for my achievements.

"If you do decide to go," Lucie said, "wear those spike heels you wore to the gala, and while you're dancing at the reception, accidentally kick Brad in the nuts."

Savannah glanced at Lucie's glass. "How much have you had to drink?"

While Savannah and Lucie argued about whether or not she was sober, I laughed. I couldn't help it. I laughed until tears prickled at the corners of my eyes, and I had to wipe them away with my sleeve.

Lucie defiantly set down her wineglass. "What's so funny?"

"We are," I said. "Thank you. You've made me feel better."

Savannah leaned over and hugged me, and her stiff-sprayed hair poked my cheek. "Anytime. Goddesses forever."

"I'm not going to the wedding," I said. "Thanks for helping me figure that out."

Tessa said, "You can count on us to always be on your side. Let's do a spa day Saturday. My treat."

A spa day with my friends didn't feel like failure at all.

"Hey." Lucie slapped her hands on her thighs. "Let's get some real food to soak up some of this wine."

"You know I don't cook." I emptied the wine into my glass and stood to get another bottle from the rack in the kitchen. "We can order something. There's a good Thai place that delivers."

"I'm on my period," Lucie said. "I need salt. Chinese? Or pizza? Do you have any ice cream, preferably chocolate?"

"We can order from Red Rover," Savannah said. "They'll bring pizza, Chinese, and ice cream, all packed in those cute thermal bags."

"No," Tessa said. "No Red Rover. Ordering directly from the restaurant is better."

"Why?" Lucie asked. "The restaurant gets our money regardless, and Red Rover will bring me a bottle of Motrin."

"They—they don't treat their employees well, okay? We'll order from the restaurant. I know an ice cream place that delivers too. I'll buy. And I've got prescription-strength ibuprofen in my bag."

Lucie held out a hand. "Gimme."

Savannah chuckled. "I don't miss that."

"What?" Lucie chased the pill with a gulp of wine. "You're already in menopause? But that's for old ladies. You're only ten years older than me."

"It's coming for you too," Savannah said. "It's not so bad."

"I can't wait," Tessa said. "I'm going to have a menopause party."

Savannah snorted. "It's not *so* bad, I said. It still sucks. Wait till you get your first hot flash."

I said, "I've had them every once in a while for the past year. The last one had me pouring sweat and then shivering for an hour."

Savannah shook her head. "Soon you'll have them every day. Getting old isn't for the weak."

I glanced at my mom's photo on the side table. "I wish my mom was still around to talk about this stuff." She'd never had a chance to go through menopause.

"Is that her?" Lucie nodded at the photo. "She was gorgeous. She rocked that eyeliner."

"She died over twenty years ago. She was entitled to that nineties eye," I said.

"I bet you miss her," Savannah said.

"Every day. She'd have some good advice for me. She was a Miss Texas, you know. She always had her eye on the prize. I still hear her sometimes, pushing me to be the best."

"I think we've all got a bit of our mothers in us. For some of us, it's something to overcome." Savannah's voice went uncharacteristically low.

"Maybe I could do a piece on it," Lucie mused. "Would either of you be willing for me to quote you?"

"I don't know." Mom used to say there were times for singing a solo and times for being in the chorus. With my business teetering on the precipice, maybe this wasn't the best time to be out front with a mic.

"Maybe." Savannah tucked a hank of blond hair behind her ear. "I usually prefer to fade into the background, you know?"

"Think about it," Lucie said. "Meanwhile, I'll do some research." She turned to Tessa. "Dial, woman. I need salt now."

"Tessa, you're on ice cream. I'll take care of the Chinese food." I picked up my phone, feeling my face stretching into another grin. Even if my business sucked right now, even if I'd made a huge mistake with Andrew, I had friends. And wine. And that made everything all right.

9

WE HAVE TO STOP MEETING LIKE THIS

CARLY

To-do list—November 9
✔ Check business budget — time to sell another bag?
✔ Set up steeper styling discount for Black Friday
Order new vibrator ~~that can do that thing Andrew did with his tongue~~
Try to relax

"Why do we put ourselves through this?" I wondered aloud at the salon on Saturday.

"Through what?" Lucie blinked her eyes open. She was sitting in the massaging pedicure chair as her feet soaked in warm, bubbly water. She lifted her glass of complimentary sparkling wine to her lips.

I wiped a trickle of sweat from my temple. Like we'd brought it on with our menopause talk the other night, my temperature was more volatile than a Real Housewife cocktail hour. I was perfectly fine one minute, but then I'd feel my body temperature rise. It would start at my stomach and prickle up my torso, then to my chest, then it would crawl up my neck, and finally, my face would flame. When it happened, I felt like an erupting volcano, an unstable one that terrorized the nearby villagers when it went off with no warning. The episodes always ended a few minutes later, leaving me chilled and shaky.

The foils the colorist was applying were like a helmet, and even my scalp was sweating. The worst part was that there was absolutely nothing I could do about it other than wait it out. And if I hated anything, it was waiting.

"Why we put ourselves through this." I pointed at my head. In the mirror, the brown ends of my hair stuck out between strips of foil.

"It's not so bad," Savannah said from the next chair over. She was going with all-over blond—again—so her hair was slicked to her head with the color cream.

"You don't like it?" Tessa asked. It looked like an effort for her to frown while the manicurist massaged her wrists. She had a few threads of gray in her thick, auburn hair, but she'd asked for only a cut and style.

"Oh, no, I mean, I'm grateful." I fanned myself. "Thanks again for treating us all. It's just...do you ever wonder why we think we need to do it? Why we need to look like we're twenty instead of forty or fifty?"

"I look like I'm fifty." Savannah wrinkled her nose at her reflection. "But a good fifty, right?"

"You're a goddess," Lucie said. "We're all beautiful."

"That's not what I—never mind." Sweat trickled from my temple. I had to get out of there. I met the colorist's gaze in the mirror. "Can I take a break, please?"

"Um, sure?" She stepped back, her gloved hands raised.

"Sorry. I'll be right back." I stood with the black cape clinging to my sweaty neck and strode toward the exit.

"Don't go out in the sun," she called after me.

I waved a glistening palm to show I'd heard her.

The salon's lobby was decorated in soothing shades of sand and ivory and softly scented with patchouli. I took a deep breath to try to cool the inferno inside me. When I fanned myself, my arms were red and blotchy. This was it. I was going to flame up from the inside out like an out-of-control nuclear reactor. Chernobyl had nothing on me.

"Carly?"

I looked up at the cringe-inducingly familiar voice.

Andrew Jones rose from the soft cognac leather sofa in the waiting area. He approached me slowly, reluctantly, looking pressed and perfect in his khaki slacks and white button-down. He probably felt obligated to say hello. I wished he'd pretended he didn't see me with my sweaty cape and red face.

"Don't you ever wear anything but Brooks Brothers?" I blurted out. The hot flash must have fried my filter.

His cheeks went pink. "It's easy. Everything coordinates."

"Like Garanimals."

"What?"

I supposed Audrey had never shopped for him at Walmart. "Never mind."

He stopped an arm's length away and scanned me from the foils on my head to the disposable flip-flops on my feet. He shook his head, bemused. "I guess I missed the memo on the dress code."

I grimaced, then tucked my hands under the cape to ensure my robe was tied at the waist. A cooling breeze reminded me I was naked underneath.

"I needed to take a break." I patted down the foils on the left side of my head. "I wish I—" I stopped. What was my runaway mouth going to say? *I wish I wasn't a sweaty, makeup-free mess...I wish I hadn't left the safety of our private room...I wish I'd gone to a different salon, maybe in another state.*

He cocked his head and smiled. "I don't know how you do it. You look beautiful even at the salon. Nat always looks like Medusa."

"I look like Medusa." I squinted at him.

"Only if Medusa were the most gorgeous woman in the city."

My cheeks heated, and that's when I realized my hot flash had ended as quickly as it had begun. Sweat cooled my body. How could he say something like that? I'd seen myself in the mirror. *Gorgeous* was not the word I'd have used.

Making me feel beautiful and strong and sexy was Andrew's superpower. He'd used it on me in Monterey, the night I'd lost my mind and slept with my frenemy's son.

But we weren't in Monterey. We were in San Francisco, and someone we knew might see us together.

I shoved my hands into the pockets of my robe. "What are you doing here?"

"I drove my mother and Natalie."

If Audrey was here, I needed to retreat, to hide, but I couldn't tear myself away from Andrew. Not yet. "Don't you have better things to do on a Saturday?"

He shrugged. "It's family. They asked. And I brought some work." When he waved at the sofa, I noticed the laptop he'd left there.

I glanced around the lobby, but the only witness was the receptionist behind her desk.

Seeming to read the thoughts on my face, he said, "We ran into each other. We're just talking. No one would read into it, I promise." He grinned, and despite my panic, those dimples weakened my knees. He tipped his head toward the sofa. "Want to join me? I could use a break from my spreadsheets."

"No, I...uh. I came out to..." I would *not* share that I was having a perimenopausal hot flash. "To make my next appointment."

"Ah."

Now I had to make an appointment at this salon, which I couldn't afford, considering the bill coming due for my new website.

I moved toward the desk, and he ambled beside me. "How have you been?"

"Fine. Good."

"And business is good?"

"Yes," I lied.

"That's great."

We reached the desk, and I turned my attention to the receptionist. "I'd like to make an appointment, please. Cut and highlights."

"In six weeks?" she asked. "That takes us to the last week of December."

"Oh, no." The last week of December reminded me of Brad's wedding.

"Is that not good?" she asked.

"It's...there's a wedding, and..." If I were going to the wedding, I'd need an earlier appointment. I'd die before I'd let Brad and all those potential clients see my roots. But I wasn't going.

"Brad's wedding?" Andrew asked. When I stared at him, he looked at his loafers. "My mother mentioned it. Only an insensitive prick would invite his ex."

"Right." Of course Brad would've invited Audrey and Charles. I couldn't stop the hurt from bubbling out. "Barcelona is where we went for our honeymoon."

"Ouch." He winced. "It's brave of you to go. Do you have a plus-one? I could take you."

I sucked in a breath. "No!" A date with Andrew? In public? Talking with him in the salon was bad enough. It made me too conscious of my lack of underwear. I pressed my thighs together. "I mean, no, I wasn't planning to go."

"Really?" One side of his mouth tipped up. "I figured you would. To prove to everyone you're the bigger person."

That smile. Those dimples. So confident, yet also inviting. It was what drew me in. It made me feel like we shared a secret. And, in fact, we did. I shuffled back half a step in my foam flip-flops.

I swallowed, remembering my friends' advice to use the occasion to prove I was over Brad and to pick up clients. "That does sound like me, doesn't it? But, surprisingly, I've got some complicated feelings about it. I think it's best if I gracefully decline."

He leaned an elbow on the tall counter. "Sure. Though Spain could be fun, especially with a date to inspire a little jealousy. Not that Brad's petty like that."

I snorted. Brad was exactly that petty.

I let myself imagine it for a minute. Walking into the reception with young, handsome Andrew. Leaning on him, his presence a support and a comfort while my ex married someone else. Dancing with him while Brad seethed.

Now who's being petty?

"Still, I think I'll pass."

"I'm looking for a date myself. Not to the wedding, but to a client dinner I've got coming up. I've asked everyone I know."

"No takers? You're joking." A handsome guy like Andrew had to have young women lined up.

"Not one. Wait a second." To the receptionist, he said, "Are you free Monday night?"

Her mouth dropped open. "Omigod. I'd love to! Go with you. Anywhere." Then her excited smile flipped over, and she regained the power of coherent speech. "But it's my mom's birthday Monday. I could…"

"No!" Andrew's expression was horrified. "Don't skip out on your mom's birthday, not for me. I'll find someone." He chuckled nervously. "Carly, I don't suppose you're free to act as my fake girlfriend?"

"It's not just a date? It's a whole fake girlfriend?"

"Unfortunately, yes. I got carried away."

I wished I could help, but a fake girlfriend? There was no way that wouldn't get back to his mother. Besides, it would be ridiculous for Andrew to pretend to date someone my age. "I don't think it's a good idea."

His shoulders slumped, but he flashed me that knee-weakening half-grin. "It was worth a shot."

"You flatter me."

"Any chance I get."

Blushing again, I turned back to the receptionist. "I'll take that appointment the last week in December, please."

After she emailed me the appointment confirmation, I said goodbye to Andrew and floated back into the salon without a second glance.

That was a lie. I did look back. And found him looking at me too.

"We have to stop meeting like this," he called out.

We definitely did. Because having Andrew call me gorgeous was a temptation I didn't trust myself to resist.

10

BIGGER BALLS

ANDREW

From: Andrew Jones
To: Victor Lynch
Sent: November 9, 8:16 am
Subject: RE: Client dinner

Hi Vic,
I'm sorry, but my girlfriend isn't able to come to the client dinner. Please let me know if you'd still like me to join you, alone.
- Andrew
Andrew Jones, Financial Engineering Lead
(saved in Drafts folder)

I watched Carly disappear into the spa, glad I'd had the chance to redeem myself after our disastrous dance at the gala. I hadn't wallowed in my hurt feelings about her leaving me. I'd simply admired her glowing face and eyes. And somehow, seeing her bare feet in her spa slippers, her toenails painted a sparkly red-orange, had helped me see things from her perspective rather than my own.

She'd just gotten divorced. Sure, it was a year ago, but I understood the pain of loss. She might not feel it every day, but whenever something reminded her of what was gone, it was as painful as the day it happened. The invitation to Brad's wedding must have hit her like that.

What an asshole. Why couldn't he get married quietly at city hall like a regular guy? Why'd he have to rub it in Carly's face by throwing a big wedding in the city where they'd honeymooned? Why'd he have to invite her?

But if she didn't go, would she have friends or family to spend the holidays with? Or had Brad taken them too?

"Why were you talking to Carly Rose?"

My mother's voice startled me from my thoughts. I glanced up and found her at the bottom of the spiral staircase from the second-floor salon suites. My sister was right behind her.

"We ran into each other."

Unlike Carly, Mother was dressed in street clothes, her Burberry trench coat belted over her black slacks, her roots blond again, her hair styled. She frowned. "Why?"

Natalie stepped off the stairs and fluffed her long hair over her coat. "We all know Carly. I'm sure Andrew was only being polite."

"It looked more than polite," Mother said. "You were leaning toward her. You weren't talking about me, were you?"

"No. We were talking about Brad Winner's wedding."

"Is she going?" Mother curled her lip.

"She said no."

"That's probably wise." Her eyes softened. "Although…"

"Although?"

"Attending his wedding might be the kick in the pants they both need. He'd see he was a fool, again. And she'd see she's better off without him. Everyone else would see what I've always known: she's too good for him."

"Really, Mother?" Natalie asked. "I thought you never liked her."

"We've never been close." She shook her hair over her shoulders as if feeling the new length. "At first, I was upset about their relationship. I was friends with Eleanor, Brad's first wife. He treated her shamefully in the divorce. I saw Carly as a home wrecker. That was before I figured out Brad had lied to her. But after that vulgar bikini boat party—"

Natalie cleared her throat and flashed me a smug grin.

"I saw her as a challenger. Our relationship was more rivalry than enmity. You respect your competition. At least, I do."

"And you think she should go to Brad's wedding?" I asked.

"I would. Not that Charles would ever treat me that despicably. But if I had the misfortune of being Brad Winner's ex-wife, I'd go and show everyone who had bigger balls."

"Mother!" Natalie gasped.

Two spots of color shone on our mother's cheekbones. "I shouldn't have accepted that glass of wine after my massage. Still, it's true. Carly's the better person."

"Are you going, Mother?" Natalie asked.

"Absolutely not. Only a third wife would plan a wedding on Christmas Day in Spain and send out the invitations only six weeks before. Outrageous."

"You think they had a reason to rush it?" Natalie asked.

"You mean to keep the attendance small? Possibly." Mother tapped a pink-painted nail against her lip. "Brad was always a cheap bastard."

"Mother!" I chuckled.

"Well, he is. I'm sure he did the same thing to Carly as he did to Eleanor. Smoke and mirrors and a ridiculous prenup. Eleanor's alimony was shameful, but at least she got child support. I'm sure Carly is struggling to build her business on what she got. It would be easier to sell her services if everyone saw who the real victor was in that divorce."

My mind spun. Everything my mother said aligned with Carly's story, except the part about Mother sabotaging her. The screw that had tightened in my chest the night we danced loosened.

Carly's success might depend on whether or not she went to her ex's wedding. Only the richest among Brad's friends could afford last-minute holiday airfare to Spain. Hayley had rich friends, too. Natalie had told me she was a model. Carly could show up in one of her elegant gowns, hold her head high, and rake in the clients.

Hell, I'd hire her to style *me*.

Which gave me an idea. One that could benefit us both.

11

A PROPOSITION

CARLY

Sitting in my car in front of my building, I closed my eyes. I inhaled through my nose and exhaled through my mouth, trying to savor the boneless feeling our spa day had given me.

Instead of tormenting myself by checking my (silent) phone, instead of scouring the fashion blogs to spot the latest trends for my (imaginary) clients, instead of obsessing over each (desperate) pixel of my website, I'd lounge on my couch watching... whatever people watched on TV these days. Or I'd read a book. Not one of the business books stacked on my bedside table. One of the romance novels Savannah had loaned me.

Nope. Scratch that.

Romance novels were highly unrealistic and pointless. I'd read the thriller Lucie had recommended at the salon. A story about terrible things happening to an innocent woman was much more realistic.

Slowly, I opened my eyes and did a double take.

Andrew Jones was leaning against the side of my building

with his hands shoved into the pockets of a charcoal wool car coat, staring intently at me.

I gathered my purse and clambered out of my car. I hit the lock on the fob, making the car beep, and slowly trudged toward the entrance. My shoulders hunched at my ears, and all my indulgent relaxation evaporated.

He held open the outer door.

I glanced around to see if any of my neighbors were nearby. Fortunately, no. But when I passed him, I caught a whiff of his clean, middle-of-the-ocean scent that had been so intoxicating in Monterey. I breathed out through my nose to clear it.

"Why are you here?" I asked.

"I need to speak with you, privately, if I may. I have a proposition."

Despite the flutter in my sad little heart, I wrangled enough control of my brain to say, "I'm not interested in another proposition like Monterey."

He ducked his head. "This is a business proposition. Nothing more."

I lifted my eyebrows. "Does that mean you're finally ready to ditch the Brooks Brothers?"

"I could be convinced."

I narrowed my eyes but saw nothing to fear in his open expression. I unlocked the inner door and climbed the stairs to my second-floor apartment. Letting him into my private space felt strangely intimate, but I'd had clients here before, which was all Andrew was claiming to be.

Pointing him to my sofa, I asked, "Can I get you something to drink?"

"Whatever you're having." He settled into the corner of the sofa, looking like he belonged there.

I shook it off as a fault in my decorating. I needed to spice it up with reds or pinks, colors that didn't belong in a menswear shop. Walking to the kitchen and flipping on the kettle, I said, "I'm having a cup of chamomile tea."

"Um, no thanks, then. I'm good."

Keeping my back to him, I smiled at my cupboards. Without a drink, maybe he'd make his proposal and take his tempting presence and expensive cologne elsewhere.

A few minutes later, I brought my mug into the living room, which was too grand a name for my one-bedroom condo's open-plan main room. I'd used a rug to visually separate it from the adjoining dining area with its table and four chairs. Only a peninsula divided it from the kitchen. It must look small and shabby to someone accustomed to wealth since birth. At least I had a humble upbringing to ground me, though it had been a challenging adjustment after living in a mansion on a private street for twenty years.

I'd expected him to be engrossed with his phone like most men of my acquaintance, but he was holding the photo of Mom and me at the Miss Texas pageant. Mom wore her winner's sash, and I wore the Miss Dallas Teen sash.

"This is you?" He turned it around to show me like I didn't have it memorized. "And your mother?"

"It is. A couple years before we moved to LA. I was into pageants," I said. "It's kind of a family legacy."

He stared at it for another moment before carefully setting it back on the table. "You were both beautiful. And you're even more beautiful now."

"Thank you." I couldn't stand the thought of sipping my tea. My cheeks burned.

"Are you still close with your mother?"

"She passed a while ago." I didn't want to talk about it. Not with Andrew. "You said you had a business proposal for me?"

Clearing the frown from his face, he straightened on the

sofa. When he rubbed his hands on his thighs, I tried not to think about those big hands spanning my skin.

"At the spa, I mentioned needing a fake girlfriend for a client dinner."

"I remember." I chuckled, low. "I still can't believe you haven't found someone to take. A nice, handsome guy like you…" I looked away. That was getting into dangerous territory.

"I'm up for a promotion at work," he said. "But they think I'm not serious enough, not settled enough to be a VP. So, I told my new boss I have a steady girlfriend."

"And he asked you to bring her to your client dinner?"

"That and"—his Adam's apple bobbed—"the bank's holiday party on New Year's Eve. I need a girlfriend until I get the promotion. And I'm asking you to pretend to be her."

"Why do you need a *fake* girlfriend? Why don't you have a *real* one?"

The tops of his cheeks turned pink. "I never met the right woman?"

"I'm not the right one either. I'm…" The reasons tripped over each other.

I'm too old.

It would look bad to your mother and her friends.

I spent the last twenty years being someone's arm candy, and the last thing I want is to reprise the role.

While I gathered my thoughts, he continued, "You need a date for Brad's wedding. Even my mother thinks you should go to show everyone you've risen above him. She says it will help everyone see that you're the better person, and they should hire you."

"She said that?" Why? That sounded like what my friends said.

"She did. So, I'm proposing a trade. You go with me to my

two events, starting Monday night, and I'll go to Brad's wedding."

"No. Absolutely not. Being seen as your date would ruin me."

"Would it?" He leaned forward, resting his elbows on his knees. "You'll have access to my network. Think of all the styling clients I could introduce you to. An entire holiday party full of bankers who dress like...bankers." He waved a hand over himself.

The bankers wouldn't have the same hang-ups as Audrey's clique. They wouldn't be offended because I was dating one of their sons. I'd be dating their coworker, which was much more acceptable. I could offer them a friends-and-family discount to appeal to their economical nature.

"To sweeten the deal, I'll pay your standard rate to style me," he added.

I grimaced. "You're terrible at this. You shouldn't add onto the offer before I've responded. Besides, you don't need to sweeten the deal. Brad's wedding is multiple days of international travel. It seems I'm getting more out of this bargain than you are."

"I need this promotion."

"You have a lot to learn about negotiation."

"And fashion. So, will you do it?"

"I go to your two parties and style you. For a fee. In exchange, you go with me to Brad's wedding."

"I'll also introduce you to as many potential styling clients as I can."

I wavered. Maybe I'd ruin my chances with my former friends, but his network of bankers had to be a lucrative bunch. "We'd have to establish new rules."

He flashed me a boyish grin. "Let's hear 'em."

"First, we're pretend-dating only at your events. At Brad's wedding, if anyone asks, we're just friends, nothing more."

"A corollary," Andrew added. "I tell my mother the truth about our arrangement."

"Your mother!" How had I forgotten about her? "She's not going to Brad's wedding, is she?"

"No. Too gauche. Anyway, I'll swear her to secrecy in case there's any crossover between the groups. I'll handle her, I promise."

"Good." The thought of appearing on her son's arm, whether or not she knew about our agreement, terrified me. "Second rule: no sex."

"Got it. No sex, real or simulated."

Wow. His too-fast agreement hurt a little. Maybe our night together hadn't been as magical for him. I mentally smacked myself. Of course it hadn't. I had wrinkles and a saggy butt. And no matter how much yoga I did, my soft stomach would never be as taut as it had been in my modeling days when I'd never let a carb pass my lips.

"Though..." He rubbed his chin. "We'll need some PDA to sell the relationship at work. So, maybe, hugs and G-rated kisses?"

I could do that. I could hug him and hold his hand during two events without falling into bed with him again. Probably.

"Fine. Third rule," I said, drawing myself up, "we set an end date. When do you think they'll give you that promotion?"

"They should decide pretty early in the new year."

"Does February first seem fair? After you win the promotion, we'll make up a story about our breakup."

"You'll run off with a younger, hotter man."

I rolled my eyes. "Too much younger, and he wouldn't be legal."

"Excuse me." Andrew set a hand on his chest. "I'm thirty-two. There's always a twenty-something spin class instructor in these stories."

"Ugh. Then I'd have to carry on a pretense with my new clients. No, thanks. I'll say your vice president hours didn't work for me. I need more of a man's time and attention." He'd given me plenty of attention in Monterey. I remembered how dark his gray-blue eyes had gone when he'd stared up at me from between my thighs.

He ran his fingers through his slightly too-long hair. "Shit, Carly. If you say those things and look at me like that, I might forget about rule two."

"I won't." If I fell into bed with Andrew again, I might never want to give him up.

"Do we have a deal?" He held out his right hand.

All the reasons I should say no spun through my head: the optics if my potential styling clients found out about our arrangement, what Audrey might think of it all, and what she might do if she didn't like Andrew's "handling" of her.

But one positive reason stood out clearly: I'd show Brad and everyone else at that wedding that I was over him, and that I'd moved past it all and come out a better woman, a woman on her way to success on her terms. And then my phone would ring.

I gripped Andrew's hand. "Deal."

He gusted out a relieved sigh. "Fantastic. I'll text you the details." He unlocked his phone and passed it to me. "Text yourself so I have your number?"

When I passed back his phone, he stood. "Thanks for this. I won't let you down. I'll be the best wedding date ever."

"Friend-date," I reminded him. But I needed the reminder too. We could never get out of control again like we'd done before. I had to keep him at arm's length and refuse to let my emotions back into the driver's seat.

New rule two would save me.

12
WE SELL IT

ANDREW

> Oliver: OMG that trig video got 100k views!

> Me: Seriously?

> Oliver: Still climbing!

> Me: That's amazing!

> Oliver: Our next video will get 150k. We're never ever going to change anything

> Me: I still think you should be on camera

> Oliver: Not a chance. Never. Changing. Anything.

> Me: But you're so pretty

> Oliver: <middle finger emoji>

I was the first to show at the restaurant, my smartwatch squealing about my elevated heart rate. Would Carly show, or would she have second thoughts again? I was picturing myself bluffing my way through this couples' dinner solo when Vic and his wife arrived.

He shook my hand. "Where's your mystery date? Ed and I have a bet that she's fictional."

The CEO and the CFO had a bet that I'd lied to them? It was a good thing I hadn't told anyone in my family about the promotion. I could imagine Mother's disappointed expression when she heard I didn't get it.

Surreptitiously, I wiped a bead of sweat from my hairline and opened my mouth to assure Vic my date would show when a familiar voice soothed my jangled nerves.

"Fictional? I've been called a lot of things but never that." Carly appeared at my side and something loosened in my chest, letting hope flutter out. Maybe I could get this promotion after all. Maybe then she'd think I was worth staying for.

She slipped her arm through mine and lifted on her toes to kiss my cheek. "Hi," she said, her voice husky.

She wore a simple, fitted black V-neck dress with a gold belt. And she wore the hell out of it. It hugged her body the way I wished I had the right to do. I settled my hand on the soft fabric covering the irresistible curve of her back.

I blinked. *Rule one.* She was my fake date. The kiss that still burned on my cheek and my hand on her back—her *upper* back—was the limit of our agreement as far as touching was concerned, per rule two.

I cleared my throat, but my voice came out as a rumble. "Carly, let me introduce you to Vic and..." What was Vic's wife's name?

"No need. I already know Yelena and Vic." She stepped

forward to kiss Yelena's cheek, then Vic's. "You didn't tell me we'd be having dinner with old friends." Her tight control slipped a bit, her eyes flashing.

Vic's forehead wrinkled. "You're dating Jones?"

"Yes, it's...new," she said.

"It's serious," I said at the same time.

"New *and* serious?" Yelena said, clutching Carly's hand. "This tea sounds hot."

"Well..." I looked at Carly, helpless. Why hadn't we made up a backstory? They always did that in spy movies. But we weren't spies. We were only lying to my boss. My breath hitched.

She tossed me a flirty smile. "When you know, you know, right?" She shrugged, which made Yelena cackle.

Vic frowned. Circling around Carly and Yelena as they crowed over each other's outfits, he crowded next to me. "You're dating Carly Winner?" he growled low enough that only I'd hear.

"Yeah. For a...for a while now." *A while* was vague enough. We'd straighten out our story later.

"She's almost my age," he said, his voice tight.

"And your wife is my age," I said. "What's the big deal? Like Carly said, when you know, you know. Also, her name is Carly Rose now."

"The big deal is that this could get complicated."

"Complicated how?" I bristled. Fuck him if he thought Carly wasn't a suitable date for a prospective vice president. "You know what? I don't care. She's incredible, and I like her. A lot." I wished I had a better vocabulary to make this fake dating thing seem more real. But my relationships had never made it to the point of introducing people I dated to my friends and colleagues.

I was much better at talking about math.

"Because the client—" Vic began.

"No," Yelena said, clutching his arm. "No talking about work until I have a cocktail in my hand. Come on, let's sit."

My heart pounded as we followed the hostess to a rectangular table for six. I wished I had something to hold on to like a graphing calculator, a sextant, or, god, Carly's hand would've been great, but we were already pushing the PDA limits of our agreement with that kiss on the cheek. Vic pointed me to one end, and he took the other. The women sat on one side, discussing some designer I'd never heard of.

The server was taking my drink order when I heard a voice I wished I didn't recognize.

"Carly? It's been a minute."

Brad Winner stood at the empty side of our table. His twenty-something fiancée stood at his side. Brad smiled, but it looked pained. The fiancée positively beamed.

Vic stood, extending his hand.

"Brad Winner is our client?" What the fuck?

"Brad, so glad you could make it." Vic's voice sounded anything but glad. "I think you know our associate, Andrew Jones, and his...um...date, Carly."

Slowly, I stood and held out my hand, steeling myself.

Brad gripped it. Hard. Like when I arm-wrestled my brother, I didn't flinch. I squeezed right back to say, *She's my date. You blew your chance.*

"Andrew Jones? Are you Jasper's son?"

"That's me."

A cool calculation tightening his eyes, Brad released my throbbing hand. "This is my fiancée, Hayley."

"Hayley Darling." She pumped my hand enthusiastically but much more gently. "Remember me?"

I caught Vic's scowl from the corner of my eye. Did he think she was a past girlfriend of mine? That was all we needed, another incestuous connection on this episode of *Game of Thrones*.

"Um...?" Her face looked a little familiar.

"St. Sulpicius Academy? I was a couple years behind Natalie." When I said nothing, she grinned. "S-U-L, P-I-C, I-Yoooou-S! Gooooo Church Mice!"

From the deepest recesses of my memory, I pulled an image of a gangly middle-schooler in a cheerleader uniform with a set of thin pompoms. The varsity squad only cheered for the soccer team when we were in the finals, so we usually got the junior squad. "Oh. Right. Nice to see you again, Hayley. Do you know my date"—I had to clear my throat—"Carly Rose?"

"Of course." She squeezed Carly's hand. "I'm so glad you're coming to the wedding. Andrew's your date? That's dank! Isn't it, babe?" She clutched Brad's arm.

He narrowed his eyes at Carly like she'd somehow engineered this disaster.

Carly's voice wavered when she said, "Brad."

Before I knew it, my arm was around her shoulders. "Excuse us a minute."

I led her to the front of the restaurant. "God, I'm so sorry. I didn't know. Are you okay?"

Her face was pale, making her orangey-red lipstick stand out. "I'm fine. It was bound to happen. In fact, since we're going to his wedding together, it's good to get this first meeting out of the way."

She straightened and shook off my arm. I could tell how unnerved she was by the slight tremor in her hand as she flicked her hair off her shoulder, but when she lifted her chin, a new challenge gleamed in her eye. She was a goddess.

I wished it were real. I wished I could hold her hand until it stopped trembling, kiss her plush lips until she forgot all about Brad and remembered how sexy, how worthy she was.

But all I could do was catch her eye and give her words she didn't need, at least not from me. She had to know she was exceptional, and Brad was nothing but an ordinary asshole, discarding what he didn't understand or appreciate. "You're spectacular. So much more precious than he knows."

She met my gaze. "You're sweet."

Sweet. The word was a stone in my belly. Sweet was a word for a kid, not someone you felt anything for. She felt nothing for me. She'd proved it when she left my hotel room as I slept.

I reminded my foolish heart it felt nothing for her. Because this was fake, and she'd leave me again on February first.

"Ready?" I asked.

She nodded.

We stopped at the bar for shots, whiskey for me and vodka for her, before we returned to the table. Brad and Hayley sat at Vic's end of the table. Separating us was a smart move on Vic's part. Not that I'd do anything with my promotion on the line, but I was feeling less than rational at the moment.

Immediately, Vic turned the conversation to business. Apparently, Brad was looking into some new investment vehicles, and Vic wanted me to share the analysis I'd done on comparative risk. Easy peasy. Explaining complex financial models to Brad was simple after I'd somehow gotten Vic to understand them last week.

Meanwhile, Carly steered the women's conversation like a professional. After all those years with Brad and his constant networking, it was probably second nature.

The trouble came when we crossed the streams.

"Darling." Yelena speared a morsel of her Dungeness crab and held out her fork, "Try this."

Vic leaned forward and took the bite from her fork. He smiled indulgently. "That's delicious. Good choice."

"I'll ask our chef if he could make it. I wouldn't know what to do with shellfish." She turned back to Carly. "I'm trying to have more meals at home so Vic can spend time with the kids. It's hard when he works so much. Do you have children, Carly?"

"No, no, we never—" She rolled her lips between her teeth. "No."

"Carly didn't want kids. She thought she'd get back to modeling one day." Brad guffawed. "Guess you've aged out of the biz now, Carl."

"Oh, no, babe." Hayley scooted Brad's wine farther away from him. "There's so much more diversity in modeling now. There's a call for mature models." I was sure she meant her smile to be reassuring, but Carly seemed anything but reassured.

"You said you didn't want more kids," Carly said. "Your two boys were enough."

"Did I?" Brad shrugged, catching Vic's gaze, then mine. *Women,* that shrug said.

Carly opened her mouth, then closed it. When she grabbed her wineglass, it sloshed a bit. She gulped it, then mumbled, "Doesn't matter."

But Brad wasn't ready to let it go. "Carly's not what you'd call domestic. She tried to cook me dinner a few weeks after we got married. She wanted to impress me. It was Southern food, fried chicken, grits, and some disgusting kale or something. She set off the smoke alarm when she got grease on the stove. The chicken was okay, but the rest of it was inedible."

Carly's cheeks reddened.

"After that, we hired a chef. But Carly can plan a good party, can't you, Carl?"

She smiled, thin and brittle as one of my mother's crystal wine globes. Then she turned to Yelena. "Speaking of parties, tell me about that dress you wore to your ten-year anniversary party last year."

"Brad, let's talk about risk modeling," I said. I smiled gratefully at the server, who took away my plate without asking if I wanted to take home my mostly uneaten steak. I wanted no reminders of this meal.

By the time they removed our dessert plates, Vic had invited Brad to the bank's charity golf scramble and asked me to join their foursome. Yelena had asked Carly to style her for the bank's New Year's Eve party, and Carly had advised Hayley on the upcoming styles for spring.

As Brad shook my hand, less crushingly this time, he said, "You've got a good head on your shoulders, kid, like your dad. Vic, I like how you manage risk. I'll call you later this week."

Vic's grin and clap on my shoulder were worth every painful moment we'd endured that evening.

I felt the euphoria of a well-executed soccer play, like the time I'd flicked the ball backward past the defender and my teammate raced past to chip it into the corner of the net. My career would follow the same well-planned trajectory. First this promotion, then another, then CFO when Vic retired or took a job at one of the big national banks. All because of Carly.

As I walked her to her car, her clingy dress hypnotized me. She took mincing steps in the narrow skirt, and with her heels, her calves flexed seductively, reminding me of how smooth they'd been when I kissed them.

It'd been a privilege to see her bare body. I knew the feel of her silky skin. I'd memorized the scent of her where her neck joined her shoulder, in the valley between her breasts, and the intoxicating spot between her legs that I'd never wanted to leave.

I shook it off. She didn't want that from me. She'd made it clear with her no-sex rule. We had a business arrangement, nothing more. She excelled at her part of it.

"You were captivating tonight," I said. "Thank you. And I'm

really sorry. Vic didn't tell me who the client was. I guess he thought it didn't matter."

"I'll be prepared next time." She stopped at an older Benz and clicked the lock.

"We've got to nail down our backstory. What did you tell Yelena about us?"

Her eyes sparkled wickedly. "That I seduced you at one of your mother's parties."

"Really?" I chuckled. "Mother would die."

"No, I stuck close to the truth. I said we'd met up by chance, and you wooed me."

Too bad my wooing hadn't stuck. I should be used to it. People didn't stick around for me.

I moved to open her car door, but her words stopped me. "I think they're watching us," she whispered.

"Who?"

She tipped her chin at the next row of cars, where Vic and Yelena lingered next to their Land Rover.

"Why are they watching us?"

In the yellow pool of the security light, the tops of her cheeks darkened. "I think they expect us to say goodnight."

"Goodnight?" I finally caught her meaning. "Oh. You mean…" I stepped closer and carefully set my hand on her waist, above her teasing belt. My voice came out as a rumble. "Goodnight."

She tipped her chin up. "You'd better kiss me to sell this."

We needed only a cursory kiss. Vic and Yelena expected us to drive our separate cars back to my place or hers and go to bed. Together. But the second my lips grazed hers, our arrangement was the last thing on my mind.

Her lips tasted like wine, like that night in Monterey. My tongue followed a familiar track, licking inside her wet warmth, her flavor more intoxicating than any alcohol.

She melted against me, allowing me to support her with my hands at the curve of her waist. I pressed forward, crushing her breasts against my chest as our kiss turned ravenous. I remembered how she looked in my hotel room bed, naked and spread out, as I'd kissed from her plush lips all the way down her body. Excitement pooled in my belly.

When she tunneled her fingers into my hair, tingles spread from my scalp to my toes. If Vic and Yelena were watching us, surely, they could see my skin glowing from the fire Carly ignited inside me.

Her car chirped, startling us apart.

She'd looked perfect all night, but now she was perfectly wrecked. Her lipstick had smeared at the edges. Her eyes were huge and glossy, the pupils blown to the very edges of her brown irises, and her breaths came fast, gusting out between her lips.

I did that to her, some caveman part of me crowed. *She likes me,* gloated that pubescent boy who'd fallen for her at that party on her yacht.

She blinked, and her gaze flicked to the next row of cars. "I think we sold it. They're gone."

The caveman shuffled back into his cave. Thirteen-year-old me slouched into his room, probably to jack off to some porn on his laptop.

Business arrangement. I should have the words tattooed on my palm so I could remind myself every time I slipped.

"I guess we did. Thanks again."

"Next stop, Brad's wedding," she said shakily. "Text me your measurements, and I'll pick up some things for you."

"You don't want me to go with you and try stuff on?"

"No. I'll have them sent to your place. You can set aside anything you don't like, and I'll pick them up and return them."

She'd practically screamed, *business arrangement.* I could take the hint.

"Goodnight, Carly. Thanks again."

"Goodnight." She got into her car, and I waited while she started it and drove away.

It was a good reminder. Carly wouldn't stay either. On February first, she'd peel out of my life, tires squealing.

13

CUFFING SEASON

CARLY

> *To-do list—November 16*
> *Volunteer shift at Success in a Dress: 9—noon*
> *Lunch with the girls*
> *~~Tell them about the arrangement~~ Do NOT tell them about the arrangement*

I frowned at a knock-off Louis Vuitton satchel. It had a scuff across the bottom, and the stitching on the pleather strap showed signs of fraying. It might last two, maybe three wearings. What if it fell apart at an interview? The women we served at Success in a Dress were just getting back on their feet after ending a stint in prison or escaping an abusive relationship. They were nervous enough. Having a wardrobe malfunction during a job interview would destroy their fragile confidence. I tossed the bag into the pile for resale. Let someone pay a dollar for it at a thrift store.

The bell above the door jingled, and three women entered laden with shopping bags. My cheeks tugged up into a smile.

"What are you doing here?" I asked. "We aren't supposed to meet for another half an hour."

"We thought we'd help you," Tessa said. "And clean out our closets at the same time." She plunked two shopping bags onto a bare spot on the long table where I'd been sorting donations.

"Ooh." I pulled out a black Alexander McQueen blazer. "This is nice. I didn't know you wore suits."

Tessa tossed her curtain of red hair. "I used to work in an office once upon a time."

"Which office?" Lucie asked.

"It was a thousand years ago." Tessa waved her hand.

"That blazer looks like it cost a thousand bucks," Lucie said. "You must've been pretty high up in that office."

Tessa rubbed at a scrape on a pink patent Jimmy Choo pump and didn't answer.

Savannah heaved her bag onto the table. "I don't know if you can use them, but I brought some casual clothes."

There had to be an entire lululemon display's worth of yoga pants and tops in there.

"Savannah, you don't have to give up stuff you can use," I said, eyeing the tunic and leggings she was wearing.

"I'm making room in my closet for more camera-friendly clothes," she said. "I, uh…" She glanced at Tessa. "I accepted some seed money to turn my blog into a YouTube show."

"Really?" I asked. "That's fabulous!"

Savannah sucked in a big breath. "Yeah, I'm nervous but excited."

When her chin trembled, I walked around the table to hug her. She was a lot like the women we served, except for her relatively stable home life and disposable income. "Want my help shopping for something to wear on camera?"

"You'd do that?"

"It would be my pleasure," I said. "We'll go shopping after lunch. We'll talk about what persona you want to present and find something that fits."

She squeezed me, hard. "Thank you."

"I've got donations too." Lucie pushed a paper bag forward with her foot. "Dresses. My mother keeps sending them to me every time my dad has some event. I never wear them. Some still have the tags."

The ones at the top of the bag were in pastel shades that would've turned her tan skin gray. She was smart to stick with black.

"Ladies, thank you so much for these. When our clients feel confident in what they're wearing, they do better in job interviews. And, uh"—I glanced at the stacks of yoga pants in Savannah's bags—"athletic pursuits."

"Can we help you sort them?" Savannah asked.

"Sure. Suits go over there." I pointed at a rack along the near wall. "Dresses over there." I gestured at the far wall. "Everything else on the tables at the back."

Savannah headed toward the back tables, and Tessa carried her bags to the rack I'd indicated.

Lucie didn't move. "So...what did you decide about your ex's wedding? Did you send back the reply card stuffed with glitter or dipped in mayonnaise?"

I winced, but I couldn't lie to my friend, not even to avoid a million follow-up questions. "Neither. I accepted."

"Bold. Do you need a plus-one? I know a guy or two."

"Thanks, that's sweet. But I already have a fake plus-one."

"What's a *fake* plus-one? Are you bringing a life-size cardboard cutout of Daniel Craig?"

"No, he's real." What would my friends think about my

agreement with Andrew? "He's playing the role of my boyfriend."

"Oh. Like in *The Proposal* or *The Wedding Date?* Is he a sex worker? Not that there's anything wrong with hiring a sex worker. We should normalize sex work."

"It's more of a professional exchange, an arrangement. I'm pretending to be his girlfriend at some of his business events."

"Ah, like cuffing season."

"No. It's nothing like cuffing season. It's all business. Real business, not funny business."

"No sex?" Her voice rang through the warehouse. "But that's the fun part of these things."

I lowered my voice. "It's not about fun. It's about building up my clientele. And he's up for a promotion at work that requires him to be in a steady relationship."

Her eyes narrowed. "Who is this guy?"

I closed my eyes so I didn't have to look at her. "Andrew Jones."

Behind me, Savannah squealed. "I knew it! I knew you'd end up together!"

I turned to face her and Tessa. "We're not together. I was explaining to Lucie that it's fake for three events. A client dinner of his, which we've already done, Brad's wedding, and his company's holiday party."

Savannah planted her hands on her hips. "Fake dating always ends up as a real relationship."

"Only in your romance novels," Lucie said. "And you've read too many of them if you confuse them with reality. Though with your sexual chemistry"—she hissed through her teeth—"you'll end up in bed for sure."

"We will not. It's rule two."

Tessa scrunched her nose. "I thought rule two was not telling anyone. That seems to contradict the whole fake-dating concept."

"We established new rules. New rule two is no sex."

"And, as I pointed out," Lucie said, "the sex is the fun part."

"As I pointed out, it's not about fun. It's business. Come on, let's wash our hands and go to lunch. I'll tell you all about our first fake date. It was a doozy."

As I led them to the sink, I resolved not to tell them how the date had ended. Because that kiss had broken all the rules.

14

I PLAY IT BALLS-OUT

ANDREW

Me: The clothes arrived. Thank you

Carly: Did you try them on?

Me: I did. They look great

Carly: Anything you want to return?

Me: No, I like them all

Carly: Wonderful. See you at the airport on the 22nd.

Me: I won't see you until then?

(a few hours later)

Me: Ok. Thanks again

I plunked a slice of Telma's sweet-potato pie in front of Natalie, then set down my plate before taking a seat.

Thanksgiving at the Jones-Hayes house wasn't much different from Mother's Sunday brunches. Jackson and his wife had brought their brood. Their son, Noah, was talking Charles's ear off about his latest graphic novel obsession, and everyone was oohing and aahing over what baby Valentine would—and wouldn't—eat. My sister Sam had made a rare visit with her fiancé, Niall, who worked hard to keep the peace between her and Mother. As usual, Nat and I were stuck in the middle. The only difference from brunch was the menu.

Until Charles stood at the foot of the table.

"We have something to celebrate today." He raised his glass.

My first thought was Jackson and Alicia. Could she be pregnant again? I glanced toward their end of the table, near Mother, but they looked calmly at Charles, waiting for what he'd say.

"The word on the street," Charles said, grinning proudly, "is that Andrew has the inside track on a promotion to bank vice president."

Fuck. There went my secret.

My siblings congratulated me and raised their glasses in the air. Even Noah raised his glass of sparkling grape juice and drank, coming away with a purple mustache.

My mother gasped. "That's wonderful, son! I knew you could do it."

My face went hot. "It's not a sure thing."

Charles raised his eyebrows. "I hear it's yours to lose."

"Really? Did you hear any details?"

He settled back in his chair. "No. Ed seemed surprised you were interested, but Vic has been pleased with your performance so far."

Being a Jones had its perks, but it also had perils. When I

was a kid, Mother was on a first-name basis with my teachers and headed almost every parent committee at my school. Now Charles knew everyone at the bank where I worked and had zero qualms about checking in with my boss's boss.

"I'm so proud of you," Mother said from the other end. "Vice president."

"I don't have the promotion yet," I warned her.

Jackson murmured something to his wife, and across the width of the table, I heard the phrase "the man." Typical Jackson. Criticizing me for not following in his entrepreneurial footsteps, or our father's.

"Making my way up at an established firm is a solid career path," I said. "It's secure."

"Safe," he scoffed. "Limiting."

"We can't all run off and be entrepreneurs. Some of us have others to take care of."

"You don't have anyone to take care of." Jackson stuffed a hunk of pie into his mouth. Alicia frowned and whispered something in his ear. His jaw bulged as he chewed.

"He takes care of me," Natalie said. "Speaking of which, I need a ride on Monday. Can you pick me up from class on your way home?"

I rolled my eyes. "Again?" I'd have to bring home the extra work from my new projects. Vic wouldn't see me working late. But family was always my first priority, so I said, "Okay."

Sam's soft voice floated to me across the table. "You're a good brother, Andrew. Thanks for always looking out for us. And thanks for watching out for Mother."

I gave a quick jerk of my chin. Three years ago, when our mother had collapsed and ended up in the hospital for bypass surgery, I'd raced across the country to be by her side. After the procedure, when she'd looked so frail in the hospital bed and asked me to stay, how could I say no? I'd quit my job in New

York, broken my lease, and spent the next month ensuring she took her meds and did her physical therapy. Charles was too soft to push past Mother's stubbornness, Nat was too young, and Sam and Jackson were occupied with school and work.

Once Mother had recovered enough to resume her normal activities, I'd found a good job at the bank. Close enough to check on her a couple of times a week, so I didn't worry as much.

"Hey," Natalie said. "Your shirt matches the dessert."

I looked down at my shirt, one of Carly's choices. This one was a casual button-down in a brown-and-orange tattersall pattern. The cuffs and inside collar had a coordinated dotted fabric that my color-averse former colleagues in New York would've frowned at, but it felt like a festive choice for Thanksgiving in California. I mumbled something noncommittal.

But she wasn't ready to let it go. "It's more color than I've seen you wear since your high school soccer uniform." Her mouth dropped open. "You got someone to style you! Was it Carly Rose?"

I glanced quickly at the head of the table. Mother paused, but then she went right back to feeding the baby a spoonful of pie.

"Let's keep our voices down, okay? Yes, she styled me. For the —" Whoops, hadn't meant to mention the wedding. "For the season," I said instead.

Nat scanned from my shirt to my pants. They weren't anything special, but they fit more snugly than my usual khakis and, magically, without constricting. "She's good if she can get you to change things up."

"Yup." I shoved a forkful of pie into my mouth to keep from saying anything else.

I had mixed feelings about my styling experience. Sure, it had been convenient to have clothes show up at my door one night after work. It was better than the catalog shopping I usually did because it took away all the decisions I hated making. But it was also impersonal. Like our terse text exchange.

On my more hopeful days, I imagined she'd thought about me when she'd gone to the store or that she'd pictured my face and my body as she picked out the shirts and pants. Had she run her hand over each garment and thought about touching it, warm from my body? The faintest trace of her perfume rose from the shirts. I hadn't washed them, only smoothed out the wrinkles with an iron. I buried my nose in my collar to catch a whiff of tart apple.

"What are you doing, weirdo?" Natalie elbowed me in the side. "You look like a turtle."

I lifted my chin. "Nothing. Had an itch," I lied. "I was afraid if I took my hands off my pie, you'd steal it."

"Oh my god," Natalie mumbled through a mouthful pie. "Why don't we eat this every week? I always forget how good it is."

I blotted my mouth with a napkin. "You should ask Telma to make it for you for Christmas."

"Mmm," she hummed. Then she swallowed. "Wait, why will she make it for *me* and not for *us*? Where are you going to be on Christmas?"

I chewed and swallowed, remembering the rules. We hadn't talked specifically about telling anyone but Mother, but Carly wanted to keep our arrangement on the down-low. "I, uh, I have plans."

"What plans do you have for Christmas?"

"I'm spending time with a friend."

"A friend? Oliver? I thought he'd go see his family in Boston." She tapped a forest-green nail against her lips. "This seems out of character. You never miss brunch, and you're the one who always made us eat dinner together after...after Dad died. Why would you ditch us on Christmas? What do you know that I don't?"

For one wild second, I thought she'd keep her question to herself. But true to her place in the birth order, she couldn't keep her nose out of my business.

Turning toward the head of the table, she called, "Mother, what are our plans for Christmas?"

Our mother wiped the baby's face with a cloth napkin. "Jackson and Alicia are spending the holiday in Texas, and Sam and Niall are going to Ohio, so Charles talked me into going to Spain for Brad Winner's wedding."

My fork froze halfway to my mouth.

"What?" Natalie squawked. "You're leaving me here alone for the holidays?"

"You're hardly a ten-year-old Macaulay Culkin," our mother said. "You'll be fine with the run of the house. And this way, you and Andrew are free to celebrate however you like."

Before I could stop her, my little sister pouted. "But Andrew's going away too."

"You are?"

When Mother's gaze swiveled to me, I shoved another bite of pie into my mouth and nodded. She was going to Brad's wedding? Carly would lose her shit. She might even change her mind about our arrangement. There was only one way to play this: balls-out.

I swallowed the pie. "I'm going to the wedding too. With Carly Rose."

Silence fell over the table. Even Valentine stopped her babbling.

Jackson broke it with a low whistle. "Way to go, little bro. You're batting above your average there."

Mother blinked. "What?" But her voice didn't rise on the question. It came out flat with disbelief.

"I—" I should've told her last weekend when it was only the four of us. "It's about the promotion. Vic told me a VP needed to look more stable. So, I made an arrangement. With Carly."

"An...arrangement?" Mother's voice sounded far away.

"She went with me to a client dinner." It was more than that, considering the client was her ex, but my strategy was to tell the story as expeditiously as possible, then distract Mother with some other topic. "She'll attend the bank's holiday party as my date. In exchange, I'm going to Brad's wedding with her. I guess we'll see each other there." I shoved my fork into my pie and stuffed a huge bite into my mouth. It tasted like failure. None of my siblings would have to fake-date someone to earn a promotion.

"When I said she should go to the wedding, I didn't mean *you* should take her." Ice crackled in Mother's tone.

I swallowed. "It's a win-win."

"She's old enough to be your mother."

My fork clattered onto my plate. "She's thirteen years older than me." I was tempted to unfasten my top button to get air to my overheated chest, but I'd gone up against Mother enough times to know that would be admitting defeat. I'd rather drown in sweat than show weakness.

She narrowed her eyes. "Consider the optics, Andrew. She's over forty and divorced. She's not fading quietly into the background like she should. Instead, she's trying to reinsert herself into *my* social circle to build that business of hers. She even had the nerve to come here last month and screech at me about it. Taking you to her ex's wedding is a ploy for gaining visibility. She'll drag you into her scandal. That's not good for your promotion."

"She was a huge help at my client dinner a couple weeks ago."

"Does Vic know it's a ruse?" she asked.

"No, and I'd appreciate it if you didn't say anything to him. Once I get the promotion, we'll split amicably. She'll have new clients for her business, and I'll have what I wanted." I pushed away the rest of my pie.

"Brad's wedding is going to be a Jerry Springer–style circus," she said. "It would be best if you weren't involved."

"Sorry, Mother. I promised. No one from the bank is going. I'm going to take a well-deserved break from work to enjoy the sunshine in Spain and hang out with my friend Carly."

She let the silence hang over the table for a few seconds. "Then I suppose we'll see you there."

I swallowed with difficulty. It seemed improbable that Mother would leave our argument unfinished. But when she held out her arms to take the baby and asked Alicia some question about her business, I reached a shaky hand for my glass of wine.

"You're in for it now," Nat said.

"You always were a troublemaker."

She snorted. "This time, you made your own trouble. Good luck with that."

15

THE PERFECT AMOUNT OF F-YOU, BRAD

CARLY

To-do list—December 7
Pick up shoes for Yelena's holiday party look
Return alternate gowns
Find something attention-grabbing to wear in Spain

I pulled the strapless dress from the rack, held it out in front of me, and squinted one eye. Mom had liked me in pink. The bright color was youthful, but was it the perfect amount of *fuck you, Brad*? I glanced at the rain pouring outside the boutique. It was winter in Barcelona too. Unless I wore a sweater, I'd freeze to death. A shawl would tip me over the line from sexy woman confidently dating a younger man to elderly lady being escorted by her nephew.

I shoved the dress back into the rack and shuffled through for one with sleeves.

"Carly! Carly!"

I turned as Hayley Darling tripped into the store, then chucked her umbrella into the stand near the door. She wore a red belted raincoat and carried a metallic Stella McCartney bag that cost more than my entire clothing budget for this trip.

She held out her arms and rushed to fold me into her embrace. "O-M-G, I was afraid this shop was too yesterday's news, but you're shopping here, so it means I can too. Are you buying stuff for Spain?"

She rocked me side to side, and I went with it. I hadn't been hugged since I'd met Tessa for coffee last week.

She released me. "Were you looking at this fuchsia? It's totally your color. Though it'd be a shame to cover it up with a coat. Maybe a faux-fur wrap? That'd be so old Hollywood. In fact, I have a baby pink one I got to keep from my last shoot. You can borrow it! I'll send it to you this afternoon. What do you think *I* should wear? Or should I not ask you since you're a stylist, and you get paid for that? Never mind. I don't want to put you in a weird spot."

She looked down at her black rubber boots, and damn it, I felt...something. Maybe not sorry for her since she was living in my house with my fucking Waterford, but a kinship, perhaps. I'd been young and in love with Brad once too.

"It's fine," I said. "Let's pretend we're a couple of friends shopping."

But that was the wrong thing to say. Tears pooled in her blue eyes, and her lip trembled.

"I'm sorry," I said, not knowing what I should be sorry about.

"It's okay." She wiped tears from her cheeks. Her mascara stayed put; she must have worn waterproof. "I cry for no reason these days. Yesterday, I cried at a dog food commercial. I don't even like dogs. Anyway, I hope we can be friends."

I tried to smile, but my face felt stiff. I'd rather walk down Market Street naked than be friends with Brad's new wife.

"I've been meaning to thank you," she said, sniffing one last time. "For being kind to me the other night at that bank dinner. Some of Brad's friends…they haven't been so nice."

My heart cracked a little.

Turning back to the racks of clothes, I said, "Navy and cherry red. Those colors will look great on you." I grabbed for a deep-blue garment and held it out to her.

It turned out to be a chunky boatneck sweater. But she took it from me. "Thanks. I'll try it on. I have most of what I'll wear on the trip, but I'm looking for one or two new pieces in a slim silhouette, something slinky, if you know what I mean?"

"Slinky." She could carry it off with her figure. Like that teeny white bikini I used to wear on the yacht.

I scanned the racks for dresses in the right texture. "Over there."

We wove our way to a rack of jewel-toned dresses in clingy fabrics. She unbelted her coat, plucked out a red dress, and held it up to her torso, smoothing the satin over her belly. "This one?"

"Yes, that red will look fabulous against your skin."

She hugged me again. "Thank you. What about this one for you?" She pulled out a jade-green wrap dress with long sleeves.

I chuckled. "Green is a little on-the-nose for an ex-wife."

"Right." Her cheeks pinked. "How about blue?" She pulled out a sapphire one with an iridescent sheen.

I tilted my head. She'd even pulled out the correct size. "That could work."

"Yay!" She clapped the sweater and the two dresses together. "This is fun."

We ended up turning the fitting rooms into an impromptu fashion show. We both sucked in our cheeks and struck runway poses. We clapped for each other every time. Surprisingly, it did turn out to be a little bit fun. By the time I changed back into my clothes, my cheeks ached from smiling.

When I emerged from the fitting room clutching the outfits I'd decided to buy, Hayley snatched them from me.

"My treat," she said. "In exchange for the professional advice." She bit her lip as she fumbled in her purse.

I shouldn't let her. Heat prickled from my chest to my cheeks. I had a clothing budget, anemic as it was, compared to hers, and plenty of pride. But when she pulled out the familiar black card, the one that used to have my name printed on it, something inside me expanded like a balloon filled with laughing gas.

"Okay." I'd let him pay for my clothes. And every time I put them on, I'd think, *Fuck you, Brad.* I grabbed a chunky statement necklace from the display. "This too."

"Yay! I love it!" She linked her arm with mine and towed me to the register.

As the clerk checked us out, Hayley leaned toward me. "I love that you're bringing Andrew Jones as your plus-one. He's such a hottie."

I looked around, but I didn't recognize any of the other shoppers. "We're keeping it on the down-low, you know?"

"Why? You're stunning and smart, and so is he. Did you know we went to the same school?"

"You mentioned it at that dinner. When you demonstrated that cheer." Cold prickles crawled down my arms. I'd been too caught up in seeing Brad again to process it. They'd gone to school together. When I was an adult. Hayley was a much more appropriate date for Andrew than I was.

She giggled. "Right. Sorry. P-p...wedding brain. Too many things whirling around up here!" She waved a hand at her sleek hair. "Anyway, he looked happy. And I bet some of that is you." Her blue eyes sparkling, she nudged my arm. "I'm always telling Brad's friends who give him shit about the age difference that age is just a number. He's your person, and it doesn't matter that he's my age."

Oh, it mattered. Brad was a man. He could get away with it. Sure, people might say something snide, but then they'd get over it. I'd been the butt of those jokes for the first year we'd been married, then never again.

When the woman was the older partner, it never went away. Like she was some sort of deviant.

I'd look ridiculous if I showed up at my ex's wedding with a younger man on my arm. People didn't hire the party joke to style them.

"What's the matter?" she asked. "You went stiff."

"Nothing, I..." I patted my pockets. "I think I left my coat in the dressing room."

I sprinted back to the dressing room where I hadn't left my coat, but I'd clearly left my sanity. What was I doing with Andrew? There was no way this would go well for me, for us. He should be dating someone his age, not escorting someone as old as me to my ex's wedding in another country.

I snagged my phone from my purse and tapped out a text to him.

> Me: The arrangement is off.

> Andrew: No, it's not. You can't just call it off

> Me: I can

> Andrew: Nope, not one of the rules. I already have my plane ticket. I'm going to the wedding with you. And I'm holding you to your promise about the holiday party

I sucked in a breath. He couldn't refuse. That's not how arrangements like these worked.

Was it?

> Me: Where are you? I want to talk face to face, not on this tiny keyboard

> Andrew: The soccer fields at St. Sulpicius Academy

I dropped my phone in my purse. I'd march over there and break our ridiculous agreement.

16

FALLING FOR MY FAKE DATE

ANDREW

From: Victor Lynch
To: All Finance Employees
Sent: December 7, 4:16 pm
Subject: Decorum

As we enter the holiday season, I'd like to remind all employees that a certain level of professional behavior is required not only at work but outside work. This includes behavior on social media and other online spaces.

Examples of unprofessional behavior include but are not limited to dressing up as a honeybee to explain the properties of hexagons.

Sincerely,
Victor Lynch, Chief Financial Officer

I dropped my phone into the pocket of my track pants, my heart pounding. I was already going against Vic's decorum directive. He'd lose his shit when I showed up dateless to the holiday party.

"What's wrong?" Oliver lowered the laser measure and started across the grass toward me.

"Nothing. It's all good." At least, I hoped it would be after I talked Carly off whatever ledge she was on. I waved him back into position. "Let's finish this shot."

"Better wipe that frown off your face then. You'll scare the kids."

"Okay, okay." I needed something positive to distract me from fears of my career implosion and the disappointment on Mother's and Charles's faces when I had to tell them I didn't get the promotion. My mind drifted toward the memory of Carly standing in my hotel room doorway. I felt my lips curling up.

"Better?" I asked.

"Hundred percent. Roll camera."

I raised the Ping-Pong paddle we were using as the target for Oliver's laser measure and spoke to his phone on the tripod.

"Today, we're talking about the Pythagorean theorem. The Pythagorean theorem describes the relationship between the sides of a right triangle." I paused so we could insert a voiceover with diagrams in editing. "My trusty assistant, Oliver, and I are going to set up a few right triangles on this soccer field and make some measurements so you can see how it works."

I was breathless from running down the sides of triangles when I saw Carly striding toward us, heels in hand.

I hadn't thought about her comfort when she'd said she wanted to meet me. Christ, I was a jerk. I held up a hand. "Just a minute," I called. "I'll come to you."

I jogged back to Oliver at the net. "We done? You got it?"

He hunched over his phone, shielding it from the glare with one hand, then he held up a thumb. "Got it. We're good. Want to meet me at my place for editing?"

"Yeah. Be there in a bit."

He glanced between Carly and me. "Good luck, man," he said, low. "I don't know what you did, but that is *not* a happy woman."

I grimaced. "I don't know what I did either."

"That's always the worst kind." He gripped my shoulders and stared into my eyes. "My life is better for having known you."

"Shut it, asshole." I shoved him, not gently.

He laughed. "See you later."

Squaring my shoulders, I trudged toward Carly, who waited at the sideline, her expression stony. I stopped just across the chalk line from her and wiped a bead of sweat from my temple. "Hi."

"Hi." Her gaze dropped to my workout shirt.

Conscious of the way it stuck to my sweaty chest, I plucked it away. "Would you be more comfortable in the parking lot? Or the car? Are you warm enough?"

She gave me a curt nod. "I'm fine. What are you doing here? Don't you need a ball to play soccer? And opponents?"

I chuckled. "We're not playing. My friend Oliver and I are…" Should I tell her about the videos? Would she think they were ridiculous like Vic did? Fuck it. She might as well know about my geeky hobby. Someone was bound to ask her about it at the holiday party, assuming I could turn this train wreck around.

"My friend and I make educational videos for kids. About math. Today we're doing one about the Pythagorean theorem. We used the lines and angles on the field to measure out different triangles and then confirmed that the hypotenuse is the square root of the sum of the squares of each side."

She squinted one eye. "That takes me back to high school geometry. Do you sell these videos to high schools?"

Fuck, I'd never thought to sell them. "No. We upload them to YouTube for free." No wonder I'd never become an entrepreneur like my brother or Carly. "According to the analytics, our viewers are a mix of kids and adults. Probably some parents watching with their precocious kids. Most of the emails we get are from tween-age kids."

"You get fan mail?"

"Yeah." I scuffed my cleat through the grass. "Kids seem to like the videos."

"God damn it," she muttered.

"What? What's wrong?" Shit, she thought the same as Vic. There went my chances at that promotion.

"I just...I came here to tell you the arrangement isn't going to work for me. And then you go and tell me *that*."

"Tell you what?" I might be a math genius, but I couldn't keep up with Carly.

"That you make videos to teach kids math. For free. On a Saturday. Most guys your age would be...I don't know. What do guys your age do on Saturday afternoons?"

I chuckled self-consciously. "Dunno. My friend and I make dorky math videos."

Her gaze dropped to my mouth, then up to my hair. "Do you always wear your hair like that in your videos?"

"Like what?" I ran a hand through it. My scalp was sweaty from all the triangles I'd run. I kept forgetting to get it cut, and it was unruly.

She rummaged in her purse and pulled out a small tub of something. "Mind if I...?"

"No." I bent my head so she could reach my hair.

She rubbed the product on her hands, then ran it through my hair. I closed my eyes, savoring the sensation of her fingertips against my scalp. When I'd gone down on her, she'd had her fingers in my hair, tugging at the roots, urging me on—

"I don't know about this arrangement," she said. "People are going to think I'm a…a cradle robber."

I blinked open my eyes. "I'm hardly a child. I'm a grown man, and I can make my own decisions. I've decided I want to date you. What's wrong with that?"

She tipped up my chin and assessed her work. "You've decided you want to *fake*-date me."

Since that kiss after dinner with Brad, I'd been wishing it were real. Even before that, in Monterey. Hell, since I'd seen her on her yacht in that bikini almost twenty years ago. But given the flash in her eyes, it didn't seem like the right time to mention my crush.

"Sure. But to everyone else, it looks like I'm dating you for real. Why wouldn't I? You're smart, ambitious, gorgeous. I'd be a fool not to want you."

I was no fool. I wanted to step across the sideline and kiss those downturned lips, stroke her back through her silky blouse, then slide my hands lower to where her narrow skirt followed the curve of her ass.

She'd made it clear she didn't want me.

She held my gaze for a moment, considering. Then she held up a mirror. "What do you think?"

I blinked at the mirror. What had she done to my hair? I didn't look like a math nerd who'd been running sprints. I looked like a movie star.

"How did you do that?"

"Just a little hair cream." She held up the tub. "Keep it. Use a light touch. This one has enough hold that it should carry you through one of your videos, even if you're running."

"That's magic. There's no way you won't get a dozen new clients at Brad's wedding."

"What if he says something cruel?" Dropping the mirror into her bag, she bit her pillowy-soft lip, and I wished I could take her into my arms and comfort her.

I shook it off. We were talking, not kissing. Our last kiss had been for show, at least for her. "If he says anything, I'll get in his face. No one messes with my date."

She pursed her lips. "What, and then you'll hit him with your caveman club? No, thanks. I meant what if he says something about you, about how young you are."

I grinned. Was that what it was about? It wasn't about me at all. It was about Carly's insecurities. "Why would he? He's older than you, and he's marrying someone younger than me. He's the ridiculous one."

"It's not the same for men. You know that."

"Where is this coming from? You seemed fine with it before."

"Fine is an overstatement. Remember our old rules?"

"Of course I do." There was gravel in my voice. I remembered everything about that night.

"I ran into Hayley today."

Oh. I could only imagine how fragile Carly's feelings were now that her ex, someone she'd given twenty years of her life to, was marrying someone else. Someone young and pretty.

I wished Carly could see herself the way I did. Strong and smart and beautiful and kind. Hayley was a pale shadow, like printouts at work when the toner ran out. Carly would see it after Brad's wedding was behind her. For now, the best way to get her there was to appeal to her business side.

"Our arrangement is working for both of us," I said. "Let me take you to this wedding. It'll be good for your business. And maybe a little fun too."

She made a face.

"Okay, fun might be overstating things. But we'll be in Spain, and if the wedding is awful, we'll head to the beach or drive to the mountains. Whatever you want."

She looked up at me from under her thick, mascara-black eyelashes, her irises clear as a glass of single-malt and just as delicate. I leaned toward her like she was a magnet and I was made of iron filings. But then I remembered how I'd felt after the last time I'd kissed her. Hurt. Ashamed of my feelings when she didn't reciprocate them.

I straightened and stuck out my hand. "Deal?"

She shook my hand. "Okay."

"Two weeks," I said. "In two weeks, we'll be in Spain. I promise, you'll have a fantastic time. Plus, everyone will beg you to style them."

She smiled. "Maybe you're right."

"I am."

As she drove away a few minutes later, I frowned. I should've mentioned my mother and Charles were going to the wedding. I couldn't blindside her like Vic had done to us when Brad joined us for dinner.

At the wedding, I'd protect her from my mother and Brad and anyone else who came for her. I clenched my fist.

I should've seen that protective impulse for the warning sign it was.

Falling for my fake date was against the rules.

17

MY EPIC MISTAKE

ANDREW

> Mother: When do you arrive in Barcelona?

> Me: The 23rd

> Mother: So late? Only two days before the wedding?

> Me: It's an arrangement. Not a vacation

> Mother: Ah, yes. The Arrangement.

> Mother: When will I see you?

> Me: You saw me last Sunday

> Mother: When will I see you IN BARCELONA?

> Me: Not until the dinner the night before

> Mother: All right. See you then.

I opened my eyes to the sun setting between the hotel curtains I'd been too tired to close. Even though we'd been in business class with seats that lay almost flat and Carly had slipped on an eye mask and nodded off, guilt had kept me awake on the flight.

She didn't know yet that my mother would be at Brad's wedding.

I sat up and scrubbed a hand through my hair. How long had I slept? Shit, was this jet lag? I'd heard of it, but I'd always thought it was a joke or something limited to those unlucky people flying in economy. I'd always been the guy ready for a meeting or a meal or a run when I landed in a new city.

Not today. I slapped my cheeks to wake myself up. I needed a shave. And the world's longest shower. And—I glanced at the tented sheets over my crotch—to take care of *that* before I saw Carly.

Earlier, after I'd trailed her through the airport and pulled her suitcases (yes, plural) from the belt, she'd found us a taxi to take us to this hotel, not the one Brad and Hayley had chosen, but a narrow building with a stone facade and wrought-iron balconies a few streets off the main tourist area. I vaguely remembered Carly telling me this was her favorite place to stay in Barcelona.

It was an older building, though considering the long history of the city, Barcelonians probably considered it new. The interior was slightly shabby but clean, the antiques polished to a lemony shine.

Carly, who'd insisted on arranging and paying for all our travel expenses, had booked too late to get us separate rooms. She'd checked with me before reserving a two-bedroom suite. After the sleepless twelve-hour transatlantic flight, I'd given the suite's living room a cursory glance, grunted, and shambled into one of the bedrooms. It had a large bed and a private bathroom, and for that, I was exceedingly grateful.

With old-man slowness, I eased out of bed, located my shave kit and fresh clothes, and trudged to the bathroom. Feeling slightly more human half an hour later, I walked out of my bedroom into the living room.

Carly sat on the claw-foot sofa, flipping through something on her tablet. Outside the window was dark. What had she done while I slept through the day like a dead man? She didn't look nearly as rough as I felt, and the lamplight gave her skin a soft glow and sparkled off the blond highlights in her hair.

"Morning," I said and winced. I might have washed the travel off my skin, but there was no rinsing the jet lag from my brain.

"Good evening." She smiled, but it didn't crinkle her eyes the way her best smiles did. "Hungry?"

When my stomach answered for me, I clapped a hand over it. "Yeah."

She stood. "Dinner is usually served later here, but we can find something to eat, especially if we go to a tourist-friendly spot. Let me—"

"Hey. Is something wrong?" She didn't usually talk this fast. Had I offended her earlier by marching like a zombie to my room? Should I have offered to escort her out? Yikes, I was a terrible wedding date so far.

"No." She bit her lip. "I guess I'm feeling…melancholy. Barcelona is one of my favorite cities, and Brad and I came here at least once a year while we were married. I walked around the neighborhood while you were asleep. I didn't think it would affect me like this."

God, I wanted to put the bastard in the ground for making her sad. "You're grieving your marriage. I get it."

"Not really. I think I'm more…bitter? Brad used to stay on US time so he could take calls from his clients, and we hardly ever did things together. I'm pissed that he's taken the city I loved and…"

"And associated bad memories with it?" I finished when she didn't.

She nodded.

"It doesn't have to be like that. We can make good memories. We'll mock Brad. What kind of loser can't come up with a unique place for his destination wedding?"

That earned me a laugh. A quick *ha,* but I'd take it and the smile that crinkled her eyes.

Twenty minutes later, we found a restaurant serving food in the off time my confused stomach had chosen to eat. We sat at a lopsided table for two on the sidewalk. The concrete still held some of the heat the winter sunshine had baked into it, but with the darkness had come a chilly breeze that the patio heater fought. Christmas lights stretched across the street from the buildings above, glowing against the inky sky. Golden reflections from lighted stars and trumpeting angels sparkled in Carly's eyes.

People strolled past us, holding heavy shopping bags or being towed by dogs. Carly patted each pup and cooed to them in Spanish. Meanwhile, I sniffed the scent of roasted meat, spice, and garlic that wafted from the restaurant's open door and let the ambiance wash through my tired brain.

When the server arrived, Carly ordered sangria, and I chose a local beer. He set a dish of olives on the table to go with our drinks. Starving, I reached for one and popped it into my mouth. The salty flavor burst on my tongue, and I rolled my eyes skyward. It was the best thing I'd ever eaten.

"Welcome to Barcelona," Carly said, smiling.

"Oh, my god. I may never leave." I grabbed another olive and moaned. "You come here every year?" I asked.

"Before the divorce."

It was my opportunity to help her make better memories, some that didn't involve that asshat, Brad. "What do you like best about Barcelona?"

"Hmm. The sangria." She toasted me and drank. "The food, the sunshine, the slower pace, the beaches, the people. Everyone here is so kind, you'll see. And the fashion." She sighed, the same way I had when I'd eaten that first olive.

"The fashion? You don't prefer Paris or New York?"

She shrugged. "Those places are better known. And I love them, too, especially New York. But Barcelona has a unique style and some up-and-coming designers I follow. But overall, I love the energy here, the sense of tradition mixed with edginess and the laid-back sense of not taking itself too seriously but still wanting to look good."

I leaned back in my chair. Even after a transatlantic flight, she looked better than good. How'd she do it? "How did you get interested in fashion?"

She traced a finger up the stem of her wine glass. "I grew up in Dallas, which has its highlights, but it isn't really a fashion mecca, you know? There's lots of fancy boots and the occasional Stetson, but it's more conservative than avant-garde.

"My mom and I didn't travel much, other than road trips for pageants. One time, she took me to New York for a long weekend. We stayed with some friends from her pageant days. And it happened to be Fashion Week. Her friends took us to watch as they unloaded racks of clothes from a truck. I didn't even see any of the models, but everyone there was so...so dazzling. Glamorous. Put together. There was this one woman..." She trailed off, a faraway look in her eyes.

I leaned forward. "What was special about her?"

"She...she was so clearly in charge. She was stylish, of course. Driven. Clearly paid attention to details and knew exactly how everything should be. Everyone listened to her.

Deferred to her. And it hit me. Right here." She tapped her chest. "I wanted to be like her. No, I wanted to *be* her."

"And now you are. You're all those things: stylish, driven, in charge." Along with her beauty, it was what had sparked my crush all those years ago.

Her forehead crinkled. "I'm nothing like her. I'm starting my stylist business from scratch. I'm begging for clients and styling people at a discount, hoping they'll tell their friends I did a good job. I'm nowhere near where I thought I'd be at forty—" She snapped her mouth shut.

Fucking rules. "You are successful. Everyone admires your fashion sense. Your intelligence. Your determination. Your management skills. When I was younger, I thought you were the most beautiful, best-dressed woman I'd ever seen. I still do."

Her cheeks pinked, but her jaw remained clenched.

"You always seem so...effortlessly confident."

"Effortless." She snorted. "There's a lot of work behind the appearance of effortlessness, from time in the gym to hours scouring the fashion blogs to introspection and assessment of one's features and sense of style. Then the years spent gaining self-confidence. The biggest lie in fashion is hashtag-woke-up-like-this. Behind every party, every outfit, every"—she made air quotes—"candid selfie, there are countless hours of preparation. Your mother knows all about it."

"Wow." I blinked. "I've never thought of that."

"You wouldn't. It's different for most men. But surely, you've worked hard to be up for a vice president position at—" Her smile was rueful. "At your age. What do you love about your job?"

"That's easy. I love math. I've always liked the precision, the unambiguousness of numbers. I can work with data to build models that we can use to make predictions."

Before I said the next thing, I took a deep breath. "My

models help people secure their futures. There was a time, right after Dad died, when we were struggling. His business was still in the startup phase, and it wasn't earning a lot. Mom had one kid in college and three more lined up behind him. She tried to hide it, but I knew she worried. So, when I got my little inheritance—it was all earmarked for my college fund—I invested it. When it did well over the first six months, I asked her if I could adjust the family's portfolio."

The server startled me when he stepped up to the table. "Ready to order?"

Carly looked at me. "Do you mind if I...?"

"Sure. Of course." I'd studied Chinese in high school, and although I knew a few Spanish words and phrases, the Catalan on the menu looked like Greek to me.

"Any food allergies, or anything you don't like?" she asked.

"No, I'm good. I mean, you're not going to make me eat brains or testicles, right?"

She exchanged a look with the server.

"Right?"

She smiled. "No. I usually skip the criadillas too." She ordered a few items in deliberate Catalan. Grinning, the server left.

Carly leaned forward. "I never knew y'all were in trouble after your dad passed. Did your plan work?"

"Yeah. It grew into a nice little nest egg. But then she married Charles, and he had enough money that no one worried anymore."

"That's impressive. And you did it all when you were, what, seventeen?"

"Sixteen." I shrugged. "In the end, it didn't really make a difference. But I liked it enough to become a financial engineer."

"And now you're rising to the executive suite." She swirled her sangria. "You've never considered going out on your own like your dad and your brother? Calling the shots and basking in the glory of victory yourself?"

"Me?" I chuckled. "No. I've seen the entrepreneur life, and I don't want any part of it. I like being a part of something bigger, working for the greater good and playing on a team. It's like when I play soccer. I can take or leave the scoring goals. What I love is passing to a teammate and celebrating after they score. Besides, I like my weekends."

She scrunched her nose. "Hmm."

"Weekends are the best," I insisted. "Sleeping in, cooking a big breakfast, maybe a soccer match or a long run. Forgetting all about work until Monday morning. My dad never took a break. And I won't work myself into the ground like he did. Though I have a ton of respect for business owners like you."

Respect? I swallowed. It wasn't only respect I had for Carly. It wasn't only lust, either. I'd had crushes before. On teammates. Classmates. College profs. I'd even had a humiliating, game-choking crush on a coach once. This wasn't that, either. I thought of Carly even when we weren't in the same room. I had fantasies that weren't only about sex, fantasies about a future together when we'd come to Barcelona and she'd take me to a fashion show or a street full of boutiques and I'd love it. Because I loved her.

Holy shit. *Did* I love her?

"Are you feeling all right?" she asked. "You're pale."

I took a shaky breath. "Fine. Must be the lighting." Our business arrangement didn't allow for anything real. Definitely not love. I tamped my burgeoning, unwelcome feelings down.

Maybe it wasn't actually love but a combination of jet lag and the romantic setting. Carly's hair sparkled with red highlights, reflecting the lights strung in the branches of the potted tree beside us. Beyond the lighted stars above, the words *Bones Festes* glowed at the end of the street. It was all so perfect that it reminded me of a theme park decorated for the holidays. All it needed was a little fake snow.

To go with our fake date.

The server bustled up with the first plates and arranged them on the table. Good. Food would be an excellent distraction.

Carly passed me the plate of tomato-topped bread. "Try this."

I lifted a slice and munched it. "Oh, my god," I mumbled between bites. "This is some kind of culinary sorcery."

She laughed. "Just fresh tomatoes, salt, good olive oil, and bread baked this morning. But it tastes magical, doesn't it? Especially when you eat it outside."

"I think I might have died on that airplane, and now I'm in heaven." I devoured the next slice, leaving the last one for Carly. I pointed at the other dish, which held a half-dozen deep-fried spheres. "What are those?"

"Fried cheese. I figured if fried foods help with hangovers, they might help with jet lag too."

Before she finished speaking, I crunched into one. The creamy cheese melted on my tongue. It came from a different universe than the fried cheese I'd eaten at bars back home. I moaned my approval.

The tapas kept coming, each dish better than the last. Well, except for the olives. I'd have to figure out how to smuggle some back home. But somehow, I knew they wouldn't taste the same in San Francisco. I understood Carly's passion for the city.

As I filled my belly, my jet-lagged brain cleared, and I remembered I had to tell her something that might ruin the Catalan Christmas magic. But I couldn't delay it any longer. I straightened and sucked in a gust of chilly air. I was too tired to put it delicately. Maybe it was best to do it quickly, like that time

Natalie enrolled in a cosmetology program and practiced waxing my eyebrows.

"So," I said, "there's been an unexpected development. My mother and Charles are coming to the wedding."

She set down her wine. "What?"

"They weren't planning on coming at first. But they changed their minds."

"When? Today?" She blinked.

"No." I looked down at the bowl of olives. They didn't look as appetizing anymore. "At Thanksgiving."

"You've known for *four weeks* and only decided to tell me now?" The women at the next table turned to stare. "What the hell, Andrew?"

Grasping her hand, I rubbed a circle on her palm with my thumb. I should've done this in private. "I was afraid you'd think it was a big deal—"

"It is a big-ass deal! If Audrey sees us together, she'll destroy me. I'll never style anyone in San Francisco again. I'll have to get a job at the fragrance counter at Bloomingdale's."

I gripped her hand. "She knows about the arrangement. She's fine with it." *Fine* was stretching things a bit, but I was certain my mother wouldn't make a scene at the wedding. "You two are friends—"

"That's absolutely not true. We're polite to each other in public."

"She respects you—"

"Another fallacy. She thinks I'm a low-class interloper."

I'd never heard those words come out of Mother's mouth. Besides, she viewed Carly as an equal; otherwise, she wouldn't have fought her so hard. "That's not true. She respects your talent and your success. She might have even envied you a little."

Carly snorted. "Envy *me?*"

"She never stops talking about that boat party."

"What boat party?"

I winced. I hadn't meant to tell her that, but here we were. "The party on your yacht on Labor Day weekend, right after you'd married Brad. You wore a bikini."

"You wear swimwear on a boat. In fact, I offered everyone swimsuits."

I chuckled. "According to my mother, you were supposed to have another stuffy hotel ballroom cocktail party." Carly would never do that. I admired her unconventional ideas. The way she twisted expectations to suit her purposes. The way I never did.

"I was?" She tilted her head. "I hosted it on the yacht because I loved going out on the water, beyond the city. Just me and the fresh air. I had no idea it'd cause such controversy. There were at least three other yacht parties that year."

"After yours, everyone wanted to host one," I said. "Mother couldn't forgive you for your success."

"Why didn't Brad tell me what everyone expected?"

I raised an eyebrow.

"Brad," she muttered. "But that was almost twenty years ago."

I shrugged. "You made an impression. You certainly did on me."

"I was so nervous. I don't even remember what I wore."

"A white bikini. With gold hardware between the—" I swallowed, remembering. Not only was her body incredible, but she carried herself with a confidence that made me see stars. "I took one look at you and had to spend the rest of the cruise inside, pretending to be interested in hearing about Derek van der Poel's trip to Amsterdam."

"I can't believe you remember."

"That bikini—and you—are impossible to forget."

She pulled her hand from mine. "That was a long time ago. And it only proves Audrey's going to make this week miserable."

I tamped down the defensiveness that rose inside me. My mother meant well, but Carly was my date, and she was my priority this week. *Because of our arrangement,* I reminded myself.

"No. We're going to have an incredible time. Not even Audrey Jones Hayes can stop us."

"Really?" She winced when her voice quivered.

Protectiveness surged in my chest. "I promise to do everything in my power to help you enjoy yourself this weekend. I'll shield you from my mother, from Brad, from anyone who threatens you. Plus, I'll be your marketing assistant while you woo the other guests and turn them into clients."

Her lips curled into a smile. "I don't need you to fight my battles or be my assistant."

"Let me take care of you." I wasn't sure where the words had come from, but they felt right. If I were at my ex's wedding, it was what I would have wanted.

"Take care of me?"

"I'll make sure you're well rested and hydrated. I'll distract you when you're worried. I'll remind you that you're a goddess." Tentatively, I reached across the table and smoothed a thumb over the crease between her eyebrows.

"That sounds...amazing."

Maybe it was the magic of the Christmas lights or the jet lag that made my voice come out as a rumble. It certainly had nothing to do with our arrangement. "You are amazing."

Clearing her throat, she moved the empty plates aside. Before she could shift it out of my reach, I snagged the bowl of olives. There were two or three left, and I was going to savor every delicious, briny bite.

"Be sure you're drinking enough water," she said with a nod

at my glass. "Those olives are salty, and rehydration is important after a long-haul flight."

"Thanks, *Mom*," I said, reaching for the last one. She stilled, and I froze, replaying my epic mistake. I cringed. "I didn't mean—"

"I know. I know." She wiped her hands on her napkin and placed it beside her plate.

I put my hand over hers. "I'm sorry. I'd have said it to any of my friends. It was a joke. A bad one."

"It's fine." She flapped her other hand like she could wave away the heaviness that had settled over our table. "Mind if I ask for our check?"

"Let me pay for dinner. Please." It was the least I could do after my gaffe.

"No. This is part of our arrangement." She waved over the server.

The server had a handheld device to take Carly's credit card at the table, and as soon as she'd paid, she stood. I fumbled to my feet and helped her put on her coat. When I rested my hands on her shoulders, she shrugged them off and with a brusque "Ready?" led the way back to our hotel.

She didn't look at me again, not when we walked into the hotel and she greeted the front-desk clerk, not when we rode the crowded elevator to the third floor, and not when she opened the door to our suite.

"I'm tired. Goodnight." With a vague wave, she shut the door.

I flopped down on the sofa, wide awake.

I'd fucked everything up, again.

18

WELCOME TO CRONE LIFE

CARLY

> *To-do list—December 24*
> ✔ *Hair and makeup (must be perfect)*
> ✔ *Shapewear (I'll regret it if I skip it)*
> *Anytime I think I'm falling for Andrew, remember I'm ~~almost old enough to be~~ frenemies with his mother*

Poking my hoop earring into my ear, I walked out of my bedroom to the living room where Andrew sat on the couch. "Can you call down to the front desk for a cab? We don't want to be…"

His *Financial Times* fluttered to the floor.

"What?"

He stammered, "You're…you're…"

"Is it too much?" I stopped fiddling with my earring and looked down at myself. The jumpsuit was from two seasons ago, but the divorce had dried up my social obligations, and I'd never worn it. It was a classic shape with long sleeves and wide legs that pooled around my espadrille wedges. The embroidery on the pale pink tulle overlay gave it structure and visual interest.

Judging by his stare, what gave Andrew the most visual interest was the deep vee neckline that plunged between my breasts.

I cleared my throat. "Too much?" I repeated.

"No." He swallowed. "Absolutely not."

I brushed at the fabric over my right thigh. "Hayley's young and beautiful, and she couldn't think I was trying to upstage her, right?"

"Carly." He kicked the paper aside and stepped around the coffee table to stand in front of me. Brushing his smooth-shaven cheek against mine, he rumbled in my ear, "You'll upstage every person in that room. It's unavoidable."

I stepped back. Hayley was a nice girl. I even liked her. I couldn't blame her for falling for Brad. He was magnetic when he wanted to be. And the last thing I wanted was to make the bride feel less-than during her wedding week.

More than that, the dangerous glint in Andrew's eyes reminded me of his slip-up last night when he'd jokingly called me Mom. Despite how much of a turn-on I found his interest in me and my business, anything romantic between us was a mistake.

People would laugh at us. At *me* for trying to use young, gorgeous, sexy Andrew to cover up my crow's feet. As my mother used to say, "In pageants and in life, they'll judge you for your appearance. Control it." Maybe fade-into-the-background black was a better choice. "Should I change?"

"No. You look exquisite. Besides, we wouldn't want to be late."

Exquisite? I smiled, not caring about the lines it carved in my face.

"Right." A late arrival would draw more attention. "Ready?"

He took the earring from my hand and, with his tongue poking out between his lips, threaded it through the piercing in my ear. "You are incredible, Carly Rose."

Warmth pooled in my chest. "Thank you," I whispered.

⁓

We weren't late, but Brad must have started the party early. In the private room in the hotel restaurant, his voice that carried over everyone else's and the red tip of his nose broadcast his buzz. Hayley hung onto his arm like he was a helium balloon and she was the only tether keeping him from floating off into the atmosphere.

"Carl!" he boomed, spreading his arms wide. Then he paused. "Can I still hug you?"

I flashed him a smile that made my face feel tight. "Sure."

When he enveloped me in his arms, the amber and cedarwood scent of Chanel Bleu reminded me of my annual Christmas gift of the fragrance. I wondered if Hayley knew to put a box of it under the tree or if he'd figured out how to buy things for himself.

When the hug went on a beat too long, Andrew cleared his throat. I gently pushed Brad's shoulder and muttered, "He's an affectionate drunk. It's only when he has too much that he—"

Brad's hand had wandered to the small of my back, and I not-so-gently shoved out of his arms. "That's enough. Do you remember—"

"Andy!" He extended a hand to my date. "I guess you're still with our Carly?"

My nostrils flared with my sharp intake of breath.

"Actually, it's Andrew," he said. "And she's my Carly now." He slipped an arm around my waist.

Arrangement or not, I couldn't let that stand. I stepped out of the circle of Andrew's arm and captured his hand in mine to keep it from roving. "He means, yes, we're here together. But I'm my own woman."

Andrew's cheeks reddened. "Of—of course you are. I didn't mean—"

"It's fine." I squeezed his hand.

"Together." Brad narrowed his bleary eyes. "I don't get it. Andy's like half your age."

"Not even close," I said as calmly as I could. "Hayley is, in fact, much closer to a third of your age than Andrew is to half mine."

Brad squinted, working out the math.

"Age doesn't matter," Hayley said. "That's what we tell everyone, right, babe? Anyway, I'm so glad you came. With all of Brad's friends here, it's great to see a friendly face. Two friendly faces."

My heart melted a little. "Thanks for including us."

Brad was still stuck in the math. "But—but Andy was in diapers when I married Carly."

"No, Brad," I said. "He was a teenager." *Barely.*

"So, while I was fucking Carly, you were, what? Listening to *NSYNC and whacking off to a poster of Jessica Simpson?"

I winced. He'd turned the corner from affectionate to mean. He'd never been physically abusive, but when he drank too much, it burned through his filter, and what he really thought came out. And Brad had some pretty low opinions of a lot of people. At this point in the evening, I used to put him to bed, though Hayley could hardly do that to her groom before we'd sat down for their prenuptial dinner.

"Hayley, Brad could use some water," I said.

"Or a punch in the nuts," Andrew growled.

"I remember!" Brad said, pointing. "That first party we had. The one on the boat. Remember, Carly? You wore a bikini even though all the other women wore dresses. You used to look hot in bikinis. And this one—" Brad frowned. "Or maybe it was his brother? Anyway, I think it might've been Andy. He said, 'Where's the bathroom?' and ran off. Must've spent the whole cruise puking in the head." He roared out a laugh.

"Brad, I'll get you some coffee," I said, my face burning. How had I stayed married to him as long as I did?

"I've got it. Sorry." Hayley fixed an all-too-familiar pained smile on her face. "We'll see you later. Once we've sobered up." Showing more force than I thought possible in her slender arms, she dragged him toward the door into the main restaurant.

"Sorry about that," I muttered.

Stepping in front of me, Andrew put his hands on my waist. "It wasn't you who said those things. It was him. You're a goddess. He's a tool."

I snorted. "I'm no goddess. I was spineless. How did I not see him for what he was?"

"Hey." He waited until I met his heated gaze. "You loved him." His throat worked on a swallow. "We forgive people we love. Your capacity for forgiveness is impressive. You're here at his wedding, aren't you?"

I chuckled and traced a circle around the button on his blue dress shirt. "That's more out of pettiness than forgiveness, but I'll take it."

He kissed the top of my head. "Regardless, you're a goddess. Don't forget it. How about a drink?"

This close, Andrew's clean, ocean scent curled around me, fuzzing my thoughts. As comforting as it was, I needed some distance. Otherwise, I'd treat this like an actual date, not a fake one. "A drink sounds great."

Later, I was glad we'd softened the edges of the party with a couple glasses of Spanish wine. Audrey and Charles came in after everyone else was seated. Apparently, she didn't mind the extra attention of a late arrival. They sat at a table in the far corner, and every time I looked up, she glared at me.

Andrew remained at my side, commenting on the delicious food, asking me about my friends, and questioning me about fashion. With his adorable distractions, Audrey's disapproval faded into the background.

Until Brad stood, clinking his glass with a knife. "Hey, everyone. Hey! I wanna say something." Everyone quieted, and he continued, "I gotta say, I'm glad Carly and me split." He tipped his glass of scotch toward me. "We had a good run, didn't we, Carl?"

Wincing, I grabbed a napkin to fan myself.

"If we hadn't ended it, I never woulda ended up with Hayley." He turned an adoring gaze on her. "And we wouldn't be having a—"

"Wedding!" Hayley popped up. "We wouldn't be having a wedding this week. Cheers!" While everyone shouted, "Hear, hear," she whispered in Brad's ear. His ears pinked, then he slipped his hand from her side to her stomach.

I didn't bother to speculate about what Brad might've said if Hayley hadn't stopped him. *A good run?* That's what he'd called our nineteen-year marriage? Then implied we'd mutually decided to end it? He'd shredded our relationship like tissue paper in the rain. After everything I'd given up for him—my career, my ambitions, my pride—*that's* how he summed it up.

Andrew leaned close. "Are you okay?"

"No." I gulped the rest of my wine.

"Want to get out of here?"

I'd intended to work the room for styling clients, but Brad had snipped my self-confidence like a wayward thread. Leaving sounded even better than drinking wine Brad had paid for. "Yes, but..."

"But?"

"Maybe we should leave separately?" I glanced at Audrey. She still glared at me. "Your mother..."

"She knows I'm your wedding date. She knows about our—" He cleared his throat. "I don't see how leaving together will change anything. Though I need to say hello. Family duty and all that. I assume you'd rather skip that?"

"Definitely." I wasn't up for talking to Audrey, not after Brad's toast.

"I'll meet you at the exit in five."

As I made my way to the front of the restaurant, I felt empty. Brad had scraped everything out of me—my equanimity, my accomplishments, my confidence—with his dismissive words.

A good run.

Twenty years of my life given to a man who summed it up in three words.

Rage bubbled up from the emptiness inside me. But not all of it was directed at Brad. No, I owned some of it too. I'd given him the best years of my life then let him create our narrative. I'd never let a man do that to me again. I'd never let myself be controlled or be the accommodating one who gave up *anything* for a man.

Never again.

Andrew and I were silent on the taxi ride back to our hotel. And when we got to our suite, I walked right into my room and closed the door, my mind churning over Brad's words.

I stared into my eyes as I washed off my makeup. I'd flown halfway around the world to prove to Brad—to everyone—that I was over him, that we could move past the divorce and be friendly and supportive of each other. Clearly, it didn't go both ways. Brad was *definitely* over me, but friendly and supportive? Not when he was drunk.

Why had I come?

I fluffed the pillow, then eased my head onto it. Nineteen

years of marriage to someone who didn't appreciate what I'd done for him. Now, I'd shown up at his wedding with a younger man, looking sad and ridiculous to everyone, including my former rival, Audrey Jones Hayes.

Who was also my date's mother.

Fucking hell.

I'd never get to sleep. I'd look old, haggard, and dried-out at my ex's wedding. Everyone would understand why Brad needed a young, dewy upgrade. Throwing off the covers, I stomped out of the bedroom to the living room's mini fridge for a bottle of mineral water.

As I lifted it to my lips, Andrew appeared at his door in plaid pajama pants and a T-shirt that clung in all the right places. He might need help with dress clothes, but his casualwear game was flawless. I'd been so distracted by his clingy shirt at the soccer field that I'd let him talk me into keeping up this farce. And now he tempted me again. I'd treated his body like an amusement park in Monterey. What I wouldn't give for a season pass.

I shook my head to rattle out the inappropriate thought.

"Sorry I woke you up," I muttered.

He squinted. We hadn't shut the drapes, and Barcelona was still lit up for a night of Christmas revelry.

"Can't sleep?" he rumbled.

"No, but it's fine."

"Fine?"

"It happens to me a lot. Now that I'm...now that I'm older."

He scratched his chest. "Want to come in here? I'm really good at sleeping. Maybe it'll rub off on you."

"You think sleep is contagious?"

He shrugged. "It's worth a try."

I remembered the last time I'd taken comfort in him. I *had* slept well after. But I was not going to sleep with Andrew Jones, neither euphemistically nor literally. Especially not out of his sense of pity.

"No, I—"

"Don't worry. I won't try anything."

That was worse. Andrew didn't find me sexy enough to want to touch me? *Welcome to crone life.* It had to be a hashtag.

"Come on." He beckoned me toward him.

I sighed. "If I can't sleep, I'm coming back out here. I don't want to keep you up too."

"Nothing can keep me up. Promise."

I followed him into the bedroom. The sheets were rumpled like he hadn't been sleeping as well as he'd claimed. He pulled them back and gestured to the bed so I could choose a side. I sat on the side closest to the door, and he circled to the other.

He waited until I lay down, stiff and straight as a valet stand. He slid in beside me and swept the comforter up to cover us both.

I stared at the ceiling. He hadn't closed the curtains completely, and a little light came in from the city outside. I could make out a fire sprinkler. I wondered if—

"This isn't going to work if you lie there like it's your job to go to sleep," Andrew grumbled.

He wrapped his arm around my waist and tugged me toward him, turning me on my side and nudging his knees behind mine. His chest expanded into my back on a long, slow breath.

"This isn't going to work," I whispered.

"Try it. Breathe with me."

I rolled my eyes. But the next time he inhaled, I did too. He exhaled, his breath hot on my neck. All of him was warm, from his chest to the arm flung over my waist to his feet, cushioning my chilly toes. My scalp prickled. What if I had a hot flash? What if he woke up covered in sweat that wasn't his?

"Breathe," he murmured in my ear.

If he woke up soaked, it was his own damn fault.

I breathed. In. Out. In. Out.

I let my heavy lids blink shut.

In. Out.

The next thing I heard was birds singing. When I opened my eyes, daylight flooded in.

Andrew Jones was still curled around me.

God damn it. I'd had my best sleep in years, and the warmth in my chest wasn't from a hot flash or from his hand on my stomach. No, I felt peaceful. Secure. Cherished. The same sensations that had terrified me that early morning in Monterey.

Again, my fake date had inspired some inconveniently real feelings.

This time, I had nowhere to run.

19

A GD GODDESS

ANDREW

From: Victor Lynch
To: Andrew Jones
Sent: December 24, 4:16 pm
Subject: RE: New model

Thanks for sending the new model before you left for vacation. The results look promising. I've shared them with the rest of the senior leadership team.

I'd like to introduce you and Carly to a few board members at the holiday party next week. You're looking like a strong VP candidate. Keep up the good work.

Sincerely,
Victor Lynch, Chief Financial Officer

For the first time, I woke up with Carly Rose in my arms, and I never wanted to wake up any other way.

Her hair smelled incredible, like coconuts and sea breezes. It reminded me of a trip I'd taken with friends to Puerto Rico. One morning, I'd gotten up while the other guys were still sleeping off their hangovers and headed to the beach, where I'd soaked up the warmth like a lizard and watched the waves as families, slathered in sunscreen, played nearby.

It had been a perfect day. I had nowhere to go and no responsibilities. I lived in the moment.

But *this* was the moment I wanted to live in forever. A moment where I believed there could be more mornings like this, waking up nestled against this incredible woman. She was steel and soft satin, wisdom and compassion, beauty and fire. Every time I was with her, she cracked open a window and let me glimpse the amazing person behind her protective wall of couture. And every time, I wanted more.

I'd never get enough. Was this what love was like?

I gazed at her shoulder, bared by her sleep tank. It was smooth and round, and I contemplated laying a kiss on the mole right above her shoulder blade. If I could do it without waking her.

Carly moved, brushing her ass against my hard-on. A shudder traveled through my body.

Scratch that, I wanted to live in *that* moment forever.

She tapped my arm, slung around her waist. "Sorry, I have to get up."

I kept my groan inside but lifted my arm. She slid out of bed, straightened her tiny silk tank and shorts, and without a backward glance, left the bedroom.

I flopped onto my back. There went the perfect moment.

I resisted reaching for my phone. I'd probably find a text

from Mother repeating what she'd hissed in my ear last night: *This arrangement of yours is ridiculous. Why choose her as your proof of stability? Brad Winner is a sinking ship, and he'll take Carly down with him. You don't want to get caught up in that.*

She had a point about Brad. He used to be friendly, but last night, he'd been an absolute ass. How had Carly stayed with him as long as she did?

I knew the answer to that rhetorical question. He was an achiever, a business owner. I lived comfortably, but I'd never reach his level of success. I could never support her in the ostentatious style he had.

Plus, I was the son of her frenemy. Despite her rules, she kept bringing up our age difference. She saw me as a kid, not an equal partner in her life. But as long as she needed me, I'd stand with her against shithead Brad and anyone else who made her feel like less than the spectacular person she was.

Because I'd made the foolish mistake of falling for her.

"Hey." She leaned against the door to my bedroom. She'd covered herself with a flowered satin robe. "Merry Christmas."

I could think of a lot of things that would make my Christmas merrier, starting with touching that silky robe. But I had to play it cool or she'd run away. Just like Monterey. "Merry Christmas."

"We have a few hours before we have to get ready for the wedding. What do you want to do? Do you need to work?"

"Nah, I'm on vacation. Besides, it's a bank holiday."

One corner of her mouth turned up into an ironic smile. "I know how you finance guys are. You're always working and always on your phone even on holidays."

"Nope." I didn't even glance at my phone on the bedside table. "Not today. Come back to bed. I can think of a better way to spend those few hours."

She stared at the tented sheets. "I don't think so."

Chuckling, I propped up onto my elbow and shifted so my erection wasn't as obvious. "Worth a shot."

She looked anywhere but at my lower half. "We can order some breakfast."

"Or...you can show me the city. We've hardly seen anything, and we leave the day after tomorrow."

"Really?" Her eyes went wide. "You want to see the Gaudi sites or Picasso? We'll have to narrow it down to show you the best—"

"I don't want to see what the tourists do. I want to see your favorite spots. I want to experience what you love about this city."

She cocked her head at me like she was trying to translate what I'd said, then she peered out the window. "Looks like a good day for walking. Wear comfortable shoes."

Fifteen minutes later, I trailed her as she moved confidently through Barcelona's subway system. After getting off the train, we walked up the steps and emerged outside. A massive red-brick archway caught my eye across the street.

"The Arc de Triomf," she said. "Like the one in Paris."

"Or like Washington Arch in Greenwich Village."

"Exactly." She headed across the street.

As we walked under it, I marveled at the artistry of the carvings, but Carly didn't linger. She continued onto a palm tree–lined promenade.

"Usually, it's crowded, but today most people are spending Christmas with family."

I wanted to slip my arm around her waist and tell her I was spending Christmas with the person I most wanted to be with, but Carly's boots tapped out a fast cadence, carrying her out of my reach.

We crossed a street and walked between two massive classical statues into a park, this one greener but just as formal.

"This is the Parc de la Ciutadella. After they demolished the city's fortress, they built it for the World's Fair. The Arc was the entrance. There's a zoo at the other end, but I prefer this side, the gardens." She took in a deep breath. "It makes me feel peaceful."

"Show me."

She took my hand, and we meandered along the tree-lined paths past more sculptures and a playground. She stopped to pet every friendly-looking dog. While I looked on, she snapped a picture for a Japanese family in front of a modernist building with turrets. When my stomach growled, she showed off her Catalan by buying coffee and pastries from a cart.

Though the flowerbeds were bare and the day was subdued, I understood why she loved the place. We had the park almost to ourselves, and the winter light filtered through the tree limbs in a timeless kind of twilight. I didn't know if we'd walked for minutes or hours when she pulled me to a stop.

"This is it. The pièce de résistance. Though that's French, and I don't know what the expression is in Spanish or Catalan. Anyway, it's what everyone comes to see. They say Gaudi worked on it while he was still in architecture school."

She gazed at the fountain, and I dutifully scanned the over-the-top structure from the clutch of golden horses pulling a chariot at the top to the stone statuary and griffins of the middle tier to the greenish water at the base. But I was less interested in the famous sight than in Carly and how she felt about it. Her gaze lingered on the trio of women in the center, her expression flat.

"What's wrong? Are you tired?"

"Always." She gave a rueful snort. "But...I don't know. It just struck me, today of all days."

I waited for her to continue.

"That's the birth of Venus, at the top. She was born when one of the Titans cut off his father's balls and tossed them into the sea."

"Gross."

"Right? She's supposed to epitomize female beauty and love. But that story's steeped in the male gaze. She is what she is because of male power."

She went silent. Was she thinking about shithead Brad? Or the patriarchy? Maybe both. I wanted to reach for her to comfort her, but she might see it as an expression of male power.

"And the two women at the sides?" She walked around to the left and pointed. I squinted at the reclining female. "That's Danae, the mother of Perseus. Zeus impregnated her in a golden shower."

"Literally? Why didn't my teachers tell me Greek mythology was so kinky?"

"Well, you never know with myths. The point is, she didn't have much of a choice."

Damn, I wished I'd listened better in school. Though I got the feeling we'd glossed over most of the patriarchal bullshit. And the kink.

"And on the other side, there's a woman with a swan. That's Leda."

"I remember her! Zeus came to her in the form of a swan… ugh." I cringed. "More rape. With a little bestiality thrown in."

"You got it. The women in these statues, these stories, they're vessels. Objects. Like I was for so long. Goddamned Brad didn't even want me to give him kids. I was only a trophy to him, until I wasn't anymore." She swiped at her cheek under her sunglasses.

I was going to murder that asshole when I saw him later today, wedding day or not. Tentatively, I touched her shoulder. When she didn't resist, I pulled her into my chest. She held herself stiffly.

"Is this okay?" I asked. "I don't mean to project my male power. I only want to...to comfort you."

"It's okay." She relaxed a bit.

"Did you want kids?" I murmured into her hair.

"Not really. Brad's kids spent weekends with us sometimes, and that was plenty. I always wanted a dog though."

"Why didn't you get one?"

"I did. A Cavalier King Charles spaniel puppy. I'd wanted one ever since I saw the photos of Blake Lively's. Shallow, I know. Anyway, I got her as a surprise for Brad."

I grunted. I couldn't imagine Brad liking any kind of surprise, especially a fluffy one that would shed its hair on his expensive suits.

"It was a terrible idea. I was young and foolish. I had her for one glorious day while he was on a business trip. I named her Gia. She was the cuddliest little thing. She slept with her head on my pillow. But she was a puppy, not house-trained yet, and when Brad walked in the front door, there was a tiny dog turd on the Aubusson. He made me take her back before he even unpacked his suitcase."

I wasn't a violent man, but I imagined myself punching Brad's smug face until he bled all over his white dress shirt.

"Hey. Hey. It's okay," she said, gently disentangling her arms from my suddenly viselike grip. She set her hands on my shoulders like I was the one who needed comforting.

Our faces were inches apart. Gold flecks as bright as the fountain's gilded statues glinted in her eyes.

"It's not okay," I said. "What he did to you. You have so much power, so much strength, so much worth. And he can't tarnish that. No one can."

She lifted a hand to my cheek. "Thank you," she whispered, "for giving back my beautiful memories of Barcelona."

I hadn't yet figured out what we were to each other. I'd been her one-night stand, and now I was her wedding date. We'd kissed, though it was only for show, and she'd slept in her sexy pajamas in my arms last night. I wanted more. But every time I thought I'd crossed the drawbridge into her fortress, she catapulted me right back out. Until now.

I held her in my arms as every one of my cells begged me to kiss her pink lips, only a breath from mine. One rational thought speared through the haze of lust. "Don't thank me. You don't need me to approve you. You don't need me at all. But Carly, I need you. I want you. You're the most amazing woman I've ever—"

Her lips landed on mine, stopping my endless flow of words before I could say something foolish like *loved*. I knew she wasn't ready to hear that. I'd worry about it sometime when Carly Rose wasn't kissing me. In public.

Maybe she'd meant to give me a quick, grateful kiss. But I wasn't having that. I threaded my fingers through her silky hair and held her to me as I plundered her with my lips and tongue. I poured all my desire, my longing, my admiration into that kiss.

And she did the same. She gripped my shoulders and returned the kiss with a wildness that matched my own. Everything disappeared around me, replaced by the rush of my pulse and desire for the woman in my arms.

I didn't realize my hands had wandered until Carly broke away from the kiss and removed them from her ass. "Maybe we should take this somewhere more private," she whispered.

I lifted my head and looked around like there was some alcove or outbuilding at the park where I could lose myself in her.

"Taxi," she said. "The hotel."

"Right." I shook my head, trying to rattle the sensible parts back into place. I grasped her hand and headed along the path toward the street.

I flagged down a taxi and let Carly pronounce the name of the hotel before I pulled her into my lap and devoured her with more kisses. Her weight against my dick made my vision go gray at the edges, so to keep myself from going off in my pants, I thought of Brad and what he'd done to Carly last night.

I gentled my kisses to show her my respect for her, to demonstrate I wouldn't take like he'd done. That I wanted the same type of partnership she'd wanted from him. That I'd never be a fool who didn't appreciate what he had.

The car stopped, and I shoved a wad of euros at the driver to compensate him for having to witness our make-out session. Then I helped Carly from the car and hustled her up the stairs to our suite.

Fuck, the key. How did a key work?

My fingers shook too hard to get the old-fashioned strip of metal into the lock.

Carly's hands were steadier as she eased the key from my fingers and turned it in the lock. I paused long enough to shove open the door, wrench out the key, and toss it to the floor before I pressed her to the inside of the heavy wood door and trailed kisses along her throat as I unwound her scarf.

I took my time at her neck, lapping at her pulse points where she'd dabbed her perfume that reminded me of tart apples in late summer. I found a spot that made her moan and thrust her chest against mine.

I pushed her coat aside and trailed my hands over the front of her blouse. "This okay?" I asked between kisses.

"Yes, I-I need..."

"What do you need?"

I started at her top button. As much as I wanted to rip and tear everything that separated our bodies, Carly cared too much about clothes for me to ruin them, so I eased the buttons loose.

"You. I need you." She palmed the front of my jeans, and I

hissed. Too much more of that, and I'd go off in my pants. And I didn't want that. I wanted to savor her for hours like we'd done in Monterey. I'd tease her while she writhed against the white sheets.

I buried my face in her cleavage to inhale her, to taste her. Then I reached behind her to unfasten her bra. My fumbling fingers were too slow, and I licked her pointed nipple through the thin fabric.

She gasped and gripped my dick through my jeans.

We weren't going to make it into the bedroom.

I finally released the bra hooks and shoved the cups up over her breasts so I could nip and lick her skin. I swirled my tongue around her rosy nipple, and she held my head to her.

"Don't stop," she moaned.

Never. But I didn't stop to say the word.

I found the fastener to her pants—thank god there was only one, and it was easier than her bra—and flicked it open. I drew down the zipper and let her pants shush to the floor.

I paused at her breast long enough to ask, "Okay?" as I slipped a finger inside the waistband of her panties.

"Yes," she whispered.

I dropped to my knees and tugged her underwear to her ankles. I worked one leg out of her panties and wide-legged pants, though I didn't bother to take off her ankle boot. Nudging her leg over my shoulder, I gazed up at my prize, glistening with arousal.

"Lean against the door," I said. "Let me know if you feel unsteady."

"I—" She gasped when I licked her with the flat of my tongue, trying to taste all of her at once. Ever since I'd sampled her in September, I'd craved more.

I refamiliarized myself with the shape of her, her scent blooming around me. Her lips, pink and swollen. Her clit nudging out of its hood. The moisture dripping down the inside of her thigh.

I lapped that up first before I traced a circle around her lips. I swiped up the center, but I didn't touch her clit. Not yet. Still, her legs trembled, and I put my hands on her hips to steady her.

"Andrew, I...I need..."

I licked her seam one more time before I smiled up at her. "What do you need, my goddess?"

Her cheeks reddened. "My clit. And you can be...a little rough."

I gusted a breath over her. "Thank you for telling me."

I did what she asked. I licked a circle around her clit. Then I did it again with more force. She cried out, and her leg shook on my shoulder. I gently took the nub between my teeth and hollowed out my cheeks, sucking for all I was worth.

She tensed and squeaked like a rusty screen door. I kept up the suction until she relaxed and nudged at my head. Releasing her, I cleaned her up with my tongue.

I sat back on my heels and gave her a playful grin. "I remember that sound from Monterey."

Her face went red. "Sorry, I...I guess I really let go. I don't usually—"

"I love your sounds. Let's hear the sounds you make when you ride me."

Her eyes glowed. She slipped her leg from my shoulder and kicked out of her pants and panties. "I want you behind me."

My blood roared in my ears at the thought of grasping her ass while I pounded into her. "You're killing me. You know that?"

She bit her lip and nodded. She slipped off her coat and dropped it to the floor. Still wearing her blouse and her boots, she sauntered to the couch and folded herself over the arm.

I followed, unfastening my belt. A little embarrassed at my

presumptiveness, but also thankful for it, I pulled the condom out of my jeans pocket.

"Such a Boy Scout," she said, tossing me a smirk over her shoulder.

"Always prepared for when my wedding date might have a need." Shoving my jeans to my hips, I rolled it on.

"A need?" Her body betrayed her. A drizzle of wetness spilled from her pussy.

"At your service, ma'am," I drawled, scooping up the wetness and rubbing it over the condom. I gasped in anticipation of her warm, wet clench.

"Ready?"

She nodded.

I thrust inside, and every nerve lit up inside me. My head floated while my feet stayed firmly planted next to hers. When my vision cleared, I backed almost all the way out and surged forward again.

She gave a high-pitched grunt, not quite the squeak I wanted to hear again. I ground into her, grasping one of her round ass cheeks while I trailed my other hand lower to her clit. I tweaked it, and she grunted again.

"Good?" I asked.

"More," she said.

I started at a steady pace that I desperately hoped would hold off my orgasm long enough for hers to build again. She was tight, squeezing around me, the friction exactly what I craved. She met each thrust, our skin slapping faster and faster, until my control slipped. I grasped her waist and used her until my vision narrowed to a pinprick and I came, roaring.

When my head cleared, I found myself slumped over her, bracing my hands on either side so she didn't bear my full weight. I replayed my foggy memory. No screen-door squeak.

The back of my neck prickled. "Did you come?"

"No, but I did before. It's—"

"Don't say fine," I growled. "Don't ever say it's fine. Not with me. Not with—" I'd almost said *with anyone,* but the thought of anyone other than me fucking Carly replaced the lingering sweetness on my tongue with bitterness. "Not ever."

I was still half-hard, and I ground my hips in a circle while I found her clit again, pinching it between my fingers, gently at first and then with determination. She gasped and pressed back against my groin. I rubbed and vibrated my fingers against her clit as her grunts lifted higher and higher in pitch.

I kept it up until, at last, she keened out that squeal I'd been chasing. She stiffened briefly before she went limp. I rucked up her blouse to expose the beautiful column of her spine, glistening with sweat, and kissed it. "You are a goddamned goddess, Carly. Never forget it."

20

ZOMBIE BRIDE

CARLY

> *To-do list—December 25*
> ✔ *Do something memorable in Barcelona*
> *Do a better job of networking at the reception*
> *Do Andrew again*

"You're radiant."

"I'm sweating." I dropped Andrew's hand and fanned my neck.

I glanced at the other wedding guests in the hotel ballroom. What a disaster. The invitation had specified "beach formal," whatever the hell that meant. The guests wore a disconcerting mix of formal gowns, flip-flops, tuxes without ties—including one without a shirt—and rumpled linen. Half looked uncomfortable about being overdressed, and the other half looked embarrassed about being underdressed.

Still, they chatted, drank champagne, and laughed like it wasn't a million degrees.

"Is it hot in here or is it just me?"

When Andrew scrunched up his nose, he reminded me of the teenager I remembered. "It's a little warm?"

"Liar. You're still wearing your blazer."

"Want me to take it off?"

That would only remind me of what we'd done in our hotel room. I didn't regret it. I'd floated through the ceremony, where my ex-husband married a woman young enough to be my daughter, on a post-orgasmic cloud. Unfortunately, I also hadn't stopped sweating. Thank the makeup gods for setting spray.

"Not unless you're hot too."

He leaned forward and whispered in my ear, "Of course I'm hot. You said it, like, three times while I was making you come." His voice rose to a high-pitched purr. "'You're so hot, Andrew.'"

"I did not!" I pushed at his chest. Not too hard; I didn't actually want him to go anywhere.

He murmured, "You thought it though."

My satisfied sex gave a happy tingle. When he'd gone to his knees, when he'd sucked my clit like it was his job, I'd given up hope I'd ever be satisfied with a vibrator again. "I did."

He kissed the side of my mouth. Anyone watching from a distance might have thought he kissed my cheek. Up close, it was anything but chaste. He *lingered.* Lingering was a big thing with Andrew Jones. After he'd railed me over the side of the couch, he'd curled up around me, sweat and all, peppering my skin with kisses and stroking my back until I fell asleep. Then he'd fallen asleep, too, and we had to sneak into a back-row seat while the ceremony was in progress.

Reluctantly, I pulled away. "Your mother's here. Let's not get carried away."

He frowned. "She'll think it's because of the fake dating. But we're real now, right? The park, the couch…that wasn't fake, was it?"

My chest felt almost too full to breathe. "I'm not sure what we are now, but that wasn't fake."

His blue eyes smoldered. "Then let her see. Let everyone see. She wants me to be happy. And I'm overjoyed right now."

My heart skipped a beat. This time, I leaned in and kissed the corner of his mouth. Quickly. No lingering. "I'm happy too. Which is not something I thought I'd say at my ex's wedding."

Time for some space. "I'm going to freshen up in the ladies'. Maybe it'll be cooler in there."

"I'll find us some drinks. What'll you have?"

"A Cava, please." I turned and headed toward the restrooms.

When the bathroom door separated me from the string quartet music and the buzz of conversation, there was a blessed moment of silence.

Until a retch came from one of the stalls.

It seemed too early for someone to have over-imbibed, but I shrugged and went to the sink and ran cool water over my hands and wrists.

The person retched again, then flushed the toilet. Good. She was done. I washed my hands and dried them on a paper towel. I'd pulled out another towel to blot my forehead when a sob came from the toilet stall.

Shit.

I walked to the stall, letting my heels click on the tile so the person would have a warning, and rapped gently on the door. "Excuse me, are you all right?" Then I remembered we were in Spain. "Disculpe, ¿está enferma?"

"Carly?" A weak voice warbled.

Damn it. I knew that voice.

The lock clicked, and the door swung inward. Hayley looked as sweaty as I did, but her face was greenish. Mascara circled her eyes and trailed down her cheek. One of the tendrils her hair stylist had left to frame her face in her half updo was wet and had something gooey stuck to it. And her white lace gown had a streak of brown on the bodice.

"Are you sick?" Of course she was. "Should I get Brad?" That was better. His bride, his problem.

"No! He can't see me like this, not on our wedding night. I'm fine. I'll be fine. Just a little...you know."

"Food poisoning? Norovirus?" I took a half step back. I did *not* want to be patient zero who spread a stomach flu to Andrew, plus a plane full of passengers on Friday.

She cradled her flat stomach with one hand. "No."

Holy. Shit. "You're *pregnant?*" I whispered.

She nodded. "No one knows except my mom and Brad."

"Brad knows?" We'd always been so careful about birth control. Brad hadn't wanted more kids. I'd been relieved that motherhood wouldn't disrupt my career. That was before I'd let marriage annihilate it.

"Yeah, he's—" She swallowed. Then she held up a finger and whirled toward the toilet. I had time to scoop up her hair, discovering that, yes, that was puke in it, before she heaved and spat into the bowl.

She coughed and flushed, then blotted her face with toilet paper. She turned to me, paler than her white gown, and smiled weakly. "He's ecstatic."

With difficulty, I kept from raising my eyebrows. "How do you feel about it?"

"Besides nauseated and sore?" She chuckled. "Over-the-moon excited. I can't wait to have a family. It's twins, you know."

"Twins?" Brad was having *two* more children? At his age? The sweat cooled on my skin, and I shivered.

It hadn't been that he didn't want more children. He hadn't wanted them with *me*.

I leaned against the side of the stall. My post-orgasmic haze evaporated. All that was left was me, unworthy of even Brad Winner's respect. Or his babymakers.

"Are you all right?" Hayley reached out a pale, trembling hand.

I straightened, my many years of practice pretending I was invulnerable kicking in. "I'm fine. How are you? Feeling any better?"

"Yeah." She looked down at herself. "I'm kind of a mess."

"Luckily, I've got my bag of tricks with me." I patted my purse, an extra-long clutch with a chain strap.

"You're the best." She reached for me as if to pull me into a hug.

I backed away. "Let's clean you up first."

We went to the sink, and while Hayley gushed about the wedding, Barcelona, and her twins—she was a twin, too, and she was hoping for girls—I washed the lank tendrils that had been caught in the crossfire. I patted them dry with a paper towel, then reshaped them using a travel packet of coconut oil.

I had a new toothbrush and toothpaste in my bag, and I waited while Hayley brushed her teeth. God, to have teeth that white again.

I used baby wipes to get the stain out of her dress and to clean up the mascara tracks on her face. A little translucent powder smoothed out her skin, and a sweep of bronzer transformed her from a zombie back into a blushing bride. I finished up with a touch of my red lipstick and another dab of coconut oil for gloss.

When I was done, she checked herself in the mirror. "O-M-G, Carly! You're a miracle worker! I look as good as I did before the wedding!"

"I imagine your stylist would disagree. But you look radiant." I took a deep breath. "I can see how happy you are."

She clutched my hands. "I am. So happy." Her lips turned

down. "I'm sorry for what Brad did to you. I hope you find love again."

"Thank you. Though I intend to focus on my career for a while before I go looking for love." Love had no place in my life anymore. Not when it could be so easily yanked away.

She flashed me a wry pout. "If that's what you want."

I'd been like her when I married Brad. Hopeful. Sure in love. I'd thought with the right partner, life would be easy. I supposed it had been. I'd never struggled for money. I'd been safe. And happy, for a while.

I was not about to ruin Hayley's joy with a warning that happiness and love were fleeting, or that she should keep a backup plan for herself so when they ended, she'd have something for herself.

The bathroom door opened, and a young, dark-haired woman strode in. "There you are, Hayley. I was worried."

When she turned her beautiful face to me, I gasped. "You're Helen Choi. From that movie. From all the movies." My friends and I had watched her entire catalog of rom-coms.

Her cheeks pinked as she smiled. "That's me."

"Helen. Meet Carly Rose. She's the stylist who helped me with my wardrobe for this trip. She's rescued me again." Hayley waved at her face.

"I've been admiring your look all night," Helen said, scanning my embroidered metallic jacquard gown from its plunging neckline to its tulle-overlaid A-line skirt. She shook my hand.

"Thank you. It has pockets." I slipped my hands inside. There was just enough room for my business cards in one and my phone—the one that still wasn't ringing—in the other.

"I love it!" Helen beamed her megawatt smile, the one she'd given her love interest in her latest film. "But are you all right, Hayley? You've been gone so long."

"I'm better now, thanks to Carly."

"Thanks for taking care of her," Helen said. With a covetous look at my sparkly, rose-gold sandals, she held out her hand to Hayley and pushed open the door. "Let's get you back to the party. It was lovely meeting you, Carly."

Hayley held out a hand for me, and I let her tug me out of the bathroom.

Andrew waited outside with my glass of sparkling wine. Shoving his phone into the breast pocket of his blazer, he said, "I thought I was going to have to send in a scout."

"We're fine. Just a fashion crisis." To Hayley, I whispered, "You're okay?"

She squeezed my hand and let go. "I am. Thanks. Helen, meet Andrew Jones. We went to the same school. Now he's a banker, but he makes these cool videos for kids too. Andrew, this is my friend Helen Choi."

The wrinkle appeared between his eyebrows. "Your name sounds so familiar."

I chuckled. "Of course she's familiar. She was an Emmy nominee this year."

Helen stuck out her hand. "It's okay. Men rarely watch my films unless their date forces them. No one blows up, and I never need a stunt double."

Andrew shook her hand, a gleam of interest in his eyes. Helen was gorgeous and much closer to his age. Was she single? A burn erupted in my stomach.

"Nice to meet you," he said. "You should keep Carly in mind whenever you need a red-carpet style. I mean, look at her." When he turned his gaze on me, the gleam turned into an inferno that ignited my cheeks.

"Do you have a card?" Helen asked.

"Oh, you don't have to—"

"I want to. I'll be dreaming of that gown all night." She grinned.

I pulled an hourglass-shaped card from my pocket and handed it to her.

She snapped a photo with her phone. "In case I lose it. Mind if I take your photo to jog my memory?"

"Oh, uh, of course not. Andrew." I beckoned him to my side.

"No." He grinned. "She wants your face, not mine. Here, I'll hold your bag." He held out his hand. I passed it to him, and he didn't say a word about how heavy it was. He tucked it under his arm.

I propped my hand on my hip and dipped my chin. Helen snapped my photo. "Thank you."

"I'd be honored to offer you a consultation," I said.

"I'll text you." She shot me a smile before she grabbed Hayley's hand. "Let's go dance."

"I'll be right there." As Helen glided to the dance floor, Hayley gave Andrew a speculative look. He still held my purse.

"You don't need to go looking for love, Carly," she said. "It looks like it's found you."

21

#COUPLEGOALS

ANDREW

> Oliver: How's Spain?

> Me: Spectacular

> Oliver: Yeah? And how's Carly?

> Me: Breathtaking

> Oliver: DETAILS man

> Oliver: Or at least more than 1 word

> Oliver: Andrew?

> Oliver: Buddy?

> Oliver: So much for living vicariously through you…

Carly stood next to the bride, who was less radiant than she'd been earlier. The contradictory scents of mint and coconuts wafted off Hayley.

I was still reeling from what she'd said: *You don't need to go looking for love, Carly. It looks like it's found you.*

Was Carly looking for love? She'd denied it. She was focused on her career. She wouldn't let another man into her life.

Certainly not a man like me. A lowly quant who had to fake-date someone to get a promotion. Though she'd agreed we were real. Did that mean she was starting to feel what I already did? That I had a chance with her?

She gave me a wry smile. A solid maybe.

I'd take maybe over no any day.

I laced my fingers with hers and leaned close to whisper in her ear, "Everything okay?"

Goosebumps rose on her bare shoulders. She smiled. "It is now."

I put my arm around her shoulder. "Cold?"

"A little. But it's fine." She held up a hand when I went to take off my suit jacket. "I'm enjoying the respite."

"Aw!" Hayley clasped her hands under her chin. "You guys are so cute. You need a picture. Carly, give me your phone."

"Mine too." I held it out to her, and the bride snapped us, first with Carly's phone, then with mine.

She grinned at my phone before she handed it back. "You two are couple goals. Carly, Andrew is just what you need. He's totally in love with you."

Shit, was it that obvious? Would it scare Carly away? I tightened my grip on her fingers.

"Don't be ridiculous," she said. "We're friends having fun."

My insides chilled to the same temperature as Carly's Cava.

"Fun? You're both glowing. The sex must be amazing," Hayley said.

Fun? Was that what Carly meant by real? As in, *Andrew's a real fun guy, but it doesn't mean anything.*

Actually, I was the only one who'd called us real. All Carly had said was that we weren't fake. Maybe she was talking about the sex, which was amazing, but I'd hoped real meant more than sex.

A voice sounded from the end of the hallway. "Andrew, I've been looking everywhere for you."

As I turned to face my mother, Carly took a step away from me.

"Hi, Audrey," Hayley said. "So glad you could make it."

"It's been an interesting event," Mother said. "I recommend you get back to your groom. He's had quite a lot of whiskey."

"Of course." Glancing at Carly, Hayley twisted her fingers together, then whirled and scurried back to the party.

"If you wouldn't mind, Carly," my mother said in a voice I knew better than to disobey, "I'd like a word."

Carly stiffened. I reached for her hand, but she shoved it into the pocket of her flared skirt. Her smile was dangerously false. "What would you like to talk about, Audrey?"

"Your relationship with my son. I've heard Andrew's perspective, and now I'd like to get yours. Could you excuse us, Andrew?"

It wasn't a request. It was a demand. But I was the one who'd insisted on the arrangement. I couldn't abandon my date now. I stood straighter. "I think I'll stay."

"It's fine, Andrew." Carly's voice was as steely as my mother's. "I'll join you in a minute."

Our talk at the fountain about male power meant I couldn't stay, not after she'd asked me to go. Though as I walked toward the bar, my heart remained behind with the two women I cared about. Two women who I wished weren't frenemies.

22

IT'S NOT SERIOUS

CARLY

"Hello, Audrey." I might not have the protection of Brad's social standing or money, but I gathered my former boldness around me like a tattered shawl. Cocking a hip, I planted my hand on my waist.

"Carly." She was shorter than me. Looking up to meet my gaze had to piss her off.

"Love your dress," I said grudgingly. Why couldn't Audrey be one of those women who fixed her style in her heyday—for Audrey, the early 2000s—and encased it in Aqua Net? No, she'd given up her bandage dresses, handkerchief hems, and box pleats. Tonight, she wore a long boatneck gown in cranberry with a shawl fold at the neckline. I'd seen the low-cut back earlier. It showed off her enviable lats. And up close, I noticed that it also had pockets.

But Audrey wasn't hiding her hands. She propped them on her hips and leaned in close to hiss, "What are you doing?"

Remembering how tightly Audrey controlled her social circle—my pool of potential clients—and also that she was my date's mother, I played innocent so she could back down with grace. "I'm here to support Brad and Hayley."

Audrey wasn't having it. "Support them? You're here to throw down. You didn't have to come to this wedding at all. You're using my son to—"

"To what?" My anger bubbled up, but I matched my whisper to hers. "To prove to Brad and everyone else that I'm not crying my eyes out in my apartment? That I don't need his validation, or frankly, yours anymore? That I'm still desirable well into my forties? Do you begrudge me any of that?"

Her voice rang out in the hallway. "I do when you involve my son!"

I kept my voice low and as even as I could. "We had an arrangement. Andrew willingly came with me." *Don't think about how he* came *with me on the hotel sofa.*

"I've heard all about this *arrangement,* and I don't like it." She looked me up and down, lingering on my boobs, showcased by the embroidered silk of the plunging neckline. "You're taking advantage of him."

"Taking advantage? He's a thirty-two-year-old man. He can make his own decisions. And he's getting as much out of this as I am." *Do* not *think about how I'm at least one orgasm ahead of him.* "I'm helping him look stable for Vic. And apparently, it's working."

Her nostrils flared. "He's a sweet boy, and you've done something nefarious to him."

"Nefarious?" Did she mean a blowjob? Because I hadn't gotten to that. Yet.

She lowered her voice. "I've seen how he looks at you. Your relationship might be only for show, but the expression on his face… I can make things easier for you. Throw some business your way. Ask my friends to do the same. If you do a good job styling them, you'll have the success you're after."

She knew me well. For months, I'd chased an in with Audrey's circle. It was what I desired most. And yet she'd stymied me every time. "What do you want in return?"

Her eyes glittered, and her voice dropped to a whisper. "Break my son's heart. Quickly. And gently." She fluttered her hands like she was dusting away the pain she was asking me to inflict. "I have my own levers to pull to get him that promotion. We both know you have no long-term future with my son. End... whatever it is you're doing to try to hurt me."

My jaw hardened. "I'm not dating Andrew to hurt you."

"Then why?" Her forehead hardly moved these days, but her right eyebrow lifted a fraction. "Why drag my family into your drama?"

"My drama?" But all I had to do was glance behind Audrey to see Brad stumbling through his wedding reception, sloshing his drink on someone's peau de soie shoes. Poor Hayley was in no condition to contain him the way I used to.

"Admit it. You came to stir up trouble."

My jaw throbbed, and I realized I was clenching my teeth. I blew out a breath and relaxed the muscles. "I came here to network. Andrew and I are having fun. It's not serious."

"Then it should be simple. Once you end this arrangement, I'll ensure business flows your way."

I should have offered to end it after his holiday party. Surely by then he'd have his promotion. We'd said we were real, whatever that meant, after he'd kissed me in front of the Cascada Monumental, but it didn't mean we were forever. Someone as young and handsome as Andrew wouldn't be infatuated with me for long. I hadn't even been able to keep crusty old Brad's attention.

But the words that came out of my mouth were, "I will not break my promise to Andrew. Not even for my business."

She narrowed her eyes and shifted her weight. "Andrew values family, you know."

"I know." How many times had he said he loved being a Jones? Was she about to threaten me with demanding he choose sides? News flash: he'd choose the Joneses over me every time.

"Sometime soon, Andrew's going to realize he wants children, a family of his own. And you can't give that to him." Her gaze burned into my middle as if she could x-ray straight through my skin to the last of my eggs rattling around in my desiccated ovaries.

A phantom ache flared in my abdomen as if her glare had vaporized one of my few remaining ova. Or, possibly, that was the Spanx again. Goddamn torture device.

I'd never wanted children. But it suddenly hurt that I'd wasted my fertile years with Brad.

Hayley would have a tiny baby—two babies—to hold. She'd teach them how to tie their shoes, ride bikes, balance a checkbook. Crap, no one balanced checkbooks anymore. Maybe she'd teach them how to fix the flipping internet router.

I'd never do any of those things.

And, if I held onto Andrew, neither would he.

Audrey nodded like she'd sunk her putt. "Think about it. Let me know when you change your mind." Whirling in a swirl of red taffeta, she strode away.

Her devil's deal remained behind, lodged like a dart in my chest.

23

CAKE? TOTALLY OVERRATED.

ANDREW

> Natalie: How's the wedding? I need all the details. What is Carly wearing?
>
> Natalie: Seriously. You all ditched me. ON CHRISTMAS! I deserve PHOTOS!
>
> Me: <sends photo>
>
> Natalie: O
>
> Natalie: M
>
> Natalie: G!!!!!!!!!!
>
> Me: What?
>
> Natalie: <heart eyes emoji>
>
> Me: Should I tell her you like her outfit?
>
> Natalie: No, doofus. It means you're totally IN LOVE

> Me: What? I didn't say that

> Natalie: You didn't have to. It's all over your faces

aces? I tried to see what my sister did, but all I saw was Carly's sparkling smile. Sure, it was one of her genuine ones with the adorable wrinkles around her eyes, but *love* was stretching it a little far. Maybe the plural *faces* was an autocorrect.

I couldn't ponder it too long because Charles found me and wanted to chat about my math videos. He and Noah had watched the one about hexagons, and he suggested I visit the hexagonal tiles on the Passeig de Gràcia. While we talked, I kept an eye on the hallway.

Finally, my mother emerged, billowing into the room like an angry, red thundercloud. Had they argued? I said a hasty goodbye to Charles and headed toward the hallway to check on Carly. Before I got there, she sailed out like a warship, guns blazing. Sparks lit her eyes, but her red lips were compressed into an angry line.

"Are you okay?" I asked through my tightening throat. Mother was a force, and I should've stayed to defend Carly, whether she'd wanted me to or not.

"We're leaving," she muttered. "Correction: I'm leaving. You stay."

My body tensed. "Why would I stay without you? I'm your date."

The lines around her mouth deepened. "Consider yourself released from any obligations concerning me."

"What are you talking about?" I grabbed her hand and threaded it through my elbow.

True to her word, she marched toward the exit. I clung to

her, mirroring the regal lift of her chin. We left her ex's wedding reception before they'd even cut the cake.

Cake? Totally overrated.

Outside the hotel, as I scanned the street for a taxi, she muttered, "Your mother thinks I'm bad for you. She's probably right."

"No!" The word rang out on the busy street. "My mother doesn't get a vote in my relationships."

"Doesn't she?" Carly tilted her head to look at me out of the side of her eye. "She's the matriarch of your family. Doesn't she have to approve anyone any of you dates? To keep the Jones family what it should be?"

"It's not like that." Or was it? Was that why I'd never brought a date to brunch? My brother, Jackson, had fallen in love with his wife without telling Mother, but of course she'd loved Alicia. Despite her humble background, she was as driven as Mother was. Then when Alicia birthed the first Jones heir, Mother had granted her the place of honor at the dining table.

My sister Samantha had fallen for Niall, a novelist, a career outside the set of respectable ones for a Jones. But his father was tech royalty, creator of the phone I had in my pocket. Even though they were estranged, Mother considered Niall part of our circle.

And so was Carly. Or she had been. What was the issue?

Finally, a taxi pulled up, and I opened the back door for Carly. I wished I could tug her to me, but an ocean of embroidered silk separated us across the seat of the taxi. She'd hate it if I wrinkled her. Instead, I leaned across it. "What did my mother say?"

She stared into my eyes for a moment. "Nothing I didn't already know." She sighed. "We're not a good fit, Andrew. We should—"

"No," I growled. "Don't say it. Are you seriously letting her decide who you should be with? Did she tell you to break it off?"

"No! Actually, yes."

My blood boiled. How did Mother think she could control my romantic relationships? A thought speared through me like a blast of chilled air. Because she was my only living parent, I'd always done what she asked. When she'd asked me to stay in California after her surgery, I hadn't hesitated to move across the country.

Not this time.

"You're not going to let her tell you what to do, are you?"

Carly folded her arms. "What are we doing? We said no sex, but we broke that rule not three days into this trip. And now everything's complicated. What's real, and what's fake?"

"We're real. This is real." Earlier, I'd been afraid to say it, but if I didn't say it now, I might not get another chance. "I always wanted it to be real. Since Monterey." I settled a hand on her forearm. "I want this. I want it all."

When she unfolded her arms, I took her hand. She didn't resist. "Your mother's right. I can't give you what you need. Your life would be easier without me."

"What I need is you. Today was special. You felt it too," I said with more confidence than I felt. Winnie's words echoed in my brain. I'd open myself up for Carly. I'd open my family to her too. "You're worth standing up to my mother for. And you won't have to do it. I will."

"But...should I?" She stared at her gown and rubbed a finger over the embroidered pattern. "I'm thirteen years older than you. Middle aged. You have so much life ahead of you. A career to grow. Maybe a family."

"I don't want a family," I said. "I want you."

When she turned her eyes up to me, they'd softened like a caramel left out in the sun. Did she want me too?

The taxi pulled up in front of our hotel, and it was time to hand over my card and work out the fare. By the time I'd finished, Carly stood out on the street, shivering.

I winced. "We forgot your coat at the hotel."

"It's fine." Goosebumps covered her bare arms.

I whipped off my suit coat and draped it over her shoulders. "I'll go back for it tomorrow."

I guided her into the hotel and up the stairs to our room. For once, I didn't fumble with the awkward key, and we were inside the suite in a matter of seconds.

"Tonight," I said, coming around to face her, "I'm going to take care of you. Tomorrow, I'll tell off my mother."

Maybe I shouldn't have mentioned my mother. Carly looked down at herself, her slim body engulfed by my suit jacket. She shrugged it off. "No."

"Fine. We'll freeze her out. We'll do whatever we want." I swallowed down the bitter taste in my mouth. "She'll come around."

"No. She won't. And I—" When she finally met my gaze, her eyes were glassy. "I won't do that to you. To your family. We're done, Andrew. I'm leaving in the morning. Don't follow me."

"But..." My stomach dropped. "What about our arrangement?"

"I'll meet you at your holiday party. I'll pretend for Vic and everyone else. But after that, it's over."

She shoved my suit coat at me and in a whirl of champagne silk, disappeared into her room.

Fuck. Me.

24

FIFTEEN MINUTES

CARLY

> *NEW To-do list—December 25*
> *Get on the first flight home*
> *Pack*
> *Burn this infernal stick-on bra*

It had to be the lowest point of my life. After being dressed down by Audrey Jones Hayes, I'd done exactly what she'd told me to do. What I'd sworn I wouldn't. Not for her. I'd broken a promise to a man I liked. Who said he cared about me.

But I hadn't done it because she'd told me to. I'd done it because it was the right thing to do. For him. Still, the stricken look on his face stuck—ugh, the irony, considering my current predicament—to the insides of my eyelids, which were currently shut against the agony.

Not from emotional pain. Physical pain.

All because of a stick-on bra.

I'd found this one online, and now I understood why it had been so cheap. It adhered with industrial-strength airplane epoxy that refused to release my skin. My left boob, the one I'd tried to free first, was red and angry looking. I couldn't spare too many more skin cells, or there'd be blood. But after losing the battle with Audrey, I wasn't ready to concede to a pair of silicone boob hammocks.

I never should have come. I hadn't made one contact at the wedding. Aside from Helen Choi, who was just being nice in front of Hayley. She'd never actually call me.

At the prenuptial dinner, I'd let Brad bully me. At the reception, Audrey had cowed me. The trip was a waste of Tessa's air miles and the proceeds from selling my last Hermès bag.

Sitting on the floor of my bathroom in my thong and the cursed bra, I yanked again. Pain sliced through me, forcing a cry out of my throat that ended in a pitiful sob. The stuck-on cup hadn't given an inch.

A tap on the bathroom door came a second before Andrew's urgent voice. "Carly, are you all right?"

"I'm fine." Sniffling, I rubbed at the inflamed skin on the top of my left breast.

"Can I come in?"

"Absolutely not." I looked like hell with red lines across my middle from my shapewear and my soft belly spilling over my panties as I curled up on the floor. I'd taken off my makeup, so nothing smoothed over my crow's feet or smile lines.

"Please? I want to see that you're okay."

"I'm fine," I repeated, my voice stronger this time.

"I don't believe you. What the hell did my mother say?"

"This has nothing to do with her." I grasped the edge of the cup and, taking a deep breath, yanked. It ceded a quarter inch of my skin. Hissing in pain, I stopped.

"Carly?" His voice wavered with concern. "I'm coming in."

All I had time to do was drape my torso over my knees to hide my red skin before he opened the door.

"Oh." His eyebrows smashed together.

"It's a fashion crisis," I said, "not an emotional one."

"How can I help?"

"You can't. Unless you're willing to give me a skin graft after I peel this bra off."

His gaze skated over the reddened skin on the side of my chest. "It's stuck to you? Like with glue?"

"It's a thing. I couldn't wear a regular bra with the low neckline of my dress. I wear these all the time. They're not usually this sticky." It would be the last time I cut corners.

He nodded. "We need a solvent. Anything alcohol-based would be irritating. Something oil-based? The hotel lotion?"

No wonder he was a rising star at his bank at thirty-two. "That's not a bad idea. There's some coconut oil in my makeup bag." I pointed to the fold-out case hanging from the back of the door. "The blue packets."

While he rummaged for it, I clambered to my feet. My creaky knee went off like a shot.

"Sorry," I said. I accidentally caught my reflection in the mirror. I hadn't taken my hair down yet, but a few strands had escaped. And not in sexy tendrils but in clumps, stuck together with hairspray.

And the silicone bra cups looked ridiculous surrounded by puffy, reddened skin.

As he turned back toward me, grasping the packets of coconut oil, I sucked in my stomach.

"What are you sorry about?" he asked.

"My knee. It creaks sometimes. These things happen when you get older."

"I've got a bad ankle. I broke it playing soccer, and it still aches in the winter."

"Not exactly the same, but thanks, I've got it from here." I reached for the packets.

"Let me."

Two words that hardly anyone ever said to me. Not Audrey or any of the other wives in my former social group. Not Brad. No one since my mother.

I'd just ended things, and Andrew Jones still offered me help.

I nodded.

He tore open the packet and squeezed out the white lotion into his palm. He looked to me for guidance.

"Rub some of it against your palm to liquefy it. Then, um, here." I pointed at the top of my right boob to give the skin on the left side time to recover.

He rubbed the oil onto the skin around the silicone, then gradually moved his fingers to the edge of the cup. The sucker didn't budge, but he kept at it.

"You know," he said conversationally like he wasn't touching my bare breast, "my mother has a lot of ideas about my life. Ideas she hasn't asked me about. But it's my life, not hers."

"Mmm?" The combination of the pain from the adhesive and the pleasure of his touch had stolen my power of intelligible speech.

"She thinks I want what my dad had. What Charles has. What my brother has. But I've never been like them. I don't need a big house, an important job with hundreds of people who depend on me, or children. I like kids, don't get me wrong, but I'm not interested in having my own."

I nodded, hypnotized. "What do you want, Andrew?"

"I..." His shoulders slumped. "For my career? I want to do fulfilling work. And I have that. Both with my job and with the videos." He paused his work on the bra cup. "Do you think the videos are ridiculous? Indecorous?"

"Indecorous?" I giggled, high on endorphins. "Who even says that?"

"Vic." His tongue stuck out between his teeth as he returned to work, and I gasped as he freed my nipple. His oiled-up fingers slid over the pebbled nub, sending a pulse of arousal straight to my sex. But he wasn't doing it to get me off, so I clung to our conversation to refocus myself.

"And what about the family part?"

"I have a family already. My mother. Charles. My little sisters. Jerk-off Jackson and his family." He sighed through his nose. "After Dad died, Mother wasn't in good shape."

"Oh, no." I'd been afraid of that. When I'd gone to her house a few days after the funeral, Andrew had accepted the fruit basket but barred my entry, saying his mother was resting.

"She got better. Eventually. But until then, I took care of my sisters and made sure they got to school and their activities and stuff. I even learned how to braid Natalie's hair. She said I sucked at it though."

I stilled his hand. "But you tried. Most teenagers wouldn't have stepped up like that."

"Sure, they would." He shrugged. "You do what you have to do. But it was a lot, and I don't want to do it again. You know?"

Interesting. Audrey had been certain he wanted children. "I get that. But you're so good in those videos, like you're talking directly to kids."

"You've seen them?"

"I—" My cheeks burned. "I may have watched one or two. After I met you that day on the soccer field."

"And you thought I was good?"

"You were brilliant, Andrew. Even I understood the Pythagorean theorem after I watched it, and I struggled in high school math."

"Thanks." He focused on the bra cup again, and with one last tug, it was off. He tossed it into the sink. "One down."

He started on the left cup, his smooth fingers working the oil into my skin and wedging under the cup with breathtaking care. As the silicone reluctantly un-stuck, he touched every newly freed inch of my breast, taking special care around the areola and over the nipple. I was so sensitized I felt the ridges of his fingerprints, and I held in a gasp. It was heaven.

But heaven was out of my reach. I cleared my throat. "My mom used to help with stuff like this in my pageant days."

He looked up into my eyes and blinked. "I saw that photo at your place."

"Mom was a former Miss Texas. I was four when she entered me into my first one and eighteen in my last. A talent scout convinced us to move to LA, and I got my first major modeling job."

"Did you like it?" He wriggled a finger underneath the silicone stuck to the lower half of my breast.

I sucked in air through my nose and focused on the sconce next to the mirror. "I liked the competition. I could've done without the unhealthy diet. But by the time I was twenty, I supported both of us on my income, and I was proud of that."

His fingers stilled. "I bet you were."

Finally, the last bit of glue released my skin, and the second cup joined its evil twin in the sink. My unsupported breasts sagged, and I covered them with my hands. Despite my attempted distraction, I was tingly all over, and my nipples were pointed, demanding peaks.

"Really? I've basically given you a breast-cancer check, and you're covering up?"

I winced. A breast-cancer check didn't sound sexy at all, yet I was turned on. "I—sorry." I dropped my hands to my sides.

"Does it hurt?" he asked.

"No, not at all." I felt floaty and shivery and *needy*. But nothing hurt.

"Good. Because, Carly, I..." He came up behind me. With his right hand, he lifted my right breast and rubbed circles across the nipple with his thumb. Then he pressed his hips to my backside, proving he was as aroused as I was.

He met my gaze in the mirror. "I heard what you said, but don't you feel what's happening between us? I've never felt so...so..."

"Turned on?" That was all this tightness in my chest and the ache in my core was.

"It's more than that. At least, for me it is. Carly, I..." He took a deep breath but stopped when he saw my expression in the mirror. "Okay, I get it. You're not ready to talk about this. Not yet."

"Andrew—"

"Coconut oil is edible, right?"

"I...what?"

He stepped in front of me, then his head descended over my throbbing left breast. He lapped at the tender, reddened skin. The warm wetness took my already oversensitive body to the next level, and I gasped.

He looked up as his tongue traced the arc of my breast. "Okay?"

"Unngh."

"I've heard human saliva is a natural painkiller...like orgasms."

The words rattled around in my brain. Fortunately, he didn't wait for me to respond.

"It's okay, darling. I've got you." He went back to work, holding up my breast in one hand while he licked the nipple. A second later, my stomach swooped when he tunneled his other hand inside my panties and found me wet and swollen.

He switched to my right breast, clamped onto my nipple, and sucked, sending a thrill of pleasure from my chest straight to my center as he nudged a finger inside me.

I moaned as my vision tunneled.

"You're a good girl," he said. "You can come."

And goddamn it. My traitorous body took that as a direct instruction. Despite the pain I'd been in only fifteen minutes ago, pleasure shot through me, and, shuddering, I came and came and came.

When I returned to awareness, Andrew nuzzled my neck. He dragged his lips up to my earlobe and whispered, "Feeling better?"

"Ye—" I swallowed to clear the gravel from my voice. "Yes. What was that, some kind of tantric technique they teach on ClickClackGo?"

He chuckled against my temple. "I think it had something to do with the extra endorphins from the pain. But, sure, I'll take some of the credit. It felt like a good one."

Nodding, I curled my fingers into the front of his shirt to hold him to me.

"Hey." He tipped up my chin. "You sure you're okay?"

"Uh-huh. It was a weird day." From afternoon sex with Andrew to my ex's wedding to finding out his new wife was pregnant to my fight with Audrey, it had been a lot, especially with my bathroom meltdown and Andrew's care to top it off.

"Let's get you to bed." Supporting me with a hand around my waist, he led me into the bedroom and pulled back the covers. Wearing only my panties, I lay down. He tucked the covers around me and bent to kiss my forehead.

"Stay," I whispered.

He sat heavily on the side of the bed. Stroking my still-crispy hair out of my face, he asked, "Are you sure?"

"Yes. I'm sorry about what I said earlier. I didn't mean it. I mean, I did at the time. I thought it was the right thing to do. Maybe it still is, but I shouldn't make those choices for both of us." I'd hated when Brad made decisions like I wasn't worthy of having an opinion. "That is, if you want to stay."

It took effort, but I kept my heavy eyelids open to take in his response.

He trailed a featherlight touch over my cheek. "Of course I want to stay. You've changed your mind about leaving tomorrow? We'll go back together on Friday?"

I turned my head to kiss his palm. "Yeah."

His cheeks lifted in an irrepressible grin. "Don't think I'm weird, but can I brush your hair? I think you'll sleep better if I brush out this hairspray. That's what Natalie says anyway."

"She's right." I started to push up on my elbow.

"Stay there. I'll grab your hairbrush."

He was gone for a minute or two, and when he walked back into the bedroom, he'd taken off his suit. He still wore an undershirt and his boxers, and he smelled minty.

"Hope you don't mind. I took a swig of your mouthwash." He helped me sit up in bed, then he squeezed in behind me, wedging me between his spread legs.

He started at the ends, holding the hair and brushing out the clumps so it didn't hurt my scalp. Slowly, he worked his way up, pulling out a hairpin every now and then.

"No one's brushed my hair like this since my mom died."

"I'm so sorry. How old were you?"

"Twenty-three." The gentle pull on my scalp was hypnotic.

"Can you tell me about it?"

I let his rhythmic brushing relax me. "We lived in LA, and she was dating a studio executive. He took her up in his helicopter, and there was an accident. They both died. And the pilot." Fleetingly, I wondered why I was spilling my history like this. Normally, I kept it buttoned up safely inside.

He paused his brushing. "That must have been terrible."

"We'd always been close. So yeah, it was a dark few months. I guess that's why it was so easy for Brad to sweep me off my feet."

He started brushing again, a little more forcefully. I shivered at the tug on my scalp.

"Was your dad around?"

"No, he was never part of my life."

"Ah." He kept up the long, rhythmic strokes. "I'm sorry. My dad worked hard, but he used to spend fifteen minutes with each of us at night. He used to brush Nat's hair. That's what she wanted."

"What did he do in his fifteen minutes with you?"

"In the summer, when there was still light, we played catch. Other times we'd play one-on-one. There was a light by the basketball hoop."

I smiled, remembering. "You were always the sporty one."

"I wish we'd talked more. We talked, but it was usually about technique or my team. I wish we'd talked about what was important."

"Hmm." I didn't remember much about his father, Jasper. He'd died two or three years after I married Brad. He was often late to his wife's parties because he was working into the evening at his startup. Though now, I mused, perhaps he was late because he was spending an hour with his kids. "I'm sure he thought your sports and your teams were important. Because they were important to you."

"Maybe. If I'd known we'd have so little time, I'd have asked him about other stuff."

"What stuff?" He'd made it to my scalp with the brush, and the gentle massage made my eyelids droop.

"About his work. About being a man. About relationships. And love."

I hummed. I'd talked about things like that with my mom.

"All done," he said, setting the brush on the bedside table. "Lean back."

I did, though his lean body wasn't as soft as a pillow. He pulled the covers over us and turned me to my side. With long strokes, he brushed his hand over my arm and my back.

"If he were still here, I think he'd tell me to suck it up and be honest."

"Hmm?" I nestled my cheek into his chest and rubbed my nose across his shirt, inhaling his scent. I loved whatever product it was that made him smell like the ocean.

Under my cheek, his heart picked up its pace. "My feelings are real, Carly. I'm falling for you."

My heart skipped a beat. I knew I should say something. But my exhausted brain couldn't come up with the right words. All I said was, "Go to sleep, Andrew."

25

A DOUBLE BLACK DIAMOND

ANDREW

From: Victor Lynch
To: All employees
Sent: December 26, 10:38 am
Subject: Holiday party

Happy holidays. Don't forget our company party on the 31st is an excellent (and mandatory) opportunity to let our hair down (figuratively, as the employee handbook's grooming standards still apply) and celebrate the end of a successful year.

Sincerely,
Victor Lynch, Chief Financial Officer

I blew at a strand of Carly's hair that tickled my nose. "How about we never leave?" I proposed, refusing to acknowledge the sunlight glinting golden in her hair or the housekeepers' voices in the hall outside our suite. I clung to the pretense of darkness. It'd been dark when she'd woken me with her hand on my dick.

She lifted her head from my chest. Her cheeks were pink, and she breathed like she'd been running sprints. She'd made that screen-door squeak sound twice. I was still inside her, and I needed to deal with the condom, but I really, *really* didn't want to change a thing. Ever.

"Never leave Spain?" she asked.

"I mean, never leave this bed."

"Like a John and Yoko thing?"

"A what? Is that a K-Drama?"

"Oh, my god." She winced. "Sometimes I forget how young you are." Gracefully, she lifted off me and settled at my side. I kept my arm around her so she wouldn't go too far.

"What about food? Exercise? Your job?" She leaned back. The fact that she didn't bring up her job poked at my heart, which was still tender after she hadn't responded to my confession about my feelings last night.

Stroking her back, I made my voice light. "You see, in the today-times, we have this fantastic thing called the internet. It comes to this device I have"—I glanced at the bedside table, but of course I'd left my phone in my room—"and it allows me to make phone calls, email my colleagues, and get almost anything I need, including food, with a click of a button."

"My generation made the internet what it is. So, screw you," she said mildly.

"Ah, speaking of screwing—" I kissed her, long and slow and ravenous. She tasted like me from the amazing blowjob she'd given me when we'd woken up. Remembering how she looked with her lips around me, I started to harden again. "I'm not in my twenties anymore, but I think I could go again in a few. Who needs a run when sex is such great cardio?"

"I think my trainer would point out that I've got muscles that aren't in my pelvic floor."

"Go for a ride on my face, and we'll give your inner thighs a workout too."

Her expression went surprisingly tender, considering my crude comment. "Are you for real?"

"About the face-sitting? Yes, please. It'll help with the refractory period." Just thinking about her pussy sent a tingle down my spine.

"No. I mean...are we really doing this? You and me?"

"Yeah." My heart galloped behind my breastbone, and I nuzzled her neck so she wouldn't see my dopey expression of love, which she clearly wasn't ready for. Though if we had a few more days in Spain like yesterday morning in the park, or another couple of nights like last night, when she'd talked about her mother, when she'd finally opened up and let me see past her picture-perfect facade, she might let me adore her.

After the scare she'd given me last night, when I thought she was crying over fucking Brad in the bathroom, I felt like I did at the top of the ski hill, all potential energy and adrenaline, my heart racing at the thought of careening down. Would this thing end in an exhilarating swoosh of my skis at the bottom of the hill, or in a face-first tumble? I'd always been so afraid of the crash that I'd broken things off before it could happen. Stayed on the intermediate runs, then taken the lift down, so to speak.

But now, I was at the top of a double black diamond, the wind whipping my face. The reward was so great I was ready to risk it all. I was acting more like my thrill-seeking brother than like the cautious second son of Jasper Jones.

I retreated, kissing down to her shoulder. "Your body is breathtaking. I think you should seriously consider the stay-here-all-day plan. Let me remind you of the benefits..." I ran my tongue over the top of her breast. It was still pink from that torture device of a bra, but the swelling was gone.

"Stop, stop," she said, laughing. "If you do that, we really will stay in bed all day, and I haven't taken you to my favorite tapas place yet."

"I'd rather eat you." I swirled my tongue around her nipple.

She put her hands on my cheeks and lifted my head so I stared into her sparkling eyes. "Tapas. Sangria. And those fish croquettes you like."

My stomach rumbled. I groaned. "Fine. You sold me with the croquetas. Do they have the potato ones too?"

"Of course. And fried brie with raspberry sauce. Plus, all the olives you can eat. We'll talk about what this is."

"Oh?" I forgot about my growling stomach. Talking had to be good, right? At least we weren't going to shove it under the rug like Monterey. "Let's talk now."

She propped her head on her hand, then tugged the covers up under her chin. "I heard you last night. I appreciate that you have feelings, but I'm not sure how I feel yet."

I wished I could take back my reckless words. "Yesterday you agreed this was real. Forget what I said last night. We'll take it as slow as you need. But let's give it a chance."

"Now is the time for me to focus on my career," she said. "Not a relationship. I made that mistake before, and, well, here I am. At his next wedding with no business to speak of."

"Helen Choi has your number."

"Sure. And maybe she'll call. But I can't wait for a long shot. I need to work as hard as I can to grow my business. Hustle. There's no room in my life for anything else. I think you need more than I can give you."

"No, I'm..." I stopped. I had to convince her I wasn't needy. I could be low maintenance. I'd give her the space she needed. And time. "Let's not decide right now. Let's see how it goes when we get back home. Maybe Helen will call you, and your business will be set forever. You can have success and a relationship."

She squinted one eye. "You know that's not how it works, right? When I'm successful, I'm busy. Even on weekends."

I knew it all too well. Fifteen minutes a day with my dad.

But those had been fifteen excellent minutes. In fifteen minutes, Carly and I could do something truly transcendent.

"I'll take it. I'd rather be with you when you're busy than with anyone else." Sitting up, I held out a hand. "Come on. We can shower together."

She bit her lip. "If I take a quick shower, I can run back to the hotel to get my coat while you're getting ready."

I flopped back onto the bed. "I forgot about your coat. I'll shower fast and get it for you."

"You wouldn't mind?"

I couldn't send her back to that hotel. What if she ran into Brad? She'd been pale at the reception when she'd come out of the bathroom with Hayley. And silent after she'd spoken with Mother. I'd protect her from another run-in with any of them.

"Course not. Now, stop trying to sex me up so I can get dressed and we can have tapas."

Laughing, she shoved a pillow at me, and I wrestled her back down, and it was a while before I got that shower.

I was a lucky guy.

~

I floated into the wedding hotel on the memory of morning sex with Carly, but that's when my luck ran out.

My post-orgasmic bubble of happiness popped when I heard Brad's booming voice. Wearing a bathrobe and slippers, he stood at the front desk in the lobby, arguing with the clerk.

"Ginger. Ale." His voice was *don't-you-understand-English?* loud. "And saltines. To my room. Stat."

The clerk said something in a quiet, soothing voice, but Brad interrupted her. "Do you have any idea how much cash I've dropped at this hotel this week? Fucking—"

Trying my best to be invisible, I skirted along the back of the lobby to the coat check. Bad luck trailed me.

"Jones!"

I felt my shoulders hunch before I turned toward him, pulling my lips into a fake smile. "Winner. What are you doing down here? You should be upstairs with your bride." God knew if I were ever lucky enough to marry Carly, I'd spend the next week between her thighs.

He chuckled. "My bride isn't feeling a hundred percent. Women, y'know?"

"Uh."

He took a few steps toward me, but his voice still carried. "So you're sleeping with Carly."

Remembering our morning in bed, the small bit of headway I'd made against her resistance, I puffed out my chest. "We're together." I refused to think about the day after tomorrow when we'd fly home and her hustle would push me aside.

He snorted. "Today, at least."

Fucking mind reader. No wonder he'd been so successful moving office square footage in San Francisco. But I was a Jones, and unlike him, I was wearing clothes. I planted my hands on my hips and sneered at his bathrobe. "What the hell's that supposed to mean?"

He crossed his arms over his chest, unfortunately spreading the lapels and exposing more of his mat of gray chest hair. "She's newly divorced. You're a rebound."

I felt the blood drain from my face. How the fuck had I not thought of that? Although she'd been divorced for a year, I was probably her first dip into the dating pool. Everyone knew what happened with rebound relationships. No wonder she'd tried to push me away.

From the smug expression on his face, Brad saw he'd won the match. "Thought so. Good luck with that, junior."

Uncurling my fingers from the fists they'd made, I shook out my hands. I wouldn't fight Brad Winner the day after his wedding. Smirking, he turned on his terrycloth slipper and strode toward the elevators.

I trudged toward the coat check. Maybe that's what Carly had been trying to tell me. She wasn't sure she could have genuine feelings for the first guy she'd dated after the end of a long marriage. I needed to do what I'd promised and take things slow, rein in my out-of-control feelings.

And protect my heart.

26

ZERO CHILL

CARLY

To-do list—December 29
✓ Catch up on sleep
✓ More Spain-style sex
Kick Andrew out, then sleep some more

"Hey." Andrew's voice was rough, and he propped his bristly chin on my bare shoulder, then handed me my phone. "Your phone was buzzing like crazy. I thought it might be important."

Important? Had I missed an appointment? No, I didn't need to take Yelena's dress to her until Tuesday, and today wasn't Tuesday...was it? We'd arrived home Friday evening and stayed in my apartment Saturday (hardly leaving my bed), so that made today Sunday. Unless we'd slept an extra day.

Frankly, it was hard to tell since every time I woke up, I melted again at Andrew's dimples. Then he did the thing with his lips that made me see stars.

"What day is it?" I tapped the phone screen.

"Sunday. Around nine." He kissed my shoulder, and I shivered.

"Mmm. Do that some more." While I unlocked my phone, he kissed down my arm. I could get used to this.

No, I couldn't.

Shouldn't.

There was no way this could last. I'd do something to screw it up—whatever I'd done with Brad—or he'd get tired and move on. Like Brad had.

I checked my notifications.

"It's just the girls' chat. I forgot I said I'd go to brunch with them today."

"You haven't missed it yet, have you?" He reversed direction with his kisses, teasing me along my clavicle.

"No. But I'm not sure I want to leave this bed."

"It is a nice bed, especially with you in it. Though brunch sounds pretty good." His stomach rumbled.

"Do you...do you want to come with me?" Where had that come from?

He was part of last week's Barcelona fantasy. I knew we'd said we were dating for real, but that didn't make him a part of my everyday life. Besides, he didn't want to come to brunch with me and my middle-aged girlfriends, did he?

Something flashed across his face, and I remembered. "Oh, no. It's Sunday. Your family has brunch on Sundays. Never mind."

"No." He squeezed my shoulder. "If you want me at the Goddess Gang's brunch, I'd be honored to go." He nodded as if making a resolution. Then his mouth quirked up in another dimple-revealing grin. "And, as I recall, your friends liked me. A lot."

Gently, I shoved him. "So full of yourself."

"It's the truth. Did they, or did they not, encourage you to come to my hotel room in Monterey?"

"Ugh, they did." They'd practically forced me to his door. "But..."

"But?" His smile faltered. "But you're not ready to introduce me as more than a hookup? As someone you're seeing?"

He was right. I was being unfair. I'd told him I'd give us a chance. So I said, "Come with me. Meet the girls. Again."

A grin spread over his face. "Excellent."

~

I'd texted ahead to warn them about my guest, but my friends had zero chill.

"Andrew!" A smug, Cheshire-cat smile spread over Lucie's face. "So glad you joined us." Hugging me, she didn't lower her voice at all. "Carly, you look very satisfied."

"Cut it out, Lucie. You're making them self-conscious." After embracing me, Savannah held out her hand to Andrew. "I'm Savannah. That's Lucie, and the redhead is Tessa. Nice to see you again."

"You two are giving me a toothache. Those blushes, I swear." Tessa shook Andrew's hand, then hugged me. "Now, let's eat. I'm starving, and the dumplings are to die for."

The hostess led us to a large round table, where the scents of ginger and roasted meat and fish made my mouth water. Savannah hip-checked Lucie away from the seat next to Andrew, so she settled for the seat next to me.

She smirked as I sat gingerly on the padded chair. "Sore?"

"Don't make me regret coming to brunch," I muttered. "I was engaged in much more pleasant activities than being harassed by you."

"I can only imagine." She waggled her eyebrows. "So this"—

she kept her voice low and cut her eyes to Andrew, who leaned over to talk to Savannah—"seems to have progressed from your arrangement to something else."

"I'm not sure exactly what to call it yet," I murmured. "We're still figuring it out."

"Looks like you're enjoying the figuring-it-out bit."

"It's got its perks." I shifted in my chair until the ache eased.

"I can only imagine." She smirked.

My phone buzzed in my skirt pocket, but I ignored it. I was with all my favorite people. Who'd be calling me?

As the waiter wheeled the cart to our table and filled our plates, my phone buzzed again. The spam caller was persistent.

After the waiter left, I looked around the table at my friends. "Did everyone have a nice Christmas?"

"Ugh, don't ask. The holidays with my folks are always painful," Lucie said. "My dad got out his Pulitzer medal for the nine millionth time and asked when I was going to write something Pulitzer-worthy. What about you, Tessa?"

"I spent it alone at home."

"Why didn't you tell me?" Savannah asked. "I'd have invited you to our place."

"Alone at home is exactly the way I like it. I stayed in my sweatpants and cuddled with my cats. They don't spout conspiracy theories or talk about the best ways to tell edible mushrooms from poisonous ones."

We all blinked at her.

"Except Anita. She has some pretty radical theories about crows." She looked around the table. "Kidding."

Andrew guffawed.

I leaned around him. "Savannah, were your kids home for Christmas?"

"Yes." She sighed. "But they left yesterday. And now..." She glanced at Andrew.

"Want me to go away for a minute while you tell them something secret?" Andrew asked.

"No, it's fine. You're one of us now."

A slow smile spread over his face, and he squeezed my knee under the table.

Savannah said, "Anyway, things aren't good between me and Jason. It's like we were performing for the kids, and now we're...not."

"Not good how?" Lucie asked, her voice sharp.

"It's not like that. He's not abusive. Not physically."

"Is he abusive in other ways?" I asked.

She winced. "He can be critical. It's nothing that isn't true though." She ran a hand over her stomach, then pushed her plate away.

I knew that move. "Did he say something about your size? Because you're beautiful just the way you are. You know that, right?"

"I..." She glanced at me. "I'm not beautiful. Not like you three."

"You are," Tessa and Lucie said at the same time.

"They're right," Andrew said. "You're gorgeous. He's a fool if he doesn't see it."

"Thank you. You're sweet." She laid a hand on his forearm.

"Don't put up with his bullshit," Lucie warned her. "Do what Carly did. Dump his ass."

"But I...I don't know. How did you know to leave your ex, Carly?"

I chuckled darkly. "His girlfriend showed up at my door asking when I was moving out."

"No!" Andrew stared at me. "Really?"

"Really."

His expression was thunderous. "If I'd known, I'd have—"

"It's fine. It turned out fine. Especially now Hayley's—" But that wasn't my secret to tell. "I'm happier." I set my hand over his, which still rested on my knee. "Anyway, Savannah, maybe don't wait as long as I did. If you think you can work it out, that's okay, too. Only you can decide what's right for you."

"If you ever need somewhere to stay, I've got plenty of room at my place," Tessa said.

"Thanks, hon." Savannah sniffed and blotted her nose with her napkin. "Enough sad stuff. Those shrimp dumplings are to die for. I've never tasted anything like them in Sacramento."

"Have you tried the sesame rice balls?" Tessa asked. "They're like heaven in your mouth."

"That's what she said," Lucie mumbled.

"I"—Savannah rubbed her stomach again—"not yet. I'll try one when the cart comes by."

When my phone buzzed, I set down my chopsticks and pulled out my phone. "I swear, these spam callers…" But it wasn't a spam caller. It was a text from Helen Choi.

> Unknown: Hi Carly, it's Helen Choi. I need a red-carpet style for my premiere in February, and I'd like a consult
>
> Unknown: Are you available this week for a video call?
>
> Unknown: And I may have given your number to a couple of friends. I hope that's OK

The phone wobbled in my numb fingertips.

"Is everything all right?" Andrew asked.

"Yes, I…I think so? It's Helen."

When he grinned, his dimples dented his cheeks adorably. "I knew she'd call."

"You scored a new client at the wedding?" Lucie asked.

I blinked at my phone to confirm I hadn't imagined it. "I think I did."

Andrew set down his chopsticks. "It's not just any client. It's Helen Choi. The actress."

My friends gasped, then peppered me with a dozen questions at once.

"Hayley's her friend," I protested. "She's being nice."

Andrew said, "Hollywood stars don't have time for nice. Your style impressed her."

After struggling for so long, I couldn't believe it. "Possibly."

"That's amazing! I'm sure it'll go great." Savannah's smile was pure confidence.

Lucie said, "She'll recommend you to ten friends. It's award season."

"Maybe." I wasn't nearly as confident. I was much surer of my ability to style middle-aged women than Hollywood stars. Why would gorgeous, successful young women like Helen Choi want to be styled by someone a loser like Brad Winner had rejected?

It had to be a mistake.

Just like whatever this was with Andrew. Pretty soon, he'd come to his senses too.

27

A CINDERELLA STORY

ANDREW

```
From: Victor Lynch
To: Andrew Jones
Sent: December 31, 2:11 pm
Subject: <none>
```

Find me at the party tonight. I'll introduce you to the chairman as our strongest VP candidate. Be sure Carly's there too.
-Vic
Victor Lynch, Chief Financial Officer

"I feel like a celebrity," I said, clutching Carly's hand as we walked into the party. Heads turned, and I knew it wasn't my new three-piece tux or even Carly's red gown, which was cut tantalizingly close to her navel, that drew their attention. It was Carly. News that my girlfriend was styling Helen Choi and her rising-star friends had blown through the bank like a tsunami. Three vice presidents had asked me if they could get on her waiting list. "Like Hugh Grant in *Notting Hill*."

"You look better in a tux than he did." She smoothed her hand over my lapel, and my heart skipped.

I slipped my arm around her waist, my fingers sliding across the smooth red silk. "Is this okay?"

"Mm-hmm." She nestled into my side. "Time to sell this."

My fingers stiffened and skidded off the fabric. Sell it? Even though we hadn't named our feelings yet, she'd taken me to brunch with her best friends. That had to mean something.

Seeming not to notice that I'd stopped breathing, Carly grasped my hand. "Should we get a drink?"

I sucked in a deep breath to say, yes, I'd very much like a drink, but Vic's wife, Yelena, and two other women flitted up to us.

"Carly." Yelena put her hands on Carly's shoulders, bumping me out of the way, and kissed her cheeks. "That gown is divine. So daring!"

"Thank you. I figured I could get away with it on the arm of this hotshot."

I wasn't so sure I was a hotshot, but her smile lit me up inside. I'd climb the corporate ladder to the top if it made me worthy to walk into every party with her.

"Vic wants to talk with you, Andrew," Yelena said. "He's over by the photo booth." She glanced at me, then did a double-take. "I love what you did with his hair. Do you think you could do something with Vic's? He hasn't changed his style since The Great Recession."

The women closed ranks around Carly, effectively dismissing me. "I'll find you later," I said, but I wasn't sure she heard me.

I trudged toward the photo booth, conveniently set up next to a bar. Vic wasn't posing for a photos, but he watched our younger employees pick up the props—masks, feather boas, novelty sunglasses with the year sticking up from the tops—and strike silly poses for the photographer. I hoped he wasn't taking notes for his next division-wide email on decorum.

"Vic," I said, reaching out to shake his hand.

"Andrew." He grasped it and, I shit you not, smiled at me. I almost stumbled back in shock but managed to keep my feet under me.

"You wanted to see me?"

"Yes, I'll introduce you to Christian Sauer in a minute," he said.

I swallowed. Being introduced to the bank's chair was a big deal.

He scanned me. "You look good. Carly must have worked her magic on you."

Self-consciously, I touched my hair, which Carly had again corralled with her magic styling product. "Yeah, she's great at that."

"Yelena's going to ask her to update my wardrobe. I can't believe I've got a connection to a dynamo like Carly Rose, stylist to the stars. You can get me the friends-and-family discount?" He elbowed me in the side.

I tried my best to smile. "Maybe. She's in high demand."

Ever since that call from Helen two days ago, she'd been up to her elbows in swatches and samples and mood boards, too busy for me to even take her out to dinner. I'd hoped to extend my time off through New Year's Day and spend a few more days figuring out what a real relationship looked like—and crowing over that sound she made when she came—but she had too much work to do.

With Carly working twenty-four-seven, I'd gone into the office both yesterday and today to pick halfheartedly at the backlog of work that had piled up while we'd been at the wedding.

"Don't I know it," he said. "By next week, it'll be easier to get a table at French Laundry than to score an appointment with your girlfriend."

I couldn't make myself laugh at Vic's joke. If my father had only been able to spare fifteen minutes a day with me, how much of Carly's valuable time could I expect? Something heavy settled into my stomach like I'd swallowed plutonium.

"Why so glum?" Vic asked. "It's New Year's Eve, you're the front-runner for that vice president position you wanted, and you'll be San Francisco's newest power couple soon enough."

My stomach lightened for a second, then dropped, even heavier. I grunted.

"I'm glad to see you've stopped making those ridiculous videos," he said.

I winced. We were only on a brief hiatus because of my trip to Spain and Oliver's travel home to the East Coast. We planned to make a video about fractions next week in Oliver's gourmet kitchen.

"Come on," Vic said. "Let's find Christian."

We found him near the stage, where the band had gone on break.

"Christian," Vic said, grasping the chair's hand, "this is Andrew Jones. I've been telling you about him. He's the financial engineer who developed that new risk model."

Sauer smiled and hit me with an unexpectedly focused gaze. "Our S&T team is salivating over that model. They tell me our clients are eating it up."

A spark flared inside me. Finally, I could talk up my work. "Thank you, sir. I discovered when I investigated the stochastic process—"

"Let's not get into the math tonight," Vic interrupted me.

So the chair wasn't into probability theory either.

He chuckled. "Thankfully, I don't need to understand the financial models. I only need to see the results. Then it becomes another arrow in the sales team's quiver."

The spark inside me flickered and died. I knew my work was sold to customers, but Sauer's words cheapened it.

Vic jumped in. "Jones is our top internal candidate for the R&D vice president position."

Sauer rocked back on his heels, pinning me with that focused gaze again. "A quant as a VP? I suppose stranger promotions have happened."

My eyelid twitched.

"He's not only a quant," Vic said. "He's a Jones. Jasper and Audrey's son."

Sauer's gaze turned calculating. "I remember your father. Brilliant man. And ambitious."

I heard what he didn't say: *what happened to you?*

At my age, my father was already a tech company vice president. That was before he poached a few of his best employees to start his company. Just like my mother, Sauer thought I should've done more with my skills and advantages.

"We need people like Andrew in leadership," he said. "Why don't you try him out in front of a client or two next week, Vic?"

"Already did." Vic's tone was smug. "He aced a meeting with Brad Winner. Guy was eating out of his hand."

Sauer tipped his chin. "Let's have him present at the board meeting next month."

The entire board? I gulped. Talking to Oliver's camera about math or explaining my models to fucking Brad Winner was nothing like talking to a group of judgmental old men who could fire me with a voice vote.

"Great idea," Vic said. "He can show them his latest model. They'll love it. Speaking of models"—he leaned in close—"Jones is dating Carly Rose, who's styling that actress everyone is talking about."

Sauer's white eyebrows shot up. "Ah, a Cinderella story."

I had a sinking feeling I was the Cinderella in that story. I glanced past Sauer to where I'd left Carly. The circle of women had grown, and I couldn't see her red dress.

"I suppose so, sir," I said.

"Let me find my wife," Sauer said, "and you can introduce us. I'll score massive points for this. Know what I mean?" He waggled his eyebrows.

"Of course." And when Sauer's wife's eyes lit up when she shook Carly's hand, Sauer earned his points. And so did I.

Vic clapped my shoulder.

But it wasn't him I wanted to impress. It was Carly, who was so busy handing out business cards she hardly spared me a glance.

She didn't need me to be successful.

Did she need me at all?

I blamed the uncomfortable weight in my belly for the foolish thing I did at midnight.

When the countdown started, I pushed my way through the crowd of client wannabes to Carly's side. She glowed as she shouted along with everyone else, "Three! Two! One! Happy New Year!"

She turned to me, a broad smile on her face. I wrapped my arms around her and kissed her. Harder than I meant to and for so long there were a few wolf whistles scattered into "Auld Lang Syne." I didn't care. I needed the connection, the proof she was still mine.

When I finally released her, her cheeks glowed pink, and we both breathed hard.

"What was that for?" she asked.

"Thought I'd remind you who you came here with." My

voice came out peevish, and I instantly regretted it all—the punishing kiss, the words, the tone.

The smile slipped from her face. "What does that mean?"

"I'm sorry." I touched her hand, and when she didn't yank it away, I curled my fingers around it. "Tonight's been stressful. I shouldn't have taken it out on you. Want to get out of here?"

The corners of her lips lifted. "Please. My feet are killing me."

I wrapped my arm around her waist and guided her toward the exit. "You can take your shoes off in the car, and I'll carry you into your place."

"To the second floor?" She laughed. "I'd like to see you try."

Challenge accepted. When we got to her place, I slung her over my shoulder in a firefighter's carry, and her voluminous skirt billowed in my face as I raced up the stairs.

She laughed the whole way up and didn't stop until I dropped her onto her bed, rucked up her skirt, and showed her with my mouth how much she meant to me.

28

THE POWER OF PUPPIES

CARLY

To-do list—January 1
~~Nothing!~~
Catch up on email and schedule responses for tomorrow

Laughing, I squirmed to the edge of my bed, out of reach of Andrew's fingertips. He'd hardly stopped touching me since that intense, hardly-safe-for-work kiss at the party last night. The many orgasms he'd given me early this morning had me feeling like the day after a core workout.

"No more cuddling!" I sat up. "It's time for breakfast. I've been ignoring your stomach rumbling for the past ten minutes."

He pouted, looking more boyish than usual. "I'd rather eat you."

How had I gotten so lucky? Andrew took care of my sexual needs like it was his job. And speaking of jobs, if even a quarter of the contacts I'd made at his party turned into business, I'd be set for months. Though they'd all have to wait until after I styled Helen and her Hollywood friends for their award shows. I was so thankful Andrew had forced my card on Helen Choi. If it had been up to me, I'd have missed out on the opportunity and everything that came with it.

"Come on," I said. "I'll make you breakfast."

"You what?" Dramatically, Andrew rubbed at his ear. "I thought I heard you say you'd cook something."

I poked his bare chest. "Don't get used to it, but I've learned a thing or two. I watched Savannah's videos."

"Wow. Okay." He blinked. "I'll take a quick shower then."

"Good." I'd be less nervous without an audience.

He launched out of bed, naked, and grabbed his phone from the table. "And I'll dial 9-1 just in case."

I tossed a pillow at his head. "Not funny. I was cooking before you were—"

Shit. I'd broken my rule not to bring up our age difference.

"I'm out of practice," I finished weakly.

He circled the bed to kiss my forehead. "I was joking. I'm sure it'll turn out great." Then he turned and sauntered toward my bathroom.

I watched his taut ass work until he shut the door behind him, then I fanned myself with my hand. I liked having Andrew in my life. Sure, I texted with my girlfriends almost every day. But their texts didn't make my stomach swoop the way Andrew's did. And when I met him at a restaurant, or when he opened the door of his place? The initial swoop gave way to tingles that raced across my skin, leaving goosebumps in their wake.

Days like this, I knew I was in dangerous waters. He was the wave, reaching up to drag me overboard while I clung to the pitching deck. I wanted to drown in Andrew's care and affection.

I couldn't envision ending our relationship on February first.

I wanted more mornings in bed and more afternoons like yesterday before the party, cuddling on the sofa and watching *When Harry Met Sally*. I'd cringed when he'd called it a classic.

I supposed that was better than old.

When I stood, my knee creaked, reminding me I wouldn't be able to squat to adjust a hem forever.

When I was twenty-five, I'd willingly given up my career to support Brad's, foolishly thinking we were partners, working together toward our future.

Older and wiser now, I knew my future rested in my own hands. I wasn't twenty-five anymore. And in a month, I wouldn't even be forty-five. I didn't have years stretching out in front of me to establish my business, to make mistakes and recover.

I couldn't lose myself in a man again. My father left before I was born. Brad? Don't even get me started. I couldn't rely on anyone else, not for all the stomach-swooping laughter in the world. Even if my skin glowed from the toe-curling orgasms.

Laughter and glowing skin didn't put clothes on my back or sock away savings for a time I'd be tired of hustling.

I tugged on leggings, a bra, and an oversized tee and made my way to my kitchen. After starting the coffee, I picked up my phone to rewatch Savannah's sunny-side-up eggs video, but there was a text from Helen.

She had questions about the initial concepts I'd sent, and I took a minute to find a few photos, then thumbed out a reply. She sent a follow-up question with her thoughts, which sent me down a rabbit hole at one of my favorite couture sites.

"Hey." Andrew stepped into my kitchen, dressed in jeans and a cable-knit sweater that made me tingle like an Irish fisherman's wife seeing her husband after a week at sea.

My cheeks hot, I set my phone on the counter and glanced at the cold stove. "Sorry, I got distracted by work."

His expression reminded me of last night at the party, when

he found me during the countdown and kissed me. It looked almost like pain, but it was gone before I could be sure.

"I'm sorry," I said. "I'll get started on breakfast."

"Don't be sorry. We'll get breakfast out."

The tension left my shoulders. This wasn't Brad, who went off the handle when I didn't meet expectations. This was Andrew, who liked me even if I didn't cook. Who thought I was a goddess despite my smile lines and unperky tits.

He stepped closer to me and put a hand on my waist. His ocean scent, combined with that sexy sweater, made my mouth go dry. Despite this morning's orgasms, my pulse throbbed between my legs.

"I have a proposal," he said.

I blinked. "A what?" He wasn't about to take a knee, was he?

"Do you have to deal with Helen right away, or do you have a few hours to spend with me? Last night was our last fake date, so I'd like to take you out on a real one."

My racing heart slowed. "Like dinner and a movie?"

He put a hand on his heart. "I may work in a bank, but I'm not that basic. I have an idea for an outdoor activity. Get your coat."

"Outdoors?" Was I prepared to date him for real where everyone could see us? The pretense had given me confidence. It was an act, same as when I'd walked out on stage in a swimsuit in my pageant days. Real meant being vulnerable. Caring what others thought of us. Even in the weak winter sun, my smile lines would be a visible contrast to Andrew's youthful skin.

"A park. Super low-key. It'll be fun." He held out a hand.

"I'm not going out like this." I waved at my leggings and T-shirt. "I have a reputation to uphold."

He chuckled. "Don't worry, no one there will care what you're wearing. And you always look beautiful to me."

"Hm." His words warmed me to the core. "Still, I need a

minute to change and do my hair." I'd learned long ago that not bothering to dress up was the surest way to run into someone you knew, perhaps a potential client.

"Okay." He shrugged. "I'll wait."

"Thanks." I lifted on my toes and kissed him. He hummed, and I turned the kiss hot and dirty, teasing my tongue along his lower lip. But when I ran my hands up the wool covering his solid chest, he backed off.

"Temptress. If we do that, we'll never get there in time."

I dropped back on my heels. "Not goddess? Now I'm a temptress?"

"Goddesses can be very tempting. Didn't Aphrodite seduce Adonis?"

"Among others, I believe." But we were getting too close to uncomfortable territory when we talked about older women as seductresses. "I'll be done in a few."

An hour later, Andrew held open the door to his Audi. He hadn't said a word about how a few minutes had turned into sixty. He only looked at me with the adoration he always did. Then he reminded me to wear a coat and shoes I didn't mind getting dirty.

He eased his car onto a grassy parking area at a suburban park. The tops of white tents poked over the surrounding shrubs. He'd pulled in next to a minivan. A family, two dads and three kids, scrambled out. Watching them, I held in a sigh. Andrew had brought me to a place that showed where he belonged. Among families. After I found the courage to let him go, he could find a nice person and settle down. In a few years, he could be driving a minivan of his own.

"Hey," he said, leaning over the console to kiss me. "What's wrong?"

"Nothing." I should enjoy him while I could, before he tired of me the way Brad had.

"Okay." But his eyebrows canted together. "Let's go. It'll be impossible to be sad once we get where we're going."

We'd barely cleared the car when the oldest kid from the minivan tugged on Andrew's sleeve. "Hey. Are you the math nerd?"

I sucked in an outraged breath. Then I remembered *The Math Nerd* was the name of his channel.

"Yeah. Do you like math?"

The kid screwed up his face. "I didn't. But then my dad found your videos, and it was kind of fun. I finally passed my nine times table."

"Did you use the hand trick?"

"Yeah!" He held up his hand and curled his right ring finger down. "Nine times nine is eighty-one!"

"That's great." Andrew beamed. "Wait until I show you something to help with elevens."

One of the dads came up behind his son, holding the toddler in one arm and extending the other for a handshake. "Thanks, man. Appreciate what you do."

Andrew's smile faltered. Why didn't he like being thanked? He loved making those videos.

"Isn't he great?" I rubbed his back. "I wish someone like him had made videos like that when I was a kid. Maybe I wouldn't have gotten a C in calculus."

Andrew shot me a wicked grin. "I don't know how you could've done that. You're the integral of e to the XY."

The dad chuckled, then looked at his son. "Thankfully, he doesn't know integrals yet. Or spelling all that well. Do you do school programs? My husband is a school superintendent, and I know he'd love to have you in his district. Wouldn't you, babe?"

The other man, who was wrangling a jacket onto the middle child, said, "Absolutely. I'm salivating over here."

"Wow, um, thanks," Andrew said. "But I, uh, I have a day job, and..."

"Sure, sure. You have a card on you, babe?" the man asked his husband.

The husband stood and dug in his pocket. "Yeah. I'd K-I-L-L to offer our students a program like that. Give me a call if you change your mind."

The oldest kid looked smug. Apparently, he wasn't as bad at spelling as his dad thought.

Pocketing the card, Andrew winced. "We're on a hiatus."

"Sorry to hear that," the first dad said.

While the second dad explained *hiatus* to the oldest son, Andrew said his goodbyes and turned toward the park.

"What was that about?" I asked.

"Ugh." He slipped an arm around me. "Vic hates the videos. If I want this promotion, I have to represent the bank *at all times.*" He frowned.

Hell. He loved making those videos. And clearly, kids loved them, too. "I'm sorry."

"Yeah. What can I do?" He shrugged. "I want that promotion." Seeming to shake it off, he said, "But today, we're celebrating us. You're going to love this."

He led me through the family festival. We passed an arts and crafts tent, face painting, a bocce tournament, and a beer pavilion and strolled to an open-sided tent at the periphery. The banner said, "Must Love (Rescue) Dogs," and barks and yips floated on the winter breeze.

When I sucked in a breath, he tugged me to a stop and positioned himself between the tent and me.

"Repeat after me: we are only here to play with the puppies. We're not taking anyone home today."

"We're playing with puppies?" My heart bounced in my chest like a Labrador.

"Repeat, please. My animal-loving sister would hurt me if we made a rash decision."

"We're only playing. We're not taking anyone home."

"Today." He smiled. "We're not taking anyone home *today*."

"Fine. We're not taking anyone home today." Hope speared through me. Would Andrew and I get a dog someday?

For the next hour, as dogs licked my face, as puppies nipped my fingers, as I buried my face in their fur, I imagined a future where Andrew Jones and I picked out one of the dogs and took it to a home we shared. We'd cuddle up on my sofa—his was an atrocious leather thing that would show scratches from the dog's nails—with a dog splayed across our laps and watch classic rom-coms. We'd go for long walks in the park, the dog pulling ahead of us as we strolled arm in arm.

It must have been the cocktail of warm dog breath and the sight of Andrew holding two wrinkled hound puppies in his lap that loosened what I'd been holding back ever since that magical day at the Parc de la Ciutadella.

After we placed the puppies back in their pen and ambled out of the tent, I cleared my throat. "I care about you, Andrew. I think I could…" The next words surged in my chest, but the lump in my throat caged them inside.

It hadn't been this hard with Brad. I'd been young and foolish. Now that I understood how the world worked, I knew what the words would mean to Andrew. I could never take them back.

"Love me?" He pulled me to a stop. Hope gleamed in his eyes. "You think you could love me? Because, Carly, I love you."

I nodded and tried to swallow. I was drowning, but it didn't feel so bad with Andrew beside me.

"You truly are a goddess." He wavered like he'd go to his knees, but then he straightened and closed the gap between us. Bending his head and gathering me toward him, he claimed my mouth right there in the park.

I didn't care.

I let everyone see that I liked Andrew Jones. That maybe I loved him. That we belonged together. No more February first. We'd see where this took us. It was a kiss of possibility, of shared hope.

He broke the kiss first, leaving me dazed and breathless. He pulled me against his cozy sweater and tunneled his fingers into my hair, messing it up.

"Holy shit," he whispered. "If I'd known about the power of puppies, I'd have taken you to the shelter months ago."

I poked my nose into the space above his sweater where I could smell his skin. "It's not the puppies. It's you. You see me. You understand me." The way Brad never did.

"Carly, I—" He slid his hands down to cup my ass, and I probably would've leaped to straddle him like Helen Choi had done at the end of that movie when she was a city slicker marketing exec who fell for a cowboy, but he pulled my phone from my back pocket. "This is buzzing like crazy."

I took it from him. A long string of texts from Helen appeared on the lock screen.

"Sorry, I..." I scanned through the texts.

"It's okay," he said. "Take a minute."

Helen's crisis would take longer than a minute. She'd been invited to replace an injured actor and present an award at the Golden Globes. She'd chosen a gown months ago, but now she needed a presenter-worthy look. I'd need to pull something together fast. Could I trust a courier? No, I'd need to fly to Los Angeles and do it personally.

I looked up from the device. "I have to deal with this. It's a fashion emergency."

"Want me to take you home?"

The fact that he didn't laugh at the idea of a fashion emergency or question me made me fall a little more. "Could you? Please?"

He took my hand, and we weaved between strollers and families toward the exit.

"I could stay at your place and help if you want," he said.

"Help? More like distract me." I chuckled, imagining how a stress-relieving neck rub might devolve into hours of naked time. "No, you'd better go home."

He made that troubling expression again.

Before we got into his car, I kissed it off his lips.

29

A MODERN-DAY PEE-WEE HERMAN

ANDREW

```
Meeting invitation: Lunch
From: Victor Lynch
To: Andrew Jones
Start time: Wednesday, January 22, 12:00 pm
End time: Wednesday, January 22, 2:00 pm
Location: La Colombe Bleue
Message: <none>
```

I pulled up to the valet stand in front of the French restaurant. This had to be it, the moment when Vic would either offer me the promotion or let me down. Gently, I hoped. For the past three weeks, his assistant had paraded a handful of external candidates past my office to Vic's. Every one of them sauntered in looking assured, and each one laughed with Vic as they came out, displaying a confidence I could never feel anywhere but in front of my computer monitor, perfecting a financial model.

The presentation to the board had gone...not great. I'd been fired up about my latest model, eager to explain it to them. I had even—I cringed a little, remembering—brought a set of dice to demonstrate the fundamental principles.

They weren't impressed. They didn't want to talk about financial modeling as much as they wanted my opinions about how to better serve the bank's customers and potential areas for growth. Topics I'd never thought about because, frankly, I didn't care. Why couldn't they let me do math and supervise the other mathematicians? Had Reva done all this?

But, if I was honest, my sense of unease over the last three weeks wasn't only because of the botched presentation or even the slate of more qualified candidates.

It was because of Carly. At the festival on New Year's Day, we'd gotten so close to where I wanted to be. When she'd almost, but not quite, said she loved me. And now she was busy. I didn't blame her. It was award season. Her phone rang nonstop. Helen and all her friends needed her opinions on their formal looks. It wouldn't end after the Oscars in March. After that, she had a long list of local clients to style.

She was like my dad, dedicated and driven. But some days, she couldn't spare even fifteen minutes for me. Sometimes it was only a text. And without the stress relief of making videos with my best friend, a text wasn't enough.

I handed the keys to the valet and strode around the back of the car to stand on the sidewalk. Vic's choice of venues didn't give me any clues about how our lunch would go. La Colombe Bleue was the kind of place my parents went for dinner. It was nice enough and popular with people at a certain income level. It was a place to see and be seen, to be sure to run into someone you knew.

Had Vic brought me here so I wouldn't make a scene if he told me he was giving the job to someone else? Cold prickles erupted in my belly, and it wasn't only because the host led me past the table where we'd had dinner with Brad that night.

I straightened my tie, the blue one Carly had told me to wear, and pulled open the door. She was in LA styling Helen for a premiere, but her text this morning had declared that lunch was good news. I almost believed her, hoping that as close as we'd become, her aura of magical success might encompass me too. Like when one of my soccer teammates was having a stellar day, we all seemed to play better.

"Here you are, sir." The host's voice startled me.

Vic was already seated, his expression giving nothing away. He stood to shake my hand. "Jones."

"Afternoon, Vic. Sorry I'm late. I was working on a model, and I lost track of time. I hope you haven't been waiting long?"

"Not too long. It's good to see your dedication to the work. Something to drink?"

Unbuttoning my suit jacket and easing into the chair, I narrowed my eyes. Was this a test? "Water's fine, thanks."

Vic waved off the server and grasped his lowball glass. "To new beginnings."

I raised my water glass. "New beginnings." Fuck, I wished he'd come out and tell me if the new beginning was a new boss for me.

He sipped his drink and gave me a steely stare. "You didn't make this easy on me, kid."

"I—I'm sorry?"

"It was hard to get a read on you. Don't get me wrong, you do excellent work. Everyone's impressed with the new risk model." He paused, his glare seeming to pierce my skin, right to my heart rabbiting in my chest. "I'd have thought someone with your background would have more...vision. You know?"

"Vision? I'm great at anticipating risk. And pretty good at predicting gains."

He waved a hand. "Not that. I mean strategic thinking. Ideas for growing the bank's position."

I kept the grimace off my face. I didn't give a shit about the bank's position, as long as it paid everyone's salary and protected our customers' assets. But Vic didn't want to hear that. "I care about the bank."

"I'll need you to work on your strategic thinking. I'm signing you up for coaching next month."

"Okay."

"Because our vice presidents can't yammer on about stok—stok—"

"Stochastic processes?"

"That. At cocktail parties."

"What are you saying, Vic?"

"I'm saying…" When he smiled, his teeth were sharp. "The promotion is yours."

It was all I could do not to whip off my shirt like I'd scored a soccer goal. "Really? That's fantastic!"

"It'll require hard work. The quants aren't the easiest to supervise. They're a bunch of prima donnas who think they can manage themselves. And you'll need to train someone to take over your work."

"Wait, I won't be continuing my modeling work?"

He shook his head. "You'll be too busy managing the team to be a quant yourself. You'll present their work to me and the rest of senior leadership. And once in a while, to the board. After you work on your soft skills, especially vision and executive presence."

Executive presence? I sat back in my chair. I didn't think I'd ever enjoy presenting to the board no matter how many workshops I attended. Building models and talking about them was fun. Could I enjoy only helping the team with their models?

"I'll need you at one hundred percent, Jones. Fortunately,

you've got Carly to help you with social events. She's good at those things."

My heart skipped in my chest. Carly. She'd be happy for me. Plus, she could help me with strategy. She had a brilliant vision for her business.

"We'll expect you to represent the bank at all times." He lowered his eyebrows meaningfully.

"Of...of course?"

He dipped his chin like he needed more.

"When I'm managing the team," I said, "I'll support all the bank's directives." Even the ridiculous ones like requiring the financial engineers to wear suits and ties. I'd lead by example and wouldn't tug my tie off as soon as I sat at my desk.

"I mean at *all times*. Including weekends."

"Weekends? I'll be working Saturdays?"

He rolled his eyes to the frescoed ceiling as if the painted blue dove could help him explain this to me. "I mean that ridiculous video series of yours. Take it down."

"Take it down?" I shook my head. He couldn't mean it. "We're already on hiatus. I haven't posted a new video in a month."

"Bank vice presidents don't make videos for children like some modern-day Pee-wee Herman. It's got to go. No new episodes. Remove the old ones. Delete the whole goddamn channel."

That kid at the festival flashed into my mind. I'd never get to show him the cool trick for multiplying by eleven like I'd promised. "But—"

"Let's talk compensation." And with that, Vic moved the conversation to incentive plans and stock grants.

I couldn't stop thinking about how disappointed Oliver would be when I told him about the videos. Would he agree to keep making them? He'd have to be the one in front of the camera, but I'd write the scripts and edit the videos. Regardless of what Vic said, we didn't have to stop. We just needed to retool. I couldn't give a hundred percent of my life to the bank. Not like my dad had done with his company.

As wonderful as Dad had been, I wouldn't repeat his mistakes. I had no intention of dying before my fortieth birthday.

But Vic wouldn't appreciate that, so I smiled and nodded and ate as much of my grilled salmon as my roiling stomach would accept. After he put the bill on his company card and we separated outside, my phone was in my hand.

It wasn't my mother's number I pulled up.

It wasn't Oliver's, either.

It was Carly's.

She was the one I cared most to impress now. The sinking sense of disappointment when she didn't answer confirmed why she'd been my first call. I wanted to share my success with her. Only her. I wanted the promotion to be our secret for a little while.

I loved her, and maybe now, as a bank vice president, I'd be worthy of her.

I left the good news on her voice mail. Unlike most of my friends, she actually checked it.

I ended my message with, "I couldn't have done it without you. Thank you. I love you."

A few hours later when my phone rang, I snatched it off my desk, excited to receive Carly's congratulations, hoping she'd tell me she loved me too.

But it wasn't Carly. It was Charles.

And when he told me the news, I flew out of the office, leaving behind both my laptop and my pride over my promotion.

30

A FASHION CRISIS

CARLY

To-do list—January 22
✓ Take up the hem in Helen's jumpsuit
✓ Triple-check the emergency bag
✓ Helen's mani-pedi at 10
✓ Hair stylist arrives at noon
Stay focused!

"Are you checking your watch?" the woman seated across from me in the limo barked. I'd been introduced to her, a combination security guard and personal assistant to Helen, but I'd forgotten her name. Maybe I was a jerk for referring to her in my head as Ms. Muscle because of the way her biceps bulged under her navy blazer.

Styling Helen Choi had taken all my mental energy. This wasn't Helen's first red carpet, but it was mine, and I wanted everything to be perfect. I hadn't balked when she'd unexpectedly asked me to come with her in the limo. I'd kneel on the carpet and fluff out the hems of her pant legs if she needed it.

I'd even delay my flight to San Francisco another day. Though I'd hoped to be home tonight. I was confident Andrew would get that promotion, and I was dying to celebrate with him. We'd toast to achieving our dreams. Then we'd fuck, and I wouldn't even worry about the cellulite on my butt. Fabulous women who styled movie stars, whose phones rang constantly, weren't troubled by nonsense like that.

Focusing on Helen, I'd left my phone on silent all day. After my success with her Golden Globe presenter gown, it had been ringing off the hook, so distracting it verged on annoying.

"I'm not checking my watch," I lied. "There was a smudge on the crystal." I swiveled to peer out the windshield at the long queue of limos outside the theater.

"You'll have plenty of time to catch your flight and get back to your man," Helen said with a knowing smile. While she was getting her nails done, she'd quizzed me about Andrew and was delighted we'd stayed together after Hayley's wedding. "It only seems late because of those clouds."

"It's so dark," I agreed. It was only four-thirty, but the cars around us had their headlights on.

"Did you see that?" Helen asked, pointing with her bottle of sparkling water. The straw was ringed with her red lipstick. She hated the feel of long-lasting lipstick, so the makeup artist had used a satiny Dior on her. "I think it was lightning."

"Sure was, Miss Helen," the driver said. He was burlier than Ms. Muscle and a decade older. "Those clouds don't look good."

I squinted up through the side window. The clouds looked heavy and dark. Lightning sliced through the sky.

"It never rains here," she said. "I'm sure it'll pass."

"Let's hope so." I bit my lip as I scanned her low-cut jumpsuit. The white silk would go sheer if it got wet. And while we were going for sexy, transparent silk that displayed her lacy bra and white thong was a bit too racy for a PG-rated movie premiere.

A sound like machine gun fire pummeled the car. Ms. Muscle was a blur of motion as she threw herself over Helen to shield her from the window, covering her with her brawny arms and shoving her flat against the seat.

I ducked and swiveled my head from side to side, trying to find the source of the noise. "What's happening?"

The driver leaned forward in his seat and tipped his face up to look through the windshield. He chuckled. "It's just rain."

Splotches the size of rouge compacts splashed against the glass. On the roof of the limo, it sounded like a jackhammer. Even though there was no danger, Ms. Muscle held on to Helen. *Interesting.* Her watch snagged my client's sleek bun, and Helen's hair stuck out on one side. But the bigger problem was what we were going to do about Helen's white outfit in the pouring rain. She'd look like a contestant in a wet T-shirt contest.

I caught Ms. Muscle's eye—I really wished I'd learned her name—and shouted over the noise, "Can you call the venue to see if they'll be able to shield her from the weather?"

She nodded and pulled her phone from the pocket of her khakis. I leaned forward to assess the damage to Helen's hair. It looked like a teacup with a thick loop jutting from the side of her head. Miraculously, Helen had managed not to spill her water. She sipped from the straw.

Ms. Muscle hung up her phone. "They've got umbrellas and a canopy. They should be able to keep her dry."

That would work for the top of her. But if rain blew in from the sides, it would be over. I had zero hope for her pant legs. We'd gone for a flared bottom that ended half an inch from the floor. Any water would soak the hem and wick up the silk, making the legs floppy and heavy. Disaster.

"What do you think, Carly? Think we'll be okay?" Helen asked, biting her lip.

"Smile," I said automatically.

She obeyed, and I checked for lipstick on her teeth. All clear.

I glanced out the window at the sheeting rain. "How long is it supposed to continue?"

"All night," the driver said. He showed us the satellite image on his phone. The splotch of red at the left edge of the screen was small and round, surrounded by wider rings of orange and yellow. "This isn't even the worst of it."

"I'll be fine." Helen nodded, decisive, making the loop of hair over her right ear wag. "I'll run to the canopy."

I blinked, envisioning the paparazzi capturing video of her running in her sky-high heels or worse, tripping over one of them and falling on her face. Surely someone would loop it into a meme. "No."

"I'll carry her," Ms. Muscle offered.

"No," Helen and I said simultaneously.

Helen smiled at her bodyguard and said, "I'd never get a role in an action movie after that. It'd be all damsels in distress."

"Then what are we going to do?" her bodyguard asked. "I'll give you my jacket, but that won't cover the rest of you." She scanned down Helen's leg to her four-inch rhinestone-covered stilettos. She tore her gaze from her employer, then stared straight ahead as she unbuttoned her blazer and started to shrug out of it.

The car lurched forward.

The catastrophe inside the car played out in slow motion. Unbalanced by the car's sudden motion, Ms. Muscle swayed, and her elbow tapped Helen's back. Helen tipped, and her sparkling water splashed onto her torso. As the cherry on top, the straw tumbled out of the bottle, and the end coated with lipstick hit her boob, leaving a red smudge across the white silk.

"Aigo!" Helen exclaimed.

"Sorry," the driver called out.

The world resumed its normal pace, and the actress looked up from the disaster of her formerly elegant outfit, her brown eyes round. "What just happened?"

Ms. Muscle stopped struggling with her jacket, her jaw slack at the see-through view of her boss. She ripped off her coat and laid it over her. "Sorry, Helen." She swallowed.

"It'll be fine," our star said, her eyes not leaving me. "Carly has something in her magic bag to fix this."

I lifted Ms. Muscle's blazer. The silk would never dry in time. And that crimson lipstick wasn't coming out even with an alcohol wipe. We'd be lucky if the dry-cleaning experts could remove it from the five-thousand-dollar jumpsuit.

But any stylist worth her cordless titanium flat iron always had a backup.

"Pop the trunk for me?" I asked the driver. "Wait here," I told Helen.

I pushed out of the limo. Immediately, the freezing-cold raindrops soaked me, each one like an ice cube pelting my head. Scurrying to the trunk, I pulled out the dress bag and sheltered it with my body as I raced back to the safety of the limo. I resisted the urge to shake off the water like a dog and pulled a black gown from the bag. "Change into this."

Despite the tinted windows, Ms. Muscle faced the window and held her thick arms across it while Helen stripped out of the white pantsuit and pulled on the black gown. It took a choking cloud of hairspray to redo her bun, but when we rolled up to the canopy where photographers huddled under their flapping ponchos, Helen looked flawless.

Ms. Muscle put her hand on the door handle.

Helen turned to me. "Thank you, Carly. You went above and beyond." She nodded at her reflection in the mirror I held. "I owe you big."

"Just doing my job," I said, my cheeks heating. In the fashion industry, there was no such thing as above and beyond. We did everything we could to make our clients look like they woke up with flawless skin and shiny hair and naturally repelled wrinkles.

"Ji-hoon, please make sure Carly gets to the airport," she said to the driver, then to me, "Say hi to Andrew for me."

"Thank you." I patted her shoulder, afraid to wrinkle her with a hug. "Don't forget to pick up your hem as you step out. One more smile?"

She beamed at me. Her teeth gleamed white.

"Stunning. Go get 'em," I said.

Ms. Muscle opened the door and, more gracefully than I'd have imagined, held the umbrella as she reached into the limo to assist Helen from the vehicle.

Clutching the skirt in her fist to keep it out of the water pooling on the sidewalk, Helen took three steps to the safety of the red carpet. There, she released the skirt. It covered her shoes, which was a shame since I'd spent hours scouting the perfect pair.

Shutters clicked, and flashes seared my retinas. Helen planted a hand on her hip, bent her knee, dipped her chin, and shot them a ferocious smile. After posing for a moment, she moved across the step and repeat backdrop. She said something to the photographers, but I couldn't hear from inside the car with the pounding rain.

When she turned to walk through the theater doors, Ji-hoon pulled away from the curb, and I dug through my satchel for my phone. The voice mail icon showed double digits of new messages, but I only cared about the one from Andrew. Make that three from Andrew. I smiled. He must have been so excited about his promotion that he'd called multiple times to tell me about his lunch with Vic.

I tapped the first one and held the phone to my ear, grinning at his good news and rubbing a circle over my heart when he closed with, "I love you." Would those words ever get old and tired before falling off completely the way Brad's had? Maybe not. Andrew was loyal and attentive in a way Brad had never been.

Immediately, his second message started to play, and I sat up at the tightness in his tone.

"I just got a call from Charles. My mother fainted. The paramedics took her to the hospital. I'm on my way to meet them. Call me, okay?"

In the third message, sent just a few minutes ago, his voice trembled. "It's a heart attack. They're doing an emergency bypass. I-I'm scared, Carly."

Of course he was scared. His dad had died of a heart attack, and I knew what it was like to lose your mother before you were ready. I hit his number to call him back.

"Carly." A sigh crackled on the line. "I'm so glad you're back from LA. Would you mind coming to the hospital? I'm at—"

"I'm sorry," I interrupted him. "I got delayed. I'm still in Los Angeles. But I'm on my way to the airport, and I should be there soon."

"Oh." The disappointment in his tone made my heart squeeze.

"Are your siblings there? And Charles?"

"Yeah. But"—he lowered his voice—"I need you."

"I know." I wished I had the superpower of teleportation. "I'll get there as soon as I can."

"Thank you," he whispered.

As Ji-hoon sped to the airport, I jammed my toe into the carpet like I had my own gas pedal and could make the limousine fly.

31

THE LEADING LADY

ANDREW

> Surgery Center: The procedure is complete. We are moving Audrey to the ICU. We will update you when she is awake.

I shifted in the cushy chair in our private waiting room. My parents' generous support of the hospital came with perks.

"Did you see?" I glanced up at Charles.

He'd stopped his pacing and stared at his phone. "How soon do you think we can get back there and see her?"

"I don't know." The talk with the surgeon earlier was a blur after six hours of worry, of glancing at my phone every five minutes to see if Carly had texted (she hadn't), and of fielding calls from Sam, who was on her way from the airport with Jackson.

From the chair beside me, Natalie's voice came out as a croak. "They didn't say how it went. How do you think it went?"

I reread the text. Shit. She was right. The hospital's fancy app might have been good at updating us without pulling a doctor or nurse off Mother's care, but it scored low on empathy and nuance. Sam and her brilliant AI skills could probably help them with that.

I was glad to have Charles and Natalie in the waiting room with me, but I wished Carly were here too. After holding Nat's hand for most of the time Mother was in surgery with only occasional breaks to pat Charles's shoulder, I needed someone to hold my hand and pat my shoulder. I was glad they relied on me to be the strong, caring one, but I'd used up all my reserves and was ready to collapse. Maybe sob for a minute.

But I'd never do it in front of Charles or Nat.

"Why don't you take a break, Charles?" I said. "Go for a walk downstairs. They have orchids growing in the atrium."

"I don't want to miss my chance to see her." He strode to the door, turned, and strode back.

"I promise you won't. I'll text you."

His gaze lingered on mine. "I won't go all the way down to the atrium. I'll just stretch my legs for a minute. You'll text me if anything happens?"

"Promise."

"You mind if I go with you?" Nat unwound her fingers from mine. "I could use a change of scenery."

"Come on," Charles said. "We'll see if we can score some chocolate from a vending machine. What about you, Andrew? Want to come?"

"No, I'll wait here in case the doctor comes in."

I watched them go, then I stood and stretched. My hands brushed the ceiling tiles. Private waiting room or not, it was still a hospital, and the smell of disinfectant crawled up my nose, reminding me of the last time Mother had been here, when her skin had looked so gray, and I'd thought I'd lose her.

When we lost Dad, we'd come to the hospital only briefly. The paramedics and then the doctors and nurses had valiantly done their best, but he hadn't lasted long. Waiting at the hospital was better than that, I reminded myself.

It didn't help.

I sank to the floor, needing something to ground me. With my back pressed to the wall, I nestled my shoulder against the chair and tucked my knees to my chest. I leaned my chin on my knees and wrapped my arms around my legs. I wasn't religious, never had been, but I sent a wish into the universe that Mother's new-and-improved vasculature would enable her to walk out of this hospital in a few days.

The door opened, and I looked up. Carly's face was like a beam of sunlight breaking through clouds. Until she saw me. "What are you doing on the floor?"

I scrambled to my feet and pulled her into my arms. "I'm so glad you're here," I murmured into her hair.

"Are you okay?" she asked.

"I am now." I inhaled, but a strong floral scent filled my nostrils, making me want to gag. "New perfume?"

"No, I—" She pulled away. "I brought these." She held out a bouquet of spotted pink lilies, which were now bruised from my embrace.

"Mmm. Thanks." People brought lilies to hospitals all the time. I'd never told her I detested them. "Let's, um..." As much as I wanted to escape the cloying stench, I couldn't leave the room in case someone came with an update. "Let's set them here and sit over there."

She laid the flowers on the table, and I led her to the chairs where Nat and I had been sitting. She wore flowy black pants and a simple black blouse. It was probably her stylist outfit, but it reminded me of Dad's funeral. I kept my gaze on her face, which was scrunched with concern.

"How's Audrey?" she asked.

"She just got out of bypass surgery. We haven't seen her yet."

"She'll be okay. She's strong." Carly clasped my hand and held it against my thigh. "So are you."

A little of her confidence trickled into me. "Thank you."

"I'm sorry I couldn't get here sooner. Helen asked me to go with her in the limousine, and I was so glad I did. You see—"

"Wait." She'd been riding in a limousine while I was at the hospital, worried out of my mind? "I called you this afternoon. You couldn't politely refuse a limousine ride to get back to—" *To me,* I wanted to say. "To get back home?"

"No, honey." She lifted her hand to my hair and smoothed it off my brow. "My phone was off. I was *working.*"

"I needed you." I caught her gaze and held it. "I needed you with me."

"I know."

"Wait." I stopped her hand in my hair and brought it back to my knee. "If you'd had your phone on or if you'd known then what had happened, would you have still ridden in that limo?"

"I—" She inhaled sharply. "I needed to be there for her. There was an accident—"

"You had an accident?" I scanned her from her smooth ponytail down to her perfectly polished shoes.

"Not a car accident. A fashion emergency. Helen spilled—"

"A fashion emergency." I could barely squeeze the words out between my clenched teeth. "My mother had a *heart attack.*"

"I understand. But you were here with your family."

"I needed you."

She sighed. "I needed to work. You'll understand that soon, especially now you're a vice president. You'll be taking early meetings with the East Coast, working late to talk to people in Asia, and going in on weekends when the work piles up."

That all sounded terrible. When would I have time to hang out with Oliver, have brunch with my family, or spend time with Carly?

Pain sharper than a surgeon's scalpel sliced through me. Maybe she didn't want to spend time with me. Maybe she was only interested in telling people she was dating a bank vice president. Did she care about me, about what I wanted? Or needed?

"What if I don't want that?" I asked.

"Sorry." She chuckled. "It goes with the territory."

"No. What if I don't want the vice president position? What if I want to keep my old job and report to someone else? What if... what if I want to quit?" If my mother's health scare taught me anything, it was that our time was limited. I wanted to enjoy the way I spent it.

Her forehead creased. "Where is this coming from? Of course you want that job. Why else would we have gone through that whole fake-dating nonsense?"

"Nonsense? Those were the best six weeks of my life because I spent them with you. I'd sacrifice almost anything to be with you. Don't you get that?"

She ripped her hands from mine. "Sacrifice?" She stood and strode to the other end of the room. "All I did when I was with Brad was sacrifice. And what did it get me? A broken heart and broken friendships. I had to start over. In my forties. I'm done sacrificing for anyone else. I'm not anyone's supporting actress anymore. I'm the leading lady in my feature film. But you're a man. You can't see that. Everything revolves around you. Well, I'm done with that bullshit."

"Bullshit?" I stood. "I'm trying to tell you what's important to me. What I need. I'm opening myself up here."

Her lip curled. "Because what's important to you is what's

important to *us*, right? I can't be the important one. Not even when I've achieved something truly great."

Somewhere in the back of my brain, a voice cried out to listen to her, but the stink of the lilies and the hospital's disinfectant crowded it out. My mother could die, and Carly was going to leave me too.

My throat constricted, and even if I'd had words, I couldn't have gotten them out.

"I've been a fool," she muttered. "I knew this couldn't work. Goodbye, Andrew. I hope Audrey feels better. I'll text Charles to check in."

And like a puff of dark smoke, she left.

Before the door closed, the intercom blared in the hallway, startling me. When it cut off and the door closed, the hum of the fluorescent lights buzzed in my ears and crawled over my skin. I was exposed, alone.

Retreating to the corner, I sank to the floor again. I folded in on myself and buried my face in my hands to block out the smell of death.

32

I OVERTHINK IT

ANDREW

> Oliver: How's your mom today?

> Me: Still in ICU. I'm allowed to see her once an hour, but she's kind of out of it

> Oliver: Would I be in the way if I came by?

> Me: PLEASE COME

I didn't realize how hungry I was until Oliver walked into our waiting room with a huge, greasy sack and my stomach rumbled.

He set the sack on the coffee table. "How're you holding up?"

"Okay, I guess." I shrugged.

"No." He put a hand on my shoulder. "How are you *really?*"

I hung my head. "Not great. They say Mother's recovering as well as we can expect, but she's always sleeping when it's my turn to go in. All this waiting's giving me too much time to think."

"You do tend to overthink. Here, have a burger." He reached into the sack and pulled out a paper-wrapped hamburger.

I unwrapped it and bit into the greasy goodness. "How did you know exactly what I needed?" I mumbled around the food.

"Easy. It's what you brought me after Simon died. When I forgot to eat." He took a much more moderate bite of his burger.

"Right." I wasn't nearly as bad as Oliver had been when his business partner died. Was I?

"Where's your family?" he asked.

"Charles doesn't leave Mother's room. The rest of us take turns. Jackson's with her now, and the girls went home to shower and rest for a while."

"And...Carly?"

I shook my head. "We're done."

"How?" He set down his burger. "Why?"

The bite I'd taken lost its flavor, but I gulped it down. "We had a fight. I said I needed her, and she said I was too demanding."

That wasn't all of it, but it was all I'd admit. I'd been too needy, too raw. Winnie had said my problem was that I didn't let people in. But when I'd opened up to Carly, she'd walked out. Winnie might be more emotionally mature than I was, but this time, she'd gotten it wrong. "She—" I cleared my throat. "She doesn't want someone like me."

"Why wouldn't she want someone like you?" he asked. "You're awesome. So you had a low moment. People who care about each other are supposed to support each other when they're sad and worried."

"She said she's kind of over that. She said she was done being the supporting partner. She compared me to her ex."

"You're nothing like that douche."

"He's a ballsy and successful douche."

"You're ballsy and successful too. You're on track for that VP position."

I shook my head. "I got it. But I'm not sure I want it. Carly didn't understand that either." Why had I deluded myself into thinking someone as successful as Carly would want someone like me? I should've known I'd never measure up. I should've never tried for more than a fake-dating fling with her. I should've left first, like I usually did.

"Wait. You don't want the promotion?"

"Vic said we have to nuke the channel."

"Fuck him."

"He's serious. He wants me not only to stop making videos but to take the whole thing down. And I realized..." I swallowed. "I realized I love making the videos, and I hate working for Vic."

"Well, duh. There's a reason we call him Vic the Prick."

"We don't call him that."

He rolled his eyes. "Everyone but you calls him that."

"So, I'm going to...turn down the promotion?" I tried out the terrifying words. What would my family think?

"Didn't you say he messaged everyone about decorum? Do you really think he'll let you keep doing the videos even in your old job?"

My stomach sank. "Probably not. Shit. I guess I need to find a new job." Maybe in a few weeks, once Mother was home from the hospital, then it wouldn't seem so overwhelming.

"Or..." Oliver waggled his eyebrows.

"Or?"

"Or you could quit and work on the channel full time." He took an aggressive bite of his burger and chewed, watching me.

"I can't do that," I scoffed. "People don't actually do YouTube full time."

"Don't they?" He picked up his phone, tapped at it, and showed me the screen of top-earning YouTubers. The numbers were astounding. "I'm not saying we'll earn that this year, but I think if we posted more often, we could continue our charitable donations at the same level *and* pay your mortgage."

"Have you been planning this?"

"Ever since that Pythagorean theorem video hit a million views. Seems like our nation's kids are looking for better ways to learn math."

I still had that school superintendent's card in my wallet. "I may have also talked to someone who wants a school program."

His eyes widened. "You could earn a good living that way too. Not that you need it, trust-funder."

"You're rich too, asshole," I mumbled. "This won't go over well with my family. We're supposed to contribute to society and make the world a better place."

"Our fan mail says we're already making the world a better place for kids."

"I'm not sure my mother would agree."

"Who's living your life, you or your mother?"

"I am," I said reflexively.

"So, you'll do it?"

I sighed. Carly would never want to be with a full-time YouTuber-slash-school-presenter. But I'd lost my chance with her. And whether I lived another ten or thirty or even fifty years, I wanted to spend it doing what made me happy.

"Yeah."

33

A FAMILY MEETING

CARLY

To-do list—February 1
✓ Finalize Helen's look for the award show
✓ Ask the girls NOT to come over
Stop watching Andrew's videos
Try to forget it's my birthday

Frosty air brushed my cheeks as I stared at the lonely carton in my freezer.

When I'd lived with Brad, our housekeeper had stocked the freezer side of the wood-paneled Sub-Zero full of nutritious choices the cook could turn into delicious meals for us. On the rare occasions I used it, the compressor whooshed after I closed the French door.

My refrigerator was a cheap, big-box-store model with the freezer on top. As little as I cooked, I couldn't justify—or afford—the expense of the top-of-the-line model. Regardless, that monstrosity wouldn't have fit in my condo. Mine was the perfect size for one tub of Double Fudge Extreme Peanut Butter Brownie ice cream.

My mouth watered, already tasting the chocolaty goodness, the sweetness cloying behind my molars, the saltiness parching my tongue.

Then my mom's warnings about calories echoed in my brain. She'd encourage me to drink a glass of water and wait thirty minutes. She'd remind me chocolate wouldn't cure my cramps. Or my emotional hangover.

That's all this was. I'd deluded myself that Andrew could support me the way I'd supported Brad all those years, that he wouldn't think my styling business was silly or unimportant.

I remembered the tic in Andrew's jaw when he'd said, "A fashion emergency," like nothing in my life could be as important as anything in his. I mean, yes, his mother was in the hospital, and he had to have been stressed about that. But in times of stress, people said what they really thought. And Andrew thought I was only good enough to be arm candy at his social events, to be his crutch when he needed one.

Never again. I reached for the carton.

In my silent kitchen, my phone rattled against the counter, making me jump like the diet police had zapped me with a cattle prod. I slammed the freezer door shut and checked my phone. Another inquiry from a friend of Helen's. I filed it so I could respond in the morning.

Just as I blanked the screen, something banged against my apartment door. I crossed the den to the front of my apartment.

Could it be Andrew coming to apologize? My phone had been buzzing nonstop since I'd walked out of the hospital a week ago but never with a call from him. A fist squeezed my heart, and it pattered giddily like I was Molly Ringwald in a John Hughes movie.

I sucked in a deep breath and peered through the peephole.

My shoulders sagged before I unlocked the door and pulled it open. "Hey, Lucie."

She pushed past me with a bottle-shaped paper bag clutched in her hand. "Happy birthday, babe. I brought the drinks."

I closed the door. "I said I was too busy to celebrate my birthday. We agreed to postpone for a few weeks."

"Too busy?" Raising her eyebrows, Lucie assessed my loungewear. Thank goodness she hadn't caught me with the ice cream.

"I'm working from home."

"Uh-huh." She pulled a bottle of tequila from the bag.

"Tequila? It's my forty-sixth birthday, not my twenty-sixth."

"Oh, you're going to want it when—"

Another knock came at my door, and I checked the peephole again. Tessa, with a stack of pizza boxes. I opened the door.

"I didn't call for a pizza," I joked weakly.

She kissed my cheek as she stepped inside. "Happy birthday."

"Thank you," I said.

"For the record, I said it wasn't fair to combine your birthday party with an inter—"

"Tessa." Lucie thumped the bottle on my counter.

Tessa scowled at her. "She'll find out soon enough." She turned to me. "Can I stash these in your oven?"

"Sure, but what's—"

Another knock stopped me, and this time, I didn't bother to look through the peephole. I opened the door to find Savannah, breathless as her hair escaped her ponytail in a halo of wild tendrils.

"Happy birthday! Am I late? I got here as fast as I could. My son borrowed my minivan, so I had to steal Jason's Porsche, and I couldn't figure out how to get the top up. But it was a blast!" Her eyes glittered.

"You stole—"

"Get in here," Lucie called. "You're just in time. What'd you bring?"

"All I had time to whip up was guacamole." She lifted a small cooler. "With homemade tortilla chips. And a movie."

"Gimme," Tessa said. "I can't get enough salt today."

Savannah kissed my cheek, then crossed to the kitchen to hug Tessa.

In a low voice, Tessa asked Savannah how she was doing. Savannah said something too soft for me to hear, but it made Tessa bite her lip and her normally steely eyes melt.

A stab of pain rocketed through my abdomen. I sank into the chair and tucked my knees against my chest.

"Are you okay?" Savannah asked.

"I'm fine." I waved a hand. "Just cramps." My periods were becoming more erratic than my junior high bestie, and after flaking on me last month, this one had hit me like a school bus.

"You want to take something?" Tessa rummaged in her bag.

"Already did," I said. "It should kick in soon."

Buzzing erupted from my phone, which I'd left on the counter. Lucie glanced at it. "Message from Yelena?"

"I'll text her later."

"Okay." Lucie nudged Tessa and Savannah into the den. "Sit down, everyone."

"Do you have news?" I asked, leaning forward. Savannah and Tessa took the sofa across the coffee table, and Lucie lowered herself into the other chair like a queen on her throne.

"Always, but that's not why we're here," Lucie said. "We're here to talk to you about what a sad sack you've been lately."

"Wait. What?" I held up a hand. I remembered what Tessa

had said. "This is an intervention? For *me?*" Anger tightened my throat. "What the hell are you intervening about?"

Savannah's gaze darted to Lucie. Tessa pivoted between Lucie and me, her mouth slightly open, like we were playing at Wimbledon.

"Look at you." Lucie flung her hand toward me. "Yoga pants. Your hair's in a ponytail. You're a mess."

"Hang on!" Savannah said. *"I'm* wearing yoga pants and a ponytail."

"It's different," Lucie said dismissively. "This is out of character for Carly."

Savannah folded her arms across her chest, obscuring her T-shirt, some faded giveaway from a 5K benefiting her kids' school.

"And if I'm not mistaken," Tessa said. "That's yesterday's ponytail and yoga pants."

I glanced down. She was right. They were my least favorite pair, a dingy gray, and they showed the wrinkles from where I'd balled them up and tossed them toward the hamper last night. "I've been too busy working on other people's looks to worry about mine. Besides, I didn't feel like doing laundry."

"I'll do your laundry." Savannah stood. "Where's your machine?"

"Sit down," Lucie barked. "We all need to be here for this."

Savannah flopped back into the chair and trapped her hands between her knees. She shot me a sympathetic expression.

I tugged the elastic out of my ponytail, wincing when it snagged. Combing my fingers through my hair, I said, "Interventions are for addicts."

"Let's call it a family meeting," Savannah said. "That sounds nicer."

"Whatever we call it"—Lucie rolled her eyes—"you need to snap out of it."

Savannah winced. "I'm sure Lucie means that it's okay to feel your feelings, but we're worried about you, sweetie. All you've done lately is work."

"I love my work," I protested. My phone buzzed again. Lucie jumped up, snatched it off the counter, and tossed it at me. I checked it—not urgent—and set it face-down on the coffee table.

Savannah stroked my hand. "You haven't responded to our group texts. You didn't even want to celebrate your birthday."

"It's not like I'm turning twenty-one or thirty or even forty. Once you pass that, birthdays are just a reminder that…"

"That you're resilient and strong and a year wiser," Lucie said.

"Hear, hear," Tessa said, holding an imaginary drink.

"Also, a reminder that my hair is going grayer, the lines on my face are getting deeper, and everything's a little less perky." Glancing at my chest, I wished I'd bothered to put on a bra.

"Who wants to be perky when you can be respected for your life experience?" Tessa asked.

"Maybe you get respect in your industry, but mine values youth and beauty," I grumbled.

"Where's all this coming from?" Lucie asked. "Is that why you broke up with Andrew? If he called you old, I'm going to march into his bank and—"

"No. He didn't. But whether or not he's thinking it now, eventually he's going to realize that I'll turn fifty while he's still in his thirties. He's going to figure out he's wasting his youth. Like I did."

"No, sweetie." Savannah patted my hand. "Life experience isn't a waste. You figured out what you wanted and grew strong enough to go after it."

I huffed out a chuckle. "It sounds a lot better when you say it."

"It's true," Tessa said. "Our lives are long—we hope—and full of mistakes. All we can do is try to do better the next day."

Writing in her notebook, Lucie hummed her agreement.

My phone buzzed again, and I checked it. I should answer, but I was with my girls. I'd get back to everyone tomorrow.

Tessa raised an eyebrow. "Did Andrew break up with you because of your phone? Because it's fucking annoying."

"Sorry." I turned off the notifications.

"You need an assistant."

"An assistant? I can't afford..." With all the new business coming in, maybe I could afford an assistant. That would free up more time to work on styling clients.

"Wait." Lucie looked up from her notebook. "Andrew broke up with Carly because of her job?"

"No," Savannah said. "It was a joke."

"Actually," I said, righteousness stiffening my spine, "I broke up with him because of it. He tried to minimize me just like Brad. And I'm not doing that again. It's my turn."

Lucie narrowed her eyes. "Your turn to do what exactly?"

"To be the important person. Not the person who's only there to support him." I crossed my arms.

"Did he say that?" Savannah asked. "That you should quit your job and support him?"

"Well, no. But he implied it. He laughed when I told him I had to stay in LA for a fashion crisis."

"He laughed at you?" Savannah seemed to expand, like a cat fluffing itself up, preparing to hiss.

"Not exactly. He just... He...he said he needed me because his mother was in the hospital, and he was worried." Saying it out loud made it seem more reasonable.

"Aw." Savannah clutched her hands to her heart. "I bet that took a lot of courage to admit. What did you say?"

"I, um..." I thought back. I'd been so proud of what I'd done for Helen when I'd walked into the hospital and then so disappointed he didn't see it. "I think I told him he'd understand when he took the VP job. Then he started talking some nonsense about not taking the job, and..." Was he serious about that?

"You know, sometimes crises make us examine what's important," Tessa said. "Maybe he was thinking about the brevity of life."

"He's only thirty-two," I scoffed. "He's not thinking about dying."

"Are you sure?" Lucie asked. "His dad died of a heart attack at forty."

I remembered how he'd said he liked his weekends and how he always made time for brunch with his family. "But—that's not what men are like. Is it?"

"Not all men," Savannah said. "Andrew sounds like one of the good ones. What did you say when he said he needed you and wanted to be with you?"

I grimaced. "I told him my life is a feature film, and I'm the leading lady."

"I love that!" Lucie scribbled a note.

"But when his mom is in the hospital might not be the best time to say it," Savannah said gently.

"Maybe not," I admitted.

"Why did you walk out without talking about it like a grownup?" Tessa leaned forward.

"Because I...because...because I was afraid if I didn't walk out, I'd stay," I whispered. "And let him hurt me like Brad did."

"Do you think he'd do that?" Tessa asked.

"Why wouldn't he?" I stood. "He's young, gorgeous, and on the rise. Why would he want someone like me?" I gestured at my saggy boobs.

"The question is, do you want him?" Tessa's green gaze bored into me.

The memory of Andrew's expression at the wedding, a mixture of awe and pride, of the tender way he'd kissed me the day he'd taken me to play with puppies, made my insides turn molten like I'd swallowed sunshine. I sank back into the chair. "I think I love him."

Lucie stopped writing and looked up. Tessa leaned back with a triumphant expression.

Savannah tucked her hands under her chin. "Aw. I knew you'd get there eventually."

"But that's bad, right?" I said. "It's one thing to have a fling with a younger guy. It's something else to fall for him. To think he could want me for the rest of my life."

Lucie paused her writing. "Isn't this just a fling? You're not marrying him."

"Of course not," I scoffed. "The age difference—"

Savannah shook her head. "Love is love, sweetie. Age doesn't matter if he makes you happy and you make him happy. Julianne Moore, Katie Couric, and Tina Turner all found love with younger men."

Lucie cocked her head. "Sounds like someone's been doing research."

Savannah's cheeks turned red. "I'm trying to be helpful."

"I'm no Tina Turner," I said.

"All those women are successful in their own right," Tessa said. "Just like you."

I shook my head. "They were all successful before they met their men. People might think I'm using him to advance my career. Audrey sure as hell did."

"But everyone knows how great you are. You're styling Helen freaking Choi," Tessa said.

"Yes, but—"

"Stella McCartney," Lucie said.

"What?" I asked.

"Stella McCartney," she repeated. "She's Paul McCartney's daughter, right?"

"Yes?"

"She probably had a lot to prove, considering her pedigree, but she made a name for herself in fashion. No one says she's only successful because of who her parents are."

"How do you know who Stella McCartney is?" I said. "You get your clothes at H&M."

"How the hell do you know where I shop?" Lucie looked down at her black cigarette pants.

Waving a hand to shush Lucie, Tessa scooted to the edge of her chair. "You're scared."

"Of course I'm scared!" The words burst out of me. "Someone who was supposed to love me humiliated me and… and demolished me. Goddamn Brad."

"Oh, Brad did more than that," Lucie said darkly. "He told everyone not to hire you."

"No, that was Audrey." Everyone knew my frenemy torpedoed my career, even before she knew I'd slept with her son.

"I've been doing some research myself," Lucie said. "Brad threatened to sabotage a real estate deal Bianca Waddingworth's husband was working on. That's why she canceled on you."

"What?"

"Yeah, I interviewed Bianca for my charitable giving project. My best guess is that Brad couldn't stand the thought of your success eclipsing his."

"What an ass," Tessa said. "I can't believe you stayed with him as long as you did."

Savannah, who'd seemed so engaged in the intervention before, picked at her yoga pants. "Sometimes…sometimes it's hard to see that you deserve more."

I reached across the coffee table and grasped her hand. "*We* deserve more."

She lifted her head and beamed at me. "We do. You do. Andrew's so much more than Brad could ever be. You deserve him. Maybe you can give him another chance to deserve you."

Could I let Andrew make me happy? He'd said he loved me. But my ex used to say he loved me. I couldn't trust Andrew not to hurt me too.

"I don't think so. Why would I need a man when I have you three?" I held out my hands. Savannah grasped one, and Lucie grasped the other.

"I'm not going to fuck you though," Lucie said. "That'd be weird."

"Lucie!" Savannah and Tessa shouted.

"Kidding. Goddesses forever," she said.

"Goddesses forever," we repeated.

What I needed was an assistant and my friends. Not another man, especially not one who wanted me to be less than I was.

34

A TWENTY-YEAR MISTAKE

CARLY

To-do list—February 9
~~Email Geraldine about the vintage Halston~~
✓ Ask Linh to email Geraldine
Ask Linh to update the website with recent work
Try to enjoy myself at the party

"It's all done," my new assistant said confidently. "Also, two new inquiries came in today. I filled out the intake form on both and sent them to your email."

"You're a lifesaver, Linh." I pulled into the parking space at the yacht club but kept the motor running to continue the call over the car's speakers.

"Just doing my job," she chirped. "I told them you'd get back to them Monday. Take today off, okay?"

"Oh, no!" Rustling my jacket next to the microphone in the ceiling, I joked, "I think you're breaking up."

"I'm serious. Tessa said twenty-five percent of my job is to get you to relax."

"Schedule me a chat with Tessa. She may have found me the world's best assistant, but that doesn't give her the right to assign you tasks."

"Will do! Anything else, Carly?"

"No. Thank you, Linh." I disconnected the call and slipped on my jacket.

I strode through the drizzle under my umbrella, avoiding the puddles in my ankle-strap heeled sandals.

I hadn't been to the yacht club since the last time Brad and I had been out on our boat. The place hadn't changed much. It was still a beautiful building, and beyond it, boats bobbed next to the dock.

I didn't look for the *Pearl,* my ex-boat. I had a brief vision of buying my own yacht, bigger and flashier than Brad's, and sailing it past him one weekend, looking fabulous while pretending not to notice him. It made me chuckle, and I walked into the room smiling.

After I'd dropped my jacket at the coat check, Bianca Waddingworth, the hostess, greeted me with kisses to both cheeks. "Carly! I'm so glad you could make it."

Okay, then. We were going to pretend she hadn't frozen me out for the last year since my divorce, that she'd never canceled her appointment with me, and we were friends again. I could play that game too. "Of course. I wouldn't miss Bob's birthday party. Remember that time he insisted on celebrating his birthday at sunrise at Mt. Davidson? I thought Brad was going to have a heart attack climbing up there."

"He's always been one of those irritating morning people."

"I half expected this to be a daybreaker."

"A what?" Her eyebrows lowered a fraction.

"It's a rave, but in the morning with no booze. All the cool kids go," I joked.

"Carl would know." A heavy arm landed on my shoulders. "She's dating one of the cool kids now."

Not wanting to make a scene, I didn't shrug off Brad's arm, but I stepped away so his arm stretched awkwardly between us.

"More than that," Bianca said, nodding. "She's got her finger on the pulse of young Hollywood. She styled Helen Choi for the Golden Globes *and* that gorgeous R&B artist at the Grammys. Who are you styling for the Oscars?"

When I named the two actresses and the actor, her eyes went round. "I have to get on your schedule. You can overlook that little mishap last fall, right?" Her eyes flicked to Brad, then back to me. "I'm terrible at managing my calendar."

"Call my assistant. We'll see what we can do." I wasn't sure I was ready to forgive her or Brad yet, but I'd let Linh string her along until I needed to plug a hole in my schedule.

"Thank you, Carly. I can't wait. I love that dress, by the way. Maybe you could find something like it for me?"

I glanced down at the red botanical Oscar de la Renta. The sleeveless boatneck would show off Bianca's toned arms. "We'll see," I repeated.

"I'll call you tomorrow." She air-kissed me again. "Thanks so much for coming. It means a lot to Bob and me." She flitted off.

Taking another step away, I shrugged off Brad's arm. "Where's Hayley?"

"Mornings aren't great for her." He shrugged.

I inhaled a sharp breath. "You left your wife at home with morning sickness?"

"Eh. She'll be fine."

I rolled my eyes, grateful we'd never had kids together.

"Where's Andy?" he asked.

Andrew would never leave someone who was sick. My heart

twinged when I remembered walking out on him at the hospital while he worried about his mother. She was back home and feeling better, I knew from Charles's text, but I regretted abandoning Andrew.

"We aren't together anymore." Straightening my shoulders, I shook out my hair.

He snorted. "I'm surprised it lasted as long as it did."

"What's that supposed to mean?"

"Men like younger women." He shrugged. "It's biology."

The pain from my heart sliced into my stomach. Brad was right. Andrew had deluded himself—and me—to think that he was any different.

"I have to say, though, Hayley isn't nearly as good as you were at taking care of me. When I was at work on Friday, my shirt ripped right at the elbow."

"You had a spare, right?" As soon as I blurted it out, I winced. Old habits. Brad wasn't my responsibility anymore.

"Nah, I wore it when I spilled coffee a few weeks ago. Forgot to replace it."

I arched my brow. "Maybe you should try taking care of yourself."

"But she's supposed to take care of me. Like you did. Anyway, I realized I need some new shirts, another suit, and a couple of ties. You can tell me what's fashionable this year."

"Wait." I held up a hand. "Are you asking me to style you?"

"No. I'm asking you to do what you used to do."

"You mean, when we were married?"

"Yeah. We're still friends, right?" He shot me the dazzling smile that used to make me go weak in the knees.

It left me cold.

Another man's smile, one with dimples, was the one I wanted to savor. Andrew would never dream of asking me to style him for free. In fact, he'd paid me to style him. He hadn't taken me for granted. When we were together, he'd told me every day how beautiful I was and showed me he cared.

I'd been furious when I'd thought he tried to minimize me and make my work secondary to his needs, but he'd been scared and alone. If I'd thought rationally about it, I'd have realized that and given him a little grace. But I hadn't thought rationally. I'd been afraid. Afraid that I'd let Andrew do what Brad had done to me.

I was still letting Brad define me. But Andrew was no Brad.

"No, Brad." I put my hands on my hips. "We're not friends. You cheated on me. And when I divorced you, you ensured I got the worst possible settlement, then you tried to sabotage my business." My voice rose, and I didn't care. "We are not friends. I will not style you. Certainly not for free. Not even if you paid me three times my normal rate."

"You styled Hayley for free."

"Hayley is my friend. You are nothing to me but a twenty-year mistake."

Someone gasped, and I realized we had an audience. People near us weren't even pretending to have their own conversations. They stared at us, mouths gaping.

I didn't care. My chest felt light. I'd freed myself from Brad's influence.

I'd made another mistake in walking out on Andrew. But it was a mistake I could correct.

If he'd let me.

35

F*** THE RULES

CARLY

```
NEW To-do list—February 9 (dictated into
voice notes)
Get to Andrew
Ask him—no, scratch that. Beg him to
forgive me
Be nice to his mother
```

As I smashed the doorbell, I tried to let the melodious chime soothe my nerves, but my heart pounded too fast. I wished I hadn't had that second cup of coffee at the Waddingworths' party. I wished I hadn't let my yoga practice fall off when my work got so busy. I wished someone would answer this fucking door.

I pounded on it. They had to be in there. Audrey prided herself in collecting her powerful, independent children around her every Sunday. Certainly, she'd have used her bypass surgery as an excuse to demand their presence.

Andrew must be here. I'd called him on the drive over, but

he hadn't answered. I deserved it after letting someone as wonderful and kind as he was—someone who wanted me the way he said he did—slip through my fingers.

I lifted my finger to press the bell again, but the door swung open. Natalie stood on the other side, and her face broke into a grin when she saw me.

"You're here!" She bounced on the toes of her pink Valentino Garavani sandals. She wore a princess-pink minidress I thought was Alexander McQueen, but I hadn't seen yet in stores. I started to ask her about it, then I remembered why I was there.

"Is your brother here? Andrew, I mean. Not the other one."

Her grin broadened. "He is, but I'll warn you, he's grumpy." Her expression cooled, and she blocked the opening. "You're here to make up, right? Not break his heart again?"

"I'm here to apologize. And ask him to take me back."

"Then come in." She opened the door wider.

I stepped over the threshold. "Did he say anything about me?" I winced. I was a forty-six-year-old professional, not a twelve-year-old passing MASH notes in class.

"No, he's been tighter than Mother's forehead after a Botox treatment, which is unusual because normally, he can't stop talking about you." As we neared the dining room, she let out a quiet, high-pitched squeal. "This is so exciting. It's like a Jane Austen adaptation, but you're Mr. Knightley, and my brother is Gwyneth Paltrow."

She threw open the door, and when the four pairs of eyes on the other side of the table met mine, the room went silent.

Audrey presided at one end of the table, wearing a flowing silk tunic. Her lips pursed when she saw me. On her right was her oldest son, his wife, and their two children. Charles anchored the other end, and he gave me a tentative smile. He nudged Andrew, who sat next to him with his back to the door.

Andrew turned, and his expression blanked.

Fair. I'd run out on him while his mother recovered from surgery for the same condition that had killed his dad. I had work to do.

"Carly, I don't recall inviting you to my home." Audrey's voice could've produced snow on a July day in Texas.

"I apologize for barging in. These are for you." I waved the bouquet of yellow roses. When no one moved, I went to the credenza, but the vases were full. I plopped them into the cut crystal water pitcher. "How are you feeling?"

She narrowed her eyes. "Stronger than ever."

From the lack of makeup on her face and the pallor of her cheeks, I doubted it. But I let her play the lioness protecting her pride. "I'm glad to hear it. Andrew, could I speak with you for a minute?"

"I, um, sure." He stood.

"Just a minute." Audrey flung out a hand to stop him. "I have something to say to Carly first."

I rolled my lips between my teeth. I supposed I deserved whatever Audrey decided to say.

"I was never in favor of your arrangement with my son. He's a sweet boy—"

"Mother!" Andrew yelped. "I'm thirty-two years old."

"Hush, Andrew. Let me speak. It might be the last chance I get to say this."

"I thought you were stronger than ever," I said.

"I had a heart attack. I'm day-to-day, dear," she said smoothly, a mischievous glint in her eye. "I thought an association with you wouldn't help him. I was wrong. And I'm sorry for what I said at Brad's reception."

"What did you say?" The knuckles of Andrew's clenched fists went white.

I thought she'd stay silent, but Audrey hadn't achieved her level of social success by playing it safe. "I asked her to break up with you. She refused. But when you two ended things last week, I saw that your feelings for her were real. And since she's here today, it seems her feelings for you are also real. So, I apologize to both of you for trying to wedge you apart."

I blinked. "Are you sure you're all right?" I glanced at Charles. "What kind of medication is she on?"

"Xanax and a blood thinner," he said.

"It's got to be the Xanax, right?" I asked.

"Definitely the Xanax," the older son muttered.

"Don't speak about me like I'm not here," Audrey said. "I'm not an invalid. And I didn't take the Xanax this morning. Now be polite and accept my apology."

"I accept," I mumbled.

"I can't believe you said that," Andrew burst out. "What gave you the right—"

"Andrew." I took a deep breath, hoping he'd do the same. "Her heart."

"Mother, don't ever try to control my life again," he said.

Natalie gasped. "Ooh, Andrew. Way to stand up."

Audrey shot her youngest daughter a glare that would've sliced leather before she turned her attention to Andrew. "Darling, I was trying to help."

"I accept your apology, but don't try it again. I'm able to stand on my own."

Audrey gave a regal nod.

"Now it's my turn to apologize," I said, stepping closer to Andrew. His face gave nothing away, so I didn't touch him. "I'm sorry I got to the hospital so late. You needed me. I never meant to make it seem like my work is more important than you. I've hired a wonderful assistant who's going to help me focus on the creative parts of my work. She takes all my business calls now, so if you decide to take me back, I'll leave my phone on for you. Even when I'm working."

"That's great, huh, Andrew?" Natalie poked him in the hip, but he didn't move. He only watched me. He was right. I owed him another apology.

"And I'm sorry I made you feel like you had to take the VP position. I want you to be happy. And if that means turning it down—"

"What?" Audrey barked.

"You didn't tell her?" I murmured.

He shook his head.

I raised my voice. "You okay, Audrey? Sure you don't want that Xanax?"

"Positive." She moved her arms like she'd cross them, winced, and let them drop back to the table.

"I support you, and I'm proud of you," I said to Andrew. "No matter what you decide to do."

"Do you love me?" he asked.

"I do." The emotion welled up inside me, blurring my vision. "I love you, Andrew."

He reached for my hand and held it. I rubbed warmth into his icy fingers.

"I love you too," he said.

The curl of his tongue and the brief flick of his teeth against his lip when he said "love" made me shiver. "No more rules," I said. "Except that we wholeheartedly support each other in whatever we do."

A tiny smile curled the corner of his mouth. "I like that one. We can do this. Together."

Turning, he said, "Mother, Charles, I quit my job."

Murmurs broke out across the table.

"You what?" Audrey's voice rang out like she hadn't had heart surgery a little over a week ago.

"I quit my job on Friday," he repeated, "to work full time on our channel and do math-related school visits. I'm going to be an entrepreneur after all."

While the murmurs crescendoed, I tugged him closer. "You're okay with that? Striking out on your own?"

"I won't be completely on my own. Oliver's my partner. And you'll be there too. This way, we can both have flexibility. We'll take our time off together, whether it's a weekend or not."

I squeezed his hand. "I like the sound of that."

Andrew raised his voice. "Carly and I'll grab some champagne from the wine cellar."

Clutching my hand, he guided me from the pandemonium of the dining room to the kitchen. He opened a door and flicked on the lights, then he followed me down an industrial-style staircase into a brick-lined room. It wasn't huge, but both walls were lined with backlit bottles. A heavy credenza anchored the far wall.

"I didn't know this was down he—"

Andrew stopped my words with a ravenous kiss.

36
I'M INCORRIGIBLE

ANDREW

From: Andrew Jones
To: Victor Lynch
Sent: February 7, 7:31 am
Subject: Resignation

Dear Vic,
Please accept this email as my formal resignation from the bank. Thank you for the opportunities you gave me. While I appreciate your confidence, I find my interests lie in another direction.

During the next two weeks, I'd be happy to help transition my responsibilities to other team members.

Sincerely,
Andrew Jones

```
From: Victor Lynch
To: Andrew Jones
CC: Human Resources
Sent: February 7, 8:11 am
Subject: RE: Resignation

Let's make this effective immediately. Pack up
your things by 9.
```

$\mathcal{C}$arly melted into our kiss. I held her in my arms, pushing her against the stair rail, never wanting to let her go. She'd faced my dragon of a mother, plus potential humiliation in front of my family, for me. She loved me just as I was, not as a bank vice president.

"I don't think you came down here for champagne at all," she murmured into my ear right before she nipped my earlobe.

"I needed to get my hands on you." Her dress had a clavicle-skimming neckline and was made of thick, embroidered fabric that kept me from touching as much of her as I wanted. I ran my fingers over the skin it revealed on her long neck and toned arms. I missed the plunging neckline she'd worn at the wedding and the New Year's Eve party. It had been easy to push aside to get my tongue on her breasts.

"Here?" But her hands were roaming too. She'd gotten my shirt untucked from my pants and halfway unbuttoned.

"Better than my childhood bedroom, don't you think?"

"Definitely." She dipped her tongue into the hollow at the base of my neck, sending tingles across my chest.

I brushed her fingers aside to finish unbuttoning my shirt. She dropped her hands to my belt and worked the buckle free.

"Don't you think someone will come looking for us?" she asked, unbuttoning my khakis.

"Don't care." I felt along the back of her dress for a zipper.

As my pants fell to the floor, she dropped to her knees. They cracked like a shot. "Sorry."

"Baby, never say sorry for that. But the floor tile will bruise your knees." My cock didn't have any consideration for the rest of her body. It pointed straight at her face, the tip already leaking.

"Don't care," she said, licking her red lips.

"Here." I stepped out of my pants and folded them into a makeshift cushion.

"They'll get wrinkled. Everyone will know what we've been doing." She settled onto my folded pants.

"They already know what we're doing," I said.

Her chest heaved. "Even your mother?"

"Definitely."

"Why is that strangely hot?"

When she took me inside her mouth, I didn't care about anything. So what if Carly's relationship with my mother would always be weird? So what if she was a stylist to the stars, and I was the nerdy host of a YouTube channel with an audience that had significant crossover to SpongeBob SquarePants? So what if she liked movies made before I was born and had been old enough to worry about Y2K?

I didn't concern myself with any of that as her lipstick smeared over my dick and her brown eyes went gold in the cellar's soft light. Stroking her hair away from her face, I touched her jaw. "I love you," I said. "I can't believe you busted into brunch to see me."

When she hummed around my dick, it set me on fire. Pleasure rocketed up my spine as she increased the suction. She gripped my ass, and heat blazed across my skin. My head fell back. How had I gotten so lucky that Carly Rose, a goddess on earth, had her mouth on my dick?

"I'm not gonna last long, baby." Bliss surged through me. "Want me to come in my hand?"

She shook her head and cupped her fingers under my balls. They tightened. I wished I could hold back, but she was on her knees on the hard floor, and my family was expecting us to return to the dining room any minute with wine. She was right. The urgency, the fear of discovery, the dirtiness of it all was incredibly hot. With a grunt, I came. She held me in her mouth until I was done, then pulled off and swallowed.

For the first time in over a week, my stomach didn't hurt and my neck didn't twinge. The orgasm must have flushed all the stress hormones from my system. I dropped to my knees and kissed her, tasting myself and her lipstick. "Baby, I... Thank you."

"Do you believe me now? That I love you? That I'm with you for...for as long as you want me?" Her eyes blinked wide.

I used the tail of my shirt to dab the smudged mascara under her eyes. "I'll always want you, Carly. You didn't have to blow me in my parents' wine cellar for me to trust you."

She smirked. "The blowjob was for me. If this dress wasn't so expensive, I'd have let a little jizz fall on it so there'd be no doubts about what we were doing when we go back upstairs."

I shook my head. "This thing with you and my mother is complicated. I think we might need to dial back the weekly brunches."

"I can be good," she said with a saucy smile. "After today, maybe she and I can be friends instead of frenemies."

"You brought her flowers."

"The woman had a heart attack. And I grew up in the South, where it's a crime to show up to someone's house empty-handed."

"You don't usually work on Sundays, right?" I asked.

"Except during award season, assuming I keep my Hollywood clients."

"How about we agree to spend every other Sunday together, just the two of us? Except during award season. We can go out for breakfast or stay in bed all day."

"Reading the newspaper?"

"They still print newspapers?"

She sighed. "Never mind. We'll read books."

"Whatever you want, baby. And on the other Sundays, when I come here for brunch, you can decide if you want to come with me."

She bit her lip. "Okay. Though I'm not sure I can stay in bed all day on a Sunday."

I grinned. "I think I can convince you. Let me give you a taste." Rising, I held out a hand.

"I've already had a taste." She licked her lips. She stood, and her knee cracked again. "Sorry."

"Stop apologizing. I love your noisy knee. I love every part of you."

Holding her hand, I led her to the credenza and hoisted her up onto it.

"Don't we need to get back?"

"Not before I make you come too. You're going to need the endorphins to get through the rest of brunch." I hiked up her skirt, but she wore something that looked like bike shorts underneath. "Um, is there a zipper on these?"

"No, you roll them down like socks. I'll do it." She slipped off the credenza.

"Let me. Hold up your skirt?"

I started at the waistband, rolling down the spandex like she'd said.

When I revealed the tops of her thighs, she groaned. "I think I could almost come from being released from that thing."

"Wait for me." I rolled it to her ankles and helped her step out of the leg openings, then I lifted her onto the credenza and spread her knees. She wasn't wet yet, but I'd take care of that.

I bent to kiss her knee. "I love this knee." I kissed the inside of her thigh along the red mark from the undergarment's seam. "I love your legs." And when I buried my face between her legs, I spelled out, "I love your incredible pussy," with my tongue. By the time I got to the last, looping Y, she was clutching my hair.

She was wet now, and I tunneled two fingers inside her. I pumped in and out, a promise of what I'd do later with my cock when we finally went home from brunch. When her breathing quickened and she gripped my hair, I found her clit and sucked it aggressively the way she liked.

She shouted out my name, too loud for the echoing space below the dining room. Neither of us cared. Stilling, she groaned out the creak that told me she'd found her peak. I let up on the suction, licking her through a shuddering aftershock.

When her fingers loosened in my hair, I straightened. She leaned her head against the wall, her eyes closing as her breathing evened out. Her cheeks were pink, and her forehead glistened. I kissed it.

I found my pants and stepped into them, grateful I'd remembered to stuff a handkerchief in the pocket. I used it to blot her forehead, tidy up the edges of her lipstick, and pat dry her pussy. Finally, I used a corner to wipe my chin.

"Such a Boy Scout," she said with a relaxed smile.

"I might not have grown up in the South, but I have some manners." I folded the handkerchief and shoved it into my pocket, then I picked up her spandex shorts from the floor. "Want me to hide these, or are you going to put them back on?"

She grabbed them from me. "I may have just fucked her son in her wine cellar, but I'm not about to show up to Audrey Hayes's dining table commando." She wrestled them on. Except for her faded lipstick and flushed cheeks, she looked as fresh as when she'd walked into the house.

"Ugh, your hair." She combed through it with her fingers. "I wish I'd brought my bag."

"Leave it." I tugged out of her reach. "Let them all see that you're a hair-puller when you come."

"Oh my god." Her cheeks flamed. "Are you sure there isn't a back door to this place?"

I wrapped my arms around her and cradled her ass with my hands. "I'm definitely not prepared for any back-door action down here."

She shoved out of my arms. "You're incorrigible."

"You love me incorrigible."

"I do."

I tugged her back to me. "And I love you driven, successful, wise, and beautiful. I'll do everything in my power to be worthy of your love."

She gazed up at me. "How'd I get to be so lucky?"

"I'm pretty sure I'm the lucky one. Promise not to leave me when my family teases us relentlessly upstairs?"

She kissed me. "I promise."

EPILOGUE

SIX MONTHS LATER

CARLY

To-do list—August 16
✓ ~~Pick up the platters from the caterers~~ (Andrew got it)
✓ Put on Chanel's picnic-print bandanna
Check for dog hair on the rug

"Oh, shit." Literally.

"Chanel, why didn't you tell me you needed to go out?" I dropped to my knees on the entryway rug and picked up the dog. Our five-year-old Cavalier King Charles spaniel was old enough to know better, but two weeks after we'd adopted her, she was still getting used to life outside a cage. She'd been rescued from a horrific life in a puppy mill, and her nipples sagged from her last litter.

I touched my nose to hers. "It's okay, baby. Everyone makes mistakes. We'll clean this up, and—"

"What happened?"

I startled at Andrew's voice and winced. The rug was new. Almost everything was new. We'd moved in together last month, and adding a dog so soon might've been too much.

"An accident. I was about to clean it up. I'm sure it won't leave a stain."

"Hey." He scooped Chanel out of my arms and extended a hand to help me up. As usual, my knee popped. "I'll take her outside, then I'll clean it up. Our friends will be here soon, and I'm sure you want to check that everything is perfect. Again."

I stroked Chanel's soft, russet ear, then I rose on my tiptoes to kiss Andrew. "Thank you."

I'm not sure how he managed it with the dog, but suddenly, his arm banded around me, and I pressed against his chest. His kiss branded me, urgent, demanding, possessive. Our hearts slammed toward each other, synchronized, reminding me of how he'd raised my pulse this morning, demonstrating the possibilities of the grab bars in our new shower. I opened to him, letting him pillage and conquer as he so clearly needed to do.

When we broke apart, breathless, I asked, "What was that about?"

He rubbed under my lip. "I needed to show you I love you more than I love that goddamn rug or anything in this house."

Bubbles rose in my chest like champagne. "Chanel too?"

She'd gone limp in his arms. Smart dog. He stroked her white blaze. "I love Chanel too. But not as much as I love you."

I scratched behind her ear and crooned, "You're only second because I don't crap on the rug, baby."

He laughed. "I'd love you even if you did."

"You sure you've got this?"

"Yeah. You'll want to fix your lipstick."

"You too." I swiped a spot of my Dior Radiant from his lower lip.

He curled his lips inside. "Leave it. I want everyone to see that you can't stop kissing me."

He was holding the dog, so I didn't swat him. Instead, I tossed my hair. "We'll see who kisses who next—"

He caught my wrist and spun me back toward him, capturing me again in a fierce kiss. I didn't fight it. I gave it right back to prove with the destruction of my lipstick that I wanted him, needed him as much as he needed me.

When he finally released me, I took Chanel from him and set her on the floor. "Really, what's going on? This is about more than the rug. Or the dog."

He ducked his head. "I'm a little nervous."

"Nervous? Not about me. 'Let me give you a tip,'" I quoted. "'I'm a sure thing, okay?'" We'd watched *Pretty Woman* a few nights ago, part of his continuing '90s education.

"Not about you. About the party. This is my first time cohosting with the lovely Carly Rose."

"It's a dozen people, honey. Our friends. Though I wish Lucie could be here."

"She's on her big trip for her book, right?"

"It's a huge interview. Though I wish..." She hadn't looked so good the day before she left. "I wish she'd done it over video."

"Her doctor said it was okay for her to travel?"

"She did. She's only twenty-six weeks. She can fly until thirty-six."

He stroked my cheek. "Don't hate me, but I invited Danny."

"I won't hate you. I like him. But Lucie will definitely have something to say about it when she gets back."

"He declined. So Lucie won't be mad at me about that." He grimaced. "She'll be furious she missed *this,* though." He slipped his hand into his pocket, and I noticed a bulge in his jeans (not that kind of bulge). This one was shaped like a cube.

"What's that?" I asked, my eyes widening.

"I—I wanted to include all of our friends, especially your friends, when I..." He pulled the distinctive sky-blue jewel box from his pocket. "But now I'm nervous."

"Andrew, are you proposing to me while I have lipstick smeared across my face and we're standing next to a pile of dog shit?"

He opened the box, flashing the diamond solitaire with smaller diamonds set into the band. "Yes?"

My first marriage had been a nineteen-year descent into misery. But Andrew was nothing like my ex. He lifted me up and supported me through the highs and lows of entrepreneurship. He never tried to diminish me and loved me as I was, even when my priorities skewed too far toward work.

"Yes, I'll marry you. But can we wait until after award season?" I was already finalizing Helen's look for the Emmys next month.

"Of course." This time, his kiss wasn't so desperate. His warm, solid lips reflected how he understood me, how he loved me despite—or possibly because of—my career ambitions. "I'll marry you whenever you're ready."

"Vegas? After the Oscars?"

"Absolutely." He slipped the ring onto my finger. "Though we'll have to have a big party afterward. Mother would never forgive us if we looked like we were trying to hide our marriage."

"Don't worry." I winked. "We'll throw something so big it'll eclipse the Vulgar Bikini Boat Party."

"I love it. And I love you." He lowered his head to kiss me but stilled when the doorbell rang.

I glanced at the rug. "Oh, shit."

Slipping Chanel under his arm, he tipped up my chin and swiped under my lip. "Team Rose-Jones. I'll take care of the dog and the rug. Distract our friends. Okay?"

I lifted to my toes and pecked his lips. "On it."

As Andrew knelt to clean the rug, I stepped to the door to welcome our guests. Teamwork. Equality. Respect. Love. This time, I'd chosen well.

∼

Thank you so much for reading *Frenemies and Lovers*. Please consider posting a review on your favorite retailer's site, BookBub, or Goodreads.

Did you catch the hint about what Lucie might be up to in her book? It's a surprise, don't-you-dare-call-it-geriatric pregnancy with her neighbor/bartender/occasional hookup, Danny, who happens to be a younger man. Read on for a sample.

And at the very end, be sure to join my newsletter to get a bonus epilogue set at Carly's very sexy 50th birthday party.

EXCERPT FROM BOOKS AND HOOKUPS

40 AND FABULOUS, BOOK 2

1

COUPLES ARE THE WORST

LUCIE

> "My legacy? Men have legacies. Women have families."
> Excerpt from interview with Savannah Lamb, recipe blogger

"Couples are the worst." I held up my hands. "There. I said it."

Andrew, who'd been gazing intently at Carly like he could Vulcan mind-meld her into leaving us all behind so he could take her home and do couple things like pick out fucking *wallpaper,* blinked slowly. "No, we're not."

At the same time, Carly said, "What? We're not a couple."

Andrew's mouth turned down as he snatched his arm from the back of Carly's barstool.

"I meant," Carly said, "we're not *that* kind of couple. Like that." She nodded at the booth closest to our high-top table, where the guy had his tongue down the woman's throat. And possibly his hand up her skirt. I leaned around Tessa to look. Yep, definitely fingering going on.

I straightened. "You're worse," I announced. "It's not just hot sex, it's *love.*"

Carly hid her blush against Andrew's soft-looking gray sweater. He stroked her arm, looking like she'd given him a gift he'd been coveting for years.

"You agree with me, right, Tessa?" I swiveled in my chair to face her. Our standing Wednesday-night happy hour was down one—our friend Savannah hadn't been able to make it from Sacramento this week—but we'd added Carly's boyfriend. I supposed this was going to be a regular thing now.

She tilted her head. "I find it fascinating how Carly has changed since she accepted Andrew as part of her life. But I don't need to judge it as better or worse. Just different."

Speaking of Vulcans. "But look at this." I picked up my glass of scotch and pointed at them with it. "They're like a couple of Care Bears. With fucking hearts shooting out of them."

"Care Bears? What are those?" Andrew's hand had moved from Carly's arm to her hip. Like they were *snuggling,* right here in the bar.

Carly looked up. "Even Lucie knows the Care Bears. You don't remember them?"

"It's like he grew up on a different planet." Dude was only seven years younger than me. I sipped my scotch, and it burned my throat on the way down. It tasted like socks someone had worn to a camp-out.

"God." Tessa rested her chin on her hand. "I'd forgotten all about Care Bears. I wanted one so bad back in the '80s. Like it was my passport to social acceptance."

"Did you ever get one?" I asked. Tessa was tighter than a nun's asshole about her past. So far, I'd figured out she'd been sheltered, or more like held back from popular culture in the

'80s and '90s. Maybe she'd come from one of those TV-rots-your-brain families. No wonder she was so smart.

"No." She drained her glass of whiskey and set it down. "Who wants another?"

"Me." I raised my hand. All this couple bullshit was stirring up something uncomfortable inside me. Not jealousy, exactly. But a weird kind of longing. I needed to either drink it away or fuck it away, and from the anemic selection of single people in the bar tonight, it was probably going to be drinking.

"Want another glass of sparkling wine?" Andrew murmured. "I'm driving."

Carly smiled up at him, her eyes practically matching the string of paper hearts hanging over the table. "Okay."

"Got it. I'll bring you a seltzer, Andrew." Tessa strode to the bar.

"What are you two doing after happy hour?" I asked. "Want to try that new Ethiopian place across the street?"

Carly's lips turned down. "Sorry, we're doing takeout at Andrew's place. I have to head down to LA the day after tomorrow, and since it's Valentine's Day..."

"Valentine's Day?" I looked up at the paper hearts. "Guess I lost track of the date." Why did February 14 raise a flag in my brain? Today had been a normal day at the paper, and I didn't have any interviews scheduled for my book until March. I lifted my phone from the table.

"Round two," Tessa announced, setting down the four drinks like a pro. She raised her glass. "To...?"

"To love," Carly said, her cheeks turning pink. "I love you all. And Savannah, too." She whispered something in Andrew's ear that made him puff out his chest like he'd won an award.

Award. It clicked into place. "Shit!" I plunked down my drink and scraped back my chair. "Gotta go. I'm late."

"Need us to drive you?" Andrew asked.

That'd be just what I needed, to give my friends a glimpse of my cringeworthy family life. "No, thanks, I'll get a rideshare." I waved as I flicked open the app and headed toward the exit.

Nope, my friends were happily deluded that I was a moderately successful journalist. I wouldn't reveal what my family knew and never hesitated to toss in my face, that I was a disappointment, destined to be forgotten.

A fact that my next stop was sure to remind me of.

"Looks like they've already started," the driver said as she cruised up the now-empty circle drive in front of the campus union hall.

I didn't have to glance at my phone to know how late I was. "Yeah."

"Sorry about the traffic." She waved a hand behind her, as if she could still see the snarl we'd fought through on our way from San Francisco.

I shrugged. "It happens." Especially when you leave late because you're drinking with your friends.

One of my dad's many mantras is that we make time for what's important. That was the one he used when he caught me pulling an all-nighter to finish a paper in college. And when I said I was busy at work and couldn't make it to whatever university event he wanted to trot me out at like a show pony. But that was before my early promise had faded like old newspaper.

When I stayed in her Tesla, staring at the closed doors of the stucco building, the driver said, "Kind of late for a funeral, isn't it?"

"Funeral?" I tilted my head.

She turned and pointed at my torso. "With that getup..."

I looked down at my black trench coat that covered my black shirtdress. "Oh. No, it's an award banquet, actually."

Her forehead scrunched, setting the barbell in her eyebrow sparkling in the building's yellow security light. "I hope you're not the one getting the award."

I chuckled. "Yeah, no. It's my father. As usual. Thanks for the ride." I pushed out of the car but paused on the sidewalk to take a deep breath. Then another. Pasting a smile on my face because he expected it, I strode to the door, heaved it open, and flung myself into the lion's den.

I smelled coffee and a muddle of foods. Potatoes, maybe, and fish. My stomach rumbled. How long ago was lunch? Oh, right, I'd skipped that. Maybe I could still scrounge a plate of something.

My father wasn't particularly tall, and he wore a dark suit like all the other men in the room. Still, he had a presence that drew my attention. Everyone's, really. His white hair and beard stood out against his brown skin. He didn't break his perpetually serious expression as he spoke with a colleague, his focus unwavering even as I approached.

My mother saw me, though. She beamed as I weaved between the round banquet tables, her strawberry-blond hair glinting in the spotlights from the nearby dais. She usually wore more muted colors, but her dress tonight was the color of one of those heart-shaped candy boxes.

"Lucie! You made it!" Her eyes crinkled, obscuring a few of her freckles.

"Sorry I'm late," I muttered as I kissed her cheek. "Traffic."

I winced as soon as I said it and glanced at Dad, hoping he hadn't heard. My hope died when he turned toward me, his jaw set.

"That old story?" he murmured. Louder, he said, "Cal, you remember my daughter, Lucie? She won an award for a seven-part series on human trafficking. How many years ago was that, Lucie?"

My cheeks burning, I shook the older white man's hand. "Fifteen or so."

"She was a brand-new reporter. No idea how she got the assignment, but she made the most of it," Dad said.

I already knew the question was coming before Cal opened his mouth. "And what have you been working on lately?"

"Moldering in the newsroom at the city paper." My father spat out the last two words like he'd say "garbage dump."

At the same time, I stood to my full height of five foot four and said, "Actually, I'm working on a book. I just signed the deal."

I'd signed it two weeks ago, but I'd wanted to look Dad in the eye when I told him.

His white eyebrow twitched upward.

"Oh, Lucie, we're so proud." Mom squeezed my shoulders.

Cal asked, "What's the book about?"

"It's about legacy. What we intend to leave behind. What we hope we're remembered for."

Cal chuckled. "You going to interview your dad, I assume?"

"It's a book about women's legacies," I said.

"Women's legacies?" Cal asked. "Like motherhood?

We all glanced at my mother in her drab Eileen Fisher suit, white silk blouse, and empty smile.

"Women can be more than mothers," I blurted. "I have some interviews lined up. A tech founder, a Hollywood stylist." I left out the facts that they were my best friends and I hadn't asked them yet. "And—"

"I'll connect you with Dr. Watts," my father said. "The university's first Black female president should have a place in your book."

Cal scratched his gray beard. "Marvin, didn't you speak on a panel recently with Senator Gu? He's got a wife who does something with refugees, I think."

"That's right," Dad said. "Eleanor. Everyone says their son is on the road to the White House. I'm sure she'll do me a favor and talk to you."

Suddenly, dinner leftovers didn't seem so appetizing.

"I've got it, Dad," I growled.

"All right." As he shrugged like he didn't care (he did), the lights flickered. "Ah. That's my cue." Without another word, he strode to the dais and took his seat next to the university president.

Cal had already disappeared, so I turned to my mother. "Did you save me a seat?"

"You can borrow your father's. He won't need it." She pointed at a chair and sat in the one next to it. The efficient servers had removed everything edible from the table. I turned the coffee cup over, hoping someone would come to fill it, and I could beg for a leftover dessert.

As the lights dimmed, Mom leaned over to whisper in my ear, "We're both so proud of you."

It was a lie. Not an intentional one; my mother was definitely proud of me, and she thought Dad was, too. But the only way my father would be proud of me was if I was sitting up on that stage, getting an award for scholarly achievement. He'd been furious the day I'd told him I'd declined my grad school acceptance to go to work for the paper. He'd told me I was throwing away my future. But I'd wanted a different future from his.

It wasn't because Dad's research into the long-term effects of racism on society wasn't valuable. It was, and politicians and activists wore out the cushions of his dining-room chairs as they begged for his advice on how to make the country a better place for all its citizens.

But I didn't care for the sanitized type of research he did, with statistics and expert interviews. No, I wanted to dig deeper into people's stories and help them share those narratives with a broader audience. Because people connected better with stories than with dry research. I'd blaze my own trail and change the world my way.

So I went to work at the newspaper, where as the new person, I took the assignments no one else wanted: city council meetings, school board meetings, the mayor's press conference announcing the city budget. Until one day, I was in the right place at the right time when a reporter called in sick, and I got to cover a bust of a human trafficking ring. Then, I'd convinced the editor to let me do a follow-up piece on some of the victims, and even Dad had noticed when a national news magazine picked it up as a feature.

Too bad I'd done nothing noteworthy in the seventeen years since.

The burst of applause startled me, and I focused on the stage just as my father stepped up to the podium. Another plaque for his wall of achievement was displayed on an easel beside him. Was there even space for it? He'd already annexed the wall in my old bedroom, the one that used to be covered in posters of Bono, Jane Goodall, and Nelson Mandela.

The speaker before him must have introduced his work because instead of talking about his research, Dad thanked the university for the honor and launched into a lengthy list of acknowledgments, from his editor at the university press to the graduate students who'd run the statistical analysis. My eyebrows crept up my forehead. Normally, Dad wasn't big on sharing credit. Some people probably thought he set the type on the printing press himself.

"...and most importantly, I'd like to thank the person who's stood by me through it all, who's supported me, who's encouraged me, who's been my partner in my journey." He paused, still unsmiling.

I was pretty sure I'd never heard him acknowledge my mother. I reached for her hand and squeezed it. She'd given up everything for him. For us both. She'd been forced out of her graduate program when her relationship with my father, who happened to be her adviser, was exposed. I was born three months later. If anyone deserved his thanks, she did.

"Dr. LaToya Watts," he said. "Without the support of our university president, my research wouldn't have received the exposure it has. Thank you." He lifted the plaque from its easel and posed next to Dr. Watts for photos as the audience applauded.

I froze, still gripping my mother's hand. Had I somehow missed his thanks to her? Judging from the forced smile on her face, no.

I leaned forward to whisper, "Are you okay?"

Her eyes crinkled at the corners. "Of course I am. This is a major achievement for your father. For us all."

One glance at my father up on the stage, shaking hands with the trustees, told me she was wrong. It was an achievement for one person only, and that was him. I hated that he couldn't love me for who I was, but ignoring the person who'd given up everything for him? No. I couldn't sit around and pretend to smile after that.

I kissed her cheek. "Bye, Mom. I've got to go."

She blinked her blue eyes wide. "You're not staying to talk to him after? Come to the house. I'll whip you up a snack."

"No, thanks. Early meeting tomorrow." As much as I longed for one of my mother's meals, listening to my father's pompous speech had ruined my appetite.

I needed another drink.

2
WHEN DO YOU GET OFF?

DANNY

Valentine's Day Manhattan
Shake 2 oz bourbon, 3/4 oz vanilla liqueur, and a dash of Angostura bitters with ice. Strain into a chilled martini glass. Garnish with a toothpick of Luxardo cherries and a ribbon of orange peel.

He was late again. I glanced at my watch, then over the bar at the light Friday-night crowd. Barb and I had managed so far, but once those desperate Valentine's-Day dates started to tank, people would pile in to drink away another lost chance at love.

Believe me, I'd been there.

Every Valentine's Day, I turned into that guy, the one who saw love everywhere. My memories of shoeboxes decorated with red and white construction paper, the cheesy jokes on the cards, and enough chocolate to put me in a sugar coma always gave me hope that the right person was out there, wanting to be my *significant otter*.

And every Valentine's Day, I was disappointed.

A lime wedge bounced off my forehead. "Look alive, Carbone." Barb nodded at the woman with the sad eyes bellied up to my end of the bar.

"Sorry." I leaped into action, tossing an extra cherry into her Manhattan. She'd need more than that to get through the rest of her date with Bud Light Guy, who couldn't be bothered to fetch their drinks.

I swiped at the bar with a cloth and straightened the garnish tray, plucking a heart-shaped piece of confetti out of the olive brine. I squinted at the door like I could make him come through it through the power of my will.

Barb rolled up beside me and threw the brake on her wheelchair. "Don't worry. He'll show. He's never let us down yet."

I gazed down into her crinkled blue eyes. "What if there was an accident?"

"Pish posh. It's much more likely your little brother lost track of time in the kitchen than a mishap on the BART. The bus might run late, but it's safe."

"I know." I pulled out my phone. There were plenty of texts in my siblings' group chat, but nothing from Leo. "I just—"

"You worry, Mother Hen," she said. "About everything. It's why I trust you with my bar."

A feeling like carbonation bubbled through my stomach. If all went according to plan, it'd be my bar this time next year. Mine and Leo's.

"Won't you miss this place?" I asked, scanning the polished wood, the well-worn high-top tables, the vintage movie posters on the wall.

Barb's gaze fell on her most prized possession in its place of honor next to the bar, the *West Side Story* poster signed by

Natalie Wood. "Of course I will. But when I'm on my world cruise, looking out at the Sydney Opera House, I don't think I'll be worrying about cockroaches in the dry storage or the rising price of tequila."

I chuckled. "Fair."

"And look." She tipped her head toward the swinging door behind me. "There he is."

My brother barreled into the tight quarters. A couple inches taller than me and rounder around the middle, he always seemed too big for it. He held one of his biodegradable clamshell containers in front of him.

"You have to try this, Danny. And Barb." His round cheeks were pink, either from the February chill or from boyish delight. He opened the box, and a mouthwatering aroma drifted out.

"You were late for french fries?" I wiped my hands on the towel that hung from my front jeans pocket and reached into the box.

"Be sure to try the garlic aioli." After Barb and I both dipped a fry in the sauce and took a bite, he said, "They're fried in truffle oil. And I shaved a little truffle on top."

I chewed the delicious morsel and swallowed. It was the best thing I'd eaten since our mom's Bolognese last Easter.

"Oh, my stars," Barb said. "My taste buds are singing."

"Good, isn't it?" Leo's tentative smile was full of hope.

"Let me try one, Leo." Walter, one of our regulars, beckoned. Leo held out the box to him.

"Shaved truffle sounds expensive," I grumbled.

"Well, yeah, the truffles cost about twenty-five each, but there's only a tiny amount on these. And the truffle oil is a little pricey. I paid two hundred for a gallon, but I could probably get a bulk discount."

"Two *hundred?*" My voice rose to an outraged squeak. "You mean it'll cost a grand to fill up the fryer? For that kind of money, we could replace the leaky ladies' room faucet with the fancy touchless kind."

"I'll try to oven-bake the next batch," he said. "That'll use a lot less oil."

"You gonna eat the rest of those?" Walter said.

Leo handed them over. "They're good, right?"

Walter nodded, his mouth full.

I lowered my voice. "I thought we were saving money, Leo."

"But it's for the bar. We'll add them to the menu."

"Walter," I said, "would you pay twenty bucks for those fries?"

He stuffed the last one in his mouth. "Twenty bucks? I could buy a burger and a beer for that. You're not going to charge me, are you?"

I hit Leo with an accusatory glare as I poured a fresh glass of water and set it in front of our customer. "That was on the house. Thanks for being our guinea pig."

"You boys can do whatever you like with the bar when it's yours," Barb said gently, "but the customers here are middle class. They might have truffle-oil taste, but they've got a peanut-oil budget."

Silently, we scanned the patrons. They were mechanics with grease on their jeans, teachers drinking off a long day with sugared-up kids, landscapers brushing grass clippings out of their hair and onto the sixty-year-old wood-plank floor. My siblings and I had gone to school with some of them. Barb had served them for years. She'd served some of their parents too. It was a place people came to connect with the community, to have a little fun after work.

In my eyes, it was perfect.

"I've been thinking," Leo said, "what if we used the kitchen to run a catering business?"

I coughed on a sip of water. "You mean on the side, in addition to the bar food?"

"Yeah. It'd bring in extra cash. And I'd manage the whole operation. It'd be my food truck on rails. Well, not literally. But I could make so much more food in a real kitchen. Banquets. Weddings. You name it."

I pictured Leo trying to share the tiny space with the cook. Norm had worked with Barb since day one, and I was pretty sure he'd rather quit than bump shoulders with an entire catering staff, including my upstart brother with his fanciful menu.

"Do you really think there's room for a catering business and Norm back there? Installing extra equipment would be—"

"Expensive, I know." Leo sighed. "Maybe we can brainstorm about it later."

"Sure." I'd always humored my little brother's nutty ideas. I'd gone along with my fair share, too. But this wouldn't be one of them. "Let's talk tomorrow. You and I are opening."

"Right. And sorry I was late tonight. Time got away from me."

It wasn't the first time. Still, I said, "Don't worry about it. Barb and I had it under control. I'm glad you're here now. Get their drinks?" I pointed at a group of nurses at the far end of the bar.

"On it." He tied an apron around his waist and strode toward them.

Barb, Leo, and I worked like a well-oiled clock that night. Barb handled the accessible end of the bar like always, and Leo and I took turns serving the rest of it and carrying cases of beer and racks of glasses to the dishwasher and back. There was a rush at eight and another at ten. We floated and replaced two kegs, and Barb arranged rides for those customers who needed them. By eleven thirty, the bar was only about half full. We'd closed the kitchen, and I'd cut two servers and carried up what I hoped was the last bucket of ice when a tingle raced across my skin. I glanced toward the door.

She'd walked in, her cheeks pink and her dark curls wild from the wind. Unwinding the scarf from her neck, she strode to Barb's end of the bar and sank onto a chair like she owned it.

I couldn't help smiling. My dad had fond memories of an old app where the person who'd visited a particular location the most often was crowned the mayor. If that app were still around, Lucie Knox would be the mayor of Barb's Bar. And she acted like it.

Flashing a queenly smile at another regular, she turned just as Barb set her drink on the coaster.

Another scotch night. After dumping the ice into the bin, I edged closer.

"...total nightmare, as usual," she said. "Hey, Danny."

Whoa. The white flash of her teeth as she smiled dazzled me. Was she wearing lipstick? I tried to be subtle as I scanned the rest of her. Black clothes, as always. She wore a dress under her black coat. My breath caught at the glimpse of her tan legs that reminded me of another night when they'd been wrapped around my waist.

She hadn't missed my checking her out. Lucie never missed anything. It was why she was such a talented reporter. She tipped her head, and even her dark pupils glittered. "What's up?" And then she glanced pointedly at my crotch.

I took half a step back and bumped into the back bar, rattling the bottle of Tito's.

"H-hi, Lucie." I bent to straighten the bottles in Barb's speed rail so the labels faced out, but that only made more blood rush to my face. Why could I never keep my cool around her?

"Busy night?"

Barb watched us, her eyes glinting with fascination.

"Yeah, I guess." I checked the garnish tray. Damn, it was full. "What with the holiday and all."

"Holiday?" Lucie crinkled her forehead.

I waved at the red and pink streamers hanging from the glass rack. "Valentine's Day?"

"Right." Slowly, she nodded, and my heart rate slowed by a few beats. Maybe she wasn't cruising for a post dating disaster hookup. Maybe she was just chatting, and I wouldn't be faced with the temptation to follow her upstairs, only to have my heart bruised when she inevitably kicked me out without so much as a cuddle.

Because even if Lucie Knox were the kind of woman who was interested in anything more than a hookup, she wouldn't choose me.

She was college educated. Brilliant. Had written that amazing piece about human trafficking when I was still in middle school. (Yes, I'd googled her.) Not to mention confident and gorgeous.

Me? I'd never been to college. I had no deep thoughts about the low value our government puts on vulnerable people like women, children, and immigrants. I was a bartender. I lived in the small apartment upstairs because Barb let me stay there for free.

I'd never be worthy of anything more than an orgasm or three to Lucie.

"Hey," she said, her teeth gleaming under that red lipstick, lipstick I was tempted to kiss off her face, "what time do you get off?"

Which, apparently, was exactly what she wanted from me.

Be sure to get your copy of *Books and Hookups* from your favorite retailer.

Want to see how Carly celebrates her 50th birthday? (Hint: the Goddess Gang are all invited.) Plus an intimate moment—or several—with Andrew. Join my newsletter at michellemccraw.com/FrenemiesBonus to download a free bonus epilogue!

ACKNOWLEDGMENTS

This book needed lots of help, and my friends and team stepped up for me. Thank you, Carla Luna and Sadira Stone, beta readers extraordinaire, who helped guide me in the right direction. (Also, everyone, check out their books. Carla writes the most adorable rom-coms, and Sadira writes some awesome older heroes and heroines!)

Thanks, also, to the Central Ohio Fiction Writers Plotters' Group for helping me brainstorm ideas to fix my character problems. I miss you guys and the excuse to shove bread in my face at Panera.

Most of all, thanks to Amy Brewer, my agent. She had the courage to tell me my book baby was ugly and offered suggestions for how to pretty her up. Y'all, she read this sucker three times (!), which is really above and beyond. And then, showing what a true partner she is, she agreed that self-publishing was the best route for it. Thank you, Amy, for your advice and support along my publishing journey.

Finally, thanks to my readers, the ones who've been with me since 2021 and the newer ones just finding me. I know there are a ton of great books out there, and I appreciate the time you've spent reading mine.

CREDITS

Edits and Proofreading

E&A Editing Services

Cover Design

Stephanie Anderson, Alt 19 Creative

Copyright © 2024 by Michelle McCraw

All rights reserved.

No part of this book may be reproduced in any form or by any electronic or mechanical means, including information storage and retrieval systems, without written permission from the author, except for the use of brief quotations in a book review. No part of this book may be used for the purpose of training artificial intelligence systems. For permissions contact help@MichelleMcCraw.com

This is a work of fiction. Names, characters, places, and incidents either are the products of the author's imagination or are used fictitiously. Any resemblance to actual persons, living or dead, businesses, companies, events, or locales is entirely coincidental.

Cover design by Stephanie Anderson at Alt 19 Creative

Made in the USA
Columbia, SC
14 February 2024